She broke into a smile, her heart soaring.

"I like you, Cece," he said plainly. "You're funny and smart, you're gorgeous, not afraid of hard work, and you keep me on my toes because I never know what you might say or do."

Cece glanced down, her cheeks on fire, but she didn't want him to stop talking.

"I know we're working together, and if this muddies things, I'll back off, but—"

"No." She cut him off. "No, you don't need to back off. I...I like you too. It's okay if this muddies things."

Dustin took her hand, tugging her that little bit closer to close the gap between them. "Literally and figuratively if we work on this yard?"

She laughed, and he caught her chin. His eyes were dark in the evening light, but she imagined fire in them. He wanted to kiss her; she could feel it in her bones.

More importantly, she wanted him to. If this was their first date, she wanted it to end with a kiss.

Also by Heather McGovern

Something Blue

Second Chance at the Orchard Inn

Home on Hollyhock Lane

Heather McGovern

FOREVER

New York Boston

Forever
Hachette Book Group
1290 Avenue of the Americas, New York, NY 10104
read-forever.com
@readforeverpub

First Edition: November 2024

Forever is an imprint of Grand Central Publishing. The Forever name and logo are registered trademarks of Hachette Book Group, Inc.

The publisher is not responsible for websites (or their content) that are not owned by the publisher.

The Hachette Speakers Bureau provides a wide range of authors for speaking events. To find out more, go to hachettespeakersbureau.com or email HachetteSpeakers@hbgusa.com.

Forever books may be purchased in bulk for business, educational, or promotional use. For information, please contact your local bookseller or the Hachette Book Group Special Markets Department at special.markets@hbgusa.com.

ISBNs: 978-1-5387-3750-7 (mass market), 978-1-5387-3748-4 (ebook)

Printed in the United States of America

BVGM

10 9 8 7 6 5 4 3 2 1

For JBG, forever our outdoorsman, carpenter, Mr. Fix-It, Renaissance Man, and big teddy bear. The world could use a million more just like you.

Home
on Hollyhock
Lane

Chapter 1

"Who do you think will draw first blood?"

Cece Shipley glanced up from her sewing pattern, spread across the floor, to find her sister Aurora looming over her with a knife. "Jeez!" She jerked upright. "Are you trying to give me heart failure?"

"Sorry." Aurora lowered the knife and blew a strand of loose reddish-blond hair from her forehead. "Chopping onions," she said, as if that explained everything.

"And?" Cece shook off the scare. They'd all been jumpy lately, in the last months leading up to their oldest sister Beth's wedding to her dream cowboy, Sawyer Silva.

Aurora imitating a slasher in some horror movie didn't help.

"I said, who do you think is going to injure themselves first in our quest to pull off the perfect wedding? Me, in the kitchen, creating a dozen different dishes until Beth decides what she wants at the reception or you"—she pointed at Cece with the knife—"cutting fabric and altering Grandma's old wedding dress?"

"I already poked myself with a needle yesterday, and it bled for five minutes. Does that count?" Cece wondered once again how on earth she was going to modernize a

midcentury wedding gown made for their vertically chal-
lenged grandmother when Beth was like five-eight.

"Nope, that was yesterday. Any injuries today?"

"Not yet."

"Then let's see if we can make it to the end of the day."
Aurora held out her free hand. "Come on."

Cece pulled both hands protectively to her chest.
"What are you going to do to me?" she teased.

"Oh, for the love—" Aurora walked over and placed
the knife on the kitchen counter. "I want you to try this
homemade dressing for the salads. I can't tell if it's got too
much kick for the average wedding guest or not enough
for the average Texan."

Cece got to her feet. "Fine, but you owe me a whole
salad after scaring me. Not just a bite."

"Deal."

"I need to take a break from the dress anyway. I've
separated the skirt from the bodice, and I know what I'm
doing as far as the silhouette of the bottom, but the neckline is still a big ole question mark hanging right about..."
Cece waved her hands above her head. "Here."

Aurora pulled two bowls from the cabinet. "Beth was
adamant she didn't want strapless."

"Exactly. But I know she doesn't want the sweetheart
neckline and cap sleeves that are on there now." Cece let
her let her head fall back with a sigh. "That only leaves,
what? Several *dozen* other options. This isn't a pillow or
curtains or decorating a living room, all of which I can do
in my sleep. This is her wedding dress. I'd rather have too
much input than not enough."

And it was very unlike Beth not to be definitive in her
decisions about a wedding. As a wedding planner for the

Inn, Beth was the definition of control freak, but with her own wedding she'd been...dare it be called *laid-back*?

Cece knew Beth's style because, while she and her sisters were very much alike with their blond hair, ranging from slightly strawberry to flax, and fair skin that burned way too easily, their vibes varied greatly. While Cece might think a flowing, twirly wedding dress with some flounce was perfect and breezy, that was simply not Beth. What if she followed her gut down the wrong path and ruined her sister's wedding dress?

"Do you feel like Beth has been too relaxed about this whole thing?" Cece asked, taking the offered bowl from her sister. "Especially considering how she usually is?"

"Uh." Aurora grabbed the blender full of her latest dressing concoction. "You think? I finally got her to decide on multiple food stations versus a plated reception. Just makes the most sense with the inn's layout and an outdoor service, indoor-and-outdoor mixed reception. But then I asked her about protein and heavy plate options. We're talking, do you want a carving station? If so, what kind? Do you want seafood plates or a shrimp cocktail station? Chicken skewers? Really, any suggestions about what kind of heavier dishes you want at the reception? She said, and I quote, 'Whatever you think is best.'"

"I think bringing bossy Beth back is best," Cece proclaimed.

She and Aurora nodded at each other.

"My thoughts exactly. Whatever *I* think is best? About *her* wedding? I got a little lightheaded and had to sit down. Maybe you should ask Sawyer if he's noticed it too? See if he'd talk to her about it." Aurora kept mixing her concoction.

Cece shook her head. "Why me?"

"Everyone knows you and Sawyer get along like a house on fire. He treated you like a little sister way before he and Beth even got engaged."

This was true, but she wasn't about to rock the boat if she and Aurora were the only ones thinking Beth was acting uncharacteristically laid-back.

"Here." Aurora held out a taste of the dressing she'd been working on.

Cece took the offered spoon and sat down. "What did you decide about the wedding food then?"

"I haven't. Are you kidding? I'm not making that call for Beth Persnickety Shipley. I think I will *gently* suggest a shrimp cocktail, a beef tenderloin carving station, some chicken options, and maybe crudités circulating with the waitstaff, but I'm still going to leave the final approval to her."

"Clever problem-solving." Cece winked at her sister before tasting her latest concoction. The dressing had citrus on the front, with a savory flavor overall, and a small bite on the back end. "Oooh, it's got a little kick. I like that. Is it horseradish?"

"Yeah, too much?"

"No, I love it. It doesn't linger like using a hot pepper. Just sort of pinches you and then runs away, and you're left wondering, did someone just run up and pinch me?"

Aurora grinned as she began putting their salads together. "You have a way with words, sis. Maybe I'll call this Lemon Pinch dressing and serve it at the restaurant."

"You should definitely call it Lemon Pinch." Cece smiled.

Aurora was almost at the one-year anniversary of

owning her successful restaurant, Lavender, in Fredericksburg. For years, everyone thought she'd make Los Angeles
her home, but when she returned to help Beth and Cece
turn around their bad luck with the family's Orchard Inn,
it seemed Aurora's home and heart were still in Texas.

She'd reconnected with her high school sweetheart,
Jude, and Cece had never seen her sister so happy.

Both of her sisters had found love, and their lives were
moving forward in the best ways, both personally and
professionally.

Cece was happy for them, of course, and she loved
Jude and Sawyer; they were perfect for her sisters. Still, a
tug of longing, or maybe even envy, pulled at her.

She loved love, but life wasn't as simple as that. Look
at their mom. She'd loved their dad and trusted him, but
he'd lied, been deceitful enough to embezzle money, and
then left his family to deal with the fallout.

Wanting to find love didn't mean you would, or that the
love would be true.

Not that Cece needed a man, because she didn't.

Right now, her focus was on building a life of her own,
something just for her. Her sisters were a blessing, and she
loved them dearly, but she wanted something of her own
too, apart from her family. Something that was hers alone.
For a while, she'd thought that meant a small place, all to
herself, but that plan fell through.

Now, she wasn't sure what having something of her
own really meant anymore.

Was it a side hustle in alterations or dressmaking?
Doing more in the way of interior decorating since she
had a knack? Or maybe it was finding another fixer-upper
and finally making her cottage-core dreams come true.

She could see it now, her in a little place in the woods—lots of wildflowers and a small garden. She'd have a cat or two, named something irresistible like Whiskers and Mittens, and she'd read by the fire at night—even though they rarely got weather conducive to needing a fire indoors.

Or maybe the future meant finding that life partner.

Ugh, no. Probably not that.

Looking for Mr. Right? That was so depressing and codependent—way too early 2000s TV show.

No. She liked her independence. To be happy and fulfilled, with a life of her own, was her goal. If, eventually, some great guy fell into her lap, fine.

Regardless, she wasn't chasing after anyone.

Cece stared down into the salad placed before her.

She'd dated plenty after high school, but for the last couple of years, she'd sworn off the dating apps and the setups from friends. When you'd kissed a few toads, you needed a break from the pond. She hadn't given up hope, but she wasn't actively looking either.

If she never met her perfect partner, then so be it. She enjoyed being a one-woman show. It might be nice to have a partner who shared in all of life's triumphs and failures, that person you longed to see at the end of the day and wake up next to and talk to each morning. And if that person happened to be strapping and strong, kind but no-nonsense, perhaps tall and bearded but definitely yummy smelling, then all the better.

"Um, sis?"

"Huh?" Cece shook her head, pulling herself back into the moment.

"The salad?"

"Right. Salad." Cece took a bite, letting the crisp

textures and full zing of flavors dance on her tongue. "Another winner." She nodded as she finished the bite. "This is amazing, but you'll have to call it something fancier if you put it on the wedding menu. I don't think Lemon Pinch suits a wedding."

Aurora laughed. "True. Not that this new, laid-back Beth would care."

"Care about what?" Beth walked into the kitchen from the private entry door with Sawyer right behind her.

"Nothing," Aurora and Cece said in unison.

"Uh-huh. Sure. What smells so good?" Beth leaned over and sniffed the blender, instantly distracted.

"New salad dressing Aurora just made," Cece answered.

"Nice." Sawyer admired their salads.

Aurora pulled her bowl a little closer. "Would you both care for some lunch?"

"I mean, if there's enough for everyone." He grinned, ever charming.

"There's plenty."

"I've got it. Don't get up." Sawyer made salads for Beth and himself, and the four of them ate at the kitchen counter.

"This is delicious. For the restaurant or the wedding?" Beth asked between bites.

Aurora shared a look with Cece. "I'm thinking both. If that's okay?"

"I think that's a great idea."

"Have you made a decision on the heavier offerings yet?" Cece tried.

"Oh." Beth pondered the question, looked to Sawyer, then her sisters, and shrugged. "What do y'all think?"

Sawyer smiled in such a way that Cece knew he'd also

noticed how calm she'd been about the wedding proceedings. "I think we can go with chicken, red meat, and a couple of seafood options. Sound good?"

"That sounds great to me." Beth returned his smile.

"Wonderful." Aurora made a checkoff motion in the air. "Yay! Done."

"Now about the dress…" Cece jumped in. "We need to discuss necklines and choose which design you want."

Beth waved one hand in the air while eating her salad with the other. "Just pick a few options, and I'll decide which one I like the best out of what you pick."

Cece considered burying her face in her salad and screaming. Apparently, making two big decisions in one day was too much to ask. "You say that now, but I don't want you freaking out days before the wedding because the dress isn't perfect."

"I'm not going to freak out."

"Can we get that in writing?"

Sawyer waved his fork in the air to get their attention as he finished chewing. "I've seen your work at the shop downtown, Cece. Beth showed me. Your pieces were always good, but *wow*."

"It's gotten better, but I still need to work on my accuracy. It takes me too long to finish a—"

"Cece." Aurora reached for her water glass. "Accept the compliment. Your work is awesome."

"Oh." She looked toward a nodding Sawyer. Her ability to accept praise and recognition without argument was a work in progress. "Thank you."

He smiled. "I bet if you put together two or three dress ideas, then it'd be easier for Beth to choose between them."

"That's a great idea!" Beth perked up.

Sawyer shared a wink with Cece. "I think you'll find choosing between a few options very helpful. Lately, too many choices equal no choice."

"Ahhh." Cece nodded. "Got it." She ate her salad, visions of dresses twirling around her brain. She did feel a lot more confident in her alterations and dressmaking abilities, but the progress had happened so fast, over the last few months.

After she'd done some sewing for interior design work around the inn, she'd gotten some offers to do alterations on dresses at a local shop. It'd been years since she'd sewn clothing, but once she got back on the bike—or the sewing machine—the skill had come back to her and then some.

But her sister's wedding dress? That was major league.

She'd sewn several day dresses, hemmed many a skirt and pair of pants. True, she had plenty of time, as long as the alterations weren't too complicated, but the idea of getting her sister's wedding dress wrong turned her stomach.

"Anyone want a refill?" Sawyer got up from the island to grab the pitcher of tea. "Oh yeah, did I tell you guys that house at the end of Hollyhock Lane finally sold the other day?"

Cece's stomach turned even more. "What?"

"The one that's been for sale forever?" Beth asked.

"Yeah, the one we all walked by a few months ago. I was beginning to think it'd sit at the end of that road and rot, but there's a sold sign on it now."

"The little two-bedroom cottage?" Cece asked, her throat dry.

"I don't know if it's two bedrooms or—"

"The one with the big porch and wisteria growing on a pergola next to it?"

Her sisters stared as Sawyer blinked at her dismay. "I think so, but I didn't take that much notice. What am I missing?"

Cece stared at her salad, her heart pounding in her stomach now.

The cottage on Hollyhock Lane. Her dream cottage. That was going to be her cottage.

Well, not really. And not legally. But in her dreams? In her dreams, the house on Hollyhock was her home. Hers to bring to code, hers to renovate, to decorate, and to caretake.

Orchard Inn would always be her family home, but that bungalow was the home of her heart. It had been part of her plan for independence, a life outside of her sisters, her own future.

It had been on the market for years but at a price she could not come close to affording. Knowing that someday it'd be sold or otherwise go into foreclosure, she'd saved for years and worked on her credit score. Still, when she'd gone to a mortgage broker months ago, the response hadn't been good. She was denied based on income. Apparently, part-time alterations work and working for your family's inn weren't the reliable sources of finances for repayment a bank wanted.

"Cece." Aurora touched her arm, drawing her from her thoughts. "Is that the—?"

"Yes." Cece put her fork down. She'd lost her appetite.

She'd told her sisters of her dream, and while they hated the idea of her not living at Orchard Inn full-time, they'd supported her goals and understood her need to have something all her own.

Then again, maybe they knew, deep down, it was never going to be.

"I'm sorry, Cece," Beth said.

Aurora rubbed her arm. "Me too."

"Oh." Sawyer's voice lifted with the realization. "You wanted to buy that house?"

"I did. I even tried, but I couldn't. Buying takes money, and a lot more of it than I have."

"But, Cece, I could've—"

She shook her head, stopping him mid-sentence. She knew what he was about to stay. He could've helped, and he would've too, because he had treated Cece like family from the day they met. Sawyer would've swooped in, loaned her the money, or cosigned the mortgage, or given her the down payment to be repaid whenever—whatever it took. That's just the kind of guy Sawyer was.

But that wasn't the point of her Hollyhock dreams. The act of suddenly having it was not what she wanted. This was supposed to be all hers, alone, from start to finish: the saving and getting a loan, the purchase, and the remodeling. The blood, sweat and tears—all hers—were part of the plan.

"I'm going to get some air." She pushed away from her lunch.

"Cece," Beth called after her.

"It's okay. Really. I just need to get out and clear my head. Go for a walk or something."

"Are you sure?" Aurora asked. "One of us could go with you."

That was the opposite of what she wanted. She needed to be alone.

"No, y'all finish lunch. You know me; I'll be fine." She wanted fresh air, nature, and silence, only her thoughts while she processed a dream lost. Sure, she'd known she couldn't buy the place soon, but in the back of her mind, she'd held out hope that if the cottage sat there long enough, empty, she'd have enough time to save more. She'd get the opportunity to show regular, steady income. Then she'd go right into a bank and sign for her new home.

Cece slid on her worn-out walking shoes and told the others goodbye. She headed out the back of the inn, through the entrance only family and friends used. From the back of the inn, she could cut through the low, sloping hills of the orchard that made up the family's farm.

Out front, they had a small section of plum trees, but the rest was all peaches.

Acres of peaches.

The Shipley sisters owned one of the smallest farms in Hill Country, but they still grew enough to sell to a few local vendors and markets. The busy season was over, summer had wound down, and fall was just around the corner.

Cece made her way up and over the rolling hills. The leaves of their orchard had barely begun to shift from a sea of green to the slightest touches of yellow, but the Texas heat still reigned supreme. Actual cool fall weather didn't hit Fredericksburg until late October or November. A person could easily work up a sweat while trick-or-treating.

Still, the subtle changes in foliage, the occasional afternoon breeze that wasn't heavy with humidity, lifted her spirits a smidge.

Most folks took walking for granted, but most folks had never had that ability jeopardized. Born with palsy, albeit a very mild case, independent walking wasn't a certainty for her. Surgeries and years of physical therapy gifted her with mobility. She didn't take a single step for granted.

Maybe that's why she loved her walks so much. She didn't want to let her luck ever go to waste, almost like if she didn't use it, she might lose it. Some would probably find that fear silly, but most had never walked in her shoes.

Walking was emotional therapy too. The action cleared her mind; being in nature brought perspective. She might not have her cottage, but she had this. Her hidden trails and pathways across the fields and meadows of her hometown. Most people didn't know about the back way to her cottage.

Correction. *The* cottage. It didn't belong to her.

With her general knowledge of the local layout, she'd blazed her own path from the back of Orchard Inn, down the side of a pasture, through a little neighborhood, and onto the winding drive of Hollyhock Lane.

Was some of this journey technically trespassing? When she started taking this path... kind of. At least the pasture part. But she'd met the family who bought the farm, and one day, eventually, she'd mentioned her walks. The owners had said it was fine, and Cece had taken it as permission granted.

She reached the edge of her family's orchard, found the little cut-through, and followed it. The cut spat her out in the pasture that ran the length of Rolling Hills Farm.

A couple had bought the land a few years back and slowly, over the last year and change, started a rehabilitation and recovery farm. Not only did they take older, injured, or unwanted domestic animals—everything from cats to cows—they provided support for people rehabilitating to visit or work the farm as part of a program.

Rolling Hills was still in its early stages, but it already had a wonderful reputation in the community, and Cece had met a family of goats when she'd met the couple who ran the farm. She wasn't sure who was more lovable between the two.

Through the tall grass of the pasture she went, hugging the dense tree line, keeping to the shade. The sky was mostly cloudy, but she was still the fairest-complexioned Shipley. The wind kicked up for a moment, rustling the trees and taller grass, and she considered turning back, in case a storm was coming. But even if a storm was missed by the forecast, it would be hours away.

She only needed another half hour, enough time to see the cottage one last time and then head back home.

Once at the end of the pasture, she hung a right onto a road that wound past a small neighborhood. Cece passed modest ranch-style homes, a few old Tudors, and a Cape Cod.

Perhaps one of these could one day be hers. Her dream Craftsman cottage might be gone, but surely something else would work out.

None of these sang to her like the house on Hollyhock Lane, but maybe they'd do.

She needed a fixed income though. Something steady and stable. Maybe she should take Beth's advice and enroll in an accounting class.

"Ugh," she groaned aloud.

The thought of learning and doing bookkeeping all day tied a knot of dread in her stomach.

Yes, a skill like that could help with the inn's finances, even with Aurora's restaurant, and she'd be successful and secure...and miserable.

"I don't want to crunch numbers," she complained aloud.

That was in Beth's wheelhouse, along with her creativity and her abilities to manage people and multitask like a goddess. Cece liked to use her hands and creativity to make things. She needed active tasks and something tangible to work toward.

Unfortunately, that didn't pay much, at least not in any way she'd been able to find.

Finally, she reached the drive, lined with the tall hollyhocks that gave Hollyhock Lane its name. The house sat at the end, with about three acres of woodland surrounding. As she turned down the lane, another big gust blew cool air across her skin, and the first drop of rain landed on her cheek.

"Uh-oh." She quickened her pace.

Then another drop fell on her nose, her shoulder, her arm. The weather lady had called for clear skies all day, but she'd been all kinds of wrong.

Cece walked a little faster toward the cottage as the drops turned into a shower. She could wait out the weather on the roomy front porch of the cottage. Summer storms were often here and gone in thirty minutes.

The rain came down faster, and within seconds, the sky opened into a downpour.

With a little squeak, Cece hurried down the lane, but by the time she reached the cottage, she was already soaked.

"Lovely," she said to herself once on the porch.

She swiped the raindrops off her face and ran her fingers through her curls. "So much for a nice walk."

Cece stepped to one side of the porch, peering into a window to give her dream home one last farewell.

A light was on inside.

Cece jerked away from the window.

The light came from the kitchen, shining into what would be the dining room. Cece knew the layout of this house. She'd had a real estate agent show it to her twice and had committed every detail to memory.

The buyer was already here?

Cece looked around and, for the first time, noticed a truck was parked under the big oak tree in the side yard.

"Fabulous," she muttered.

Number 4 Hollyhock Lane was supposed to be hers. Now she didn't even feel comfortable seeking shelter on the porch.

Cece stared out at the front yard, the driveway, and down the lane. Lightning cracked nearby, followed by rolls of thunder seconds later. All around her, the wind blustered and moaned, bending treetops to its will. She couldn't stand outside in this deluge, but it'd be too risky trying to get home in the high winds. Tornadoes were never completely outside the realm of possibility.

She had the protection of the porch and no other options.

For a little while, she huddled away from the windows and front door to remain unseen. Still, curiosity nibbled at her wet feet, making her peek through the window that looked into the living room.

Who was in her cottage?

Whoever they were, she resented them on principle.

They'd taken her dream, and there was no way they'd be the kind of loving steward she would have been.

People nowadays bought historical homes only to gut them and redo them in farmhouse gray or boring beige. They wouldn't put the time and energy into reclaiming this house's intended charm and nuance. They wouldn't travel far and wide to antique malls and thrift shops to find the perfect art nouveau lamp or Stickley furniture.

Whoever they were, she hoped she never had to meet them or look them in the eye.

As she moved away from the window to find a better hiding place, the front door opened.

Chapter 2

H ello?" Dustin Long asked the empty doorway.

He swore someone was just standing there. He'd had a long day, but he wasn't exhausted to the point of delusion.

Yet.

Dustin stepped out onto the porch. "Hello?" he repeated.

His pit-lab mix, Bruce, took this greeting as the opportunity to be a welcome wagon of his own. Bruce bounded out onto the porch with a bark, his nub wagging in eager anticipation of a visitor.

The problem was, Bruce appeared to many to be a man-eater. He looked more pitty than Labby, and he was no longer a puppy. Most people were convinced he'd swallow them whole.

He wouldn't, of course. He was named for the star animatronic in *Jaws*, but Bruce was a lover, not a fighter, made for snuggles, snacks, and snoozing.

Bruce did his excited tippy taps across the porch until he spotted his new friend. He bounded for a woman, petite in stature and wearing bright green shorts and a T-shirt with multicolored polka dots. She crowded into one corner of the porch, looking for all the world like she wanted to climb the railing and jump off to run for her life.

"Bruce!" Dustin called. "Brucey! He's friendly, I promise. I'm sorry." Dustin grabbed his dog's collar and eased him away from the woman. "Chill, dude. Not everyone wants to be pounced on. Sorry," he said again.

"It's...it's okay," she managed, arms wrapped around herself.

"You sure? He can be a lot, but he's not mean. Overly friendly. Apologize to the nice lady."

The woman took a deep breath, dropping her arms to her sides. "I'm fine. He surprised me is all."

Dustin chuckled. He and Bruce had that effect on people.

Both big and burly, they tended to present in such a way that people took one look and thought *rough-and-tumble trouble*. Appearances served them well when it came to anyone who meant them ill, but being a contractor and businessman, Dustin had learned he had to quickly smooth out the edges if he wanted to be successful or even acceptable to most people.

This skill also served him well with terrified women who'd wandered up on his porch.

"May I help you with something?" he offered. "Are you lost? Selling solar panels?"

"What?" She looked genuinely confused.

Genuinely confused and very pretty.

Petite, but fit, big brown eyes, fair skin, and curly blonde hair...that was mostly wet.

"You're wet," he blurted.

"Yeah." She gestured vaguely toward the torrential downpour. "It's raining."

Dustin shook off the spell. Beautiful women had a way of making him stupid. He looked around the porch for clues about this contextless meeting. "Then you got caught out in the rain?"

"Yes," she answered quickly. Almost too quickly. "I was out for a walk, and it started to storm, so I ran up on your porch to get out of the rain." She nodded.

The private road was awfully long for someone to choose to run up it to escape the rain, but who was he to judge?

"Okay, um, I have some towels." He went back inside, leading the way.

She remained rooted to the spot.

"Or I can bring you something." Why would she come into a stranger's house? This was the twenty-first century. She had no reason to trust a stranger, especially not a big, scary stranger with a big, scary dog.

"Hang on." He ran into the house, taking Bruce with him.

"No, that's okay," she called after him. "I just needed a little shelter from the storm. I didn't mean to bother you."

"You're not." He found the towels he'd thrown in his duffel. "That storm came out of nowhere. No wonder you got caught out in it."

He left Bruce inside and closed the front door behind him as he walked back out onto the porch and handed her a towel.

"Thank you. I'm really sorry about this," she said.

"It's okay. Can't help the weather. I'm Dustin."

"I'm Cece." She patted her face dry and rubbed at her arms. "We're sort of neighbors, I guess. I live a few blocks away. Country blocks."

He laughed. "Important distinction."

"Are you from the city?"

A crack of lightning struck, and inside, the lights flickered. Concern furrowed Cece's brow.

"Listen," he tried. "I know you don't know me, but I don't think it's a good idea for us to be out here with this storm."

She glanced around at the whipping wind and pouring rain.

"You're welcome to wait just inside the door if you feel safer. I can, I don't know, lock myself in a bedroom, but we can't just stand out here."

Cece shook her head. "No, I know. I'm the one who wandered up on your porch, so you don't need to lock yourself in a room, but I did just drop a pin on my location so my sisters know where I am. Just so you know."

He nodded and opened the front door to let her in. "Noted." He went through the dining room and into the kitchen, and she followed.

Another crack of lightning split the sky, and this time, the lights flickered and went out.

Even though it was still technically daytime, the house grew as dark as the stormy skies.

"Uh-oh." Dustin racked his brain. "I have a battery-operated lantern for work. Hang on." He went out to the back porch, where he'd dropped a lot of his work gear that morning. A small toolbox, tarps, buckets, various lighting equipment, including the cordless kind for when you had to cut the power for safety. He dug around in his pile of supplies until he found a couple of lantern-style lights. "Got 'em," he called.

He got back to the kitchen to find Cece standing by the counter, arms crossed protectively.

Bruce had begun barking in the nearest bedroom.

"Here we go." Dustin turned on the lanterns. "Okay if I let Bruce out?"

"Of course. Yeah, sorry. I'm just—"

"Don't apologize. It's been a weird afternoon. Hang on, buddy," he shouted to Bruce before letting him out.

Bruce trotted into the kitchen, a little calmer now, and nudged Cece with his nose.

She uncrossed her arms long enough to pet him and give him a scratch behind one of his floppy ears.

Bruce leaned into her touch shamelessly.

"I think he likes you."

She gave him one more pat. "He's sweet."

Not a compliment Bruce heard often, but she was correct.

Another crack of lightning, and this time, the roll of thunder shook the house.

Two lines etched between Cece's brows.

Dustin found he wanted to comfort her in some way. "It'll be okay. Probably pass over us pretty soon. Here, you want to sit?" He motioned toward the folding table and chairs he'd set up in the little dining area of the kitchen.

"Might as well." She eased over to a seat and hung the towel over the back.

"I don't have any real food, but I've got some snacks and a thermos of coffee."

"Coffee would be nice."

"Coffee it is." He found the sleeve of paper cups he'd stuck in a cabinet and poured two cups full of the coffee he'd brought with him that morning.

He always kept a Stanley thermos with him. True to its

reputation, the coffee he'd made at the hotel this morning was still steaming when he poured it.

"Here you go." He slid into the chair across from Cece.

"So...you bought this place."

Her words were more statement than question, and they carried a heaviness that seemed out of place in a casual conversation.

"I did. Closed on it yesterday. Hence the temporary furnishings and paper cups." He smiled to lighten the mood.

"I didn't think anyone would want it. It was on the market forever."

That was exactly why he'd wanted it.

This little cabin was not hot on the market, so no high demand or bidding war. He'd used almost all his savings but had paid a very reasonable price for what he'd gotten in return, and the rest he could fix up with sweat equity.

"Yeah? Well, it is a bit of a fixer-upper, but I'm up for it."

Dustin was more than up for the challenge. This was his profession, after all. Other people had paid him to do remodels for years, and now he could finally do one for himself.

Cece took a small sip of her coffee. "You'll have your work cut out for you."

"True, but I had this place thoroughly inspected, and the bones are good. Plumbing needs a little work, but not as much as you might think. These old houses were built better. They hold up."

"I'm aware." She placed the cup down on the table and laced her fingers around it. "What are your plans?"

"I'll take care of the wiring that needs updating. See

if I need an electrician, which I doubt. Take care of the plumbing and then the floors. First, though, I'll dig into the details of what needs work and see how much to budget for the place to get something out of it."

Cece sat up a little straighter. "What do you mean, 'get something out of it'?"

"Profit." He hadn't bought the house to live in. This was an investment intended to produce a good return. "See what kind of profit I can make on the house."

"You—you're going to flip it?"

"That's the plan." All he needed was two hundred thousand, free and clear, and he'd be able to buy into his half of a new construction business in Florida.

Her eyes darkened as she shook her head and pulled her arms off the table. "Why would you do that?"

Why did he suddenly feel like he was being interrogated? She'd gone from curious stranger to local detective in a minute flat.

He sat back, completely baffled. "Why? Because that's what people do with investment properties."

The scowl deepened, and she looked like an angry doll with all the golden curls framing her face. "But this house has been here since the 1920s."

"Obviously."

Her mouth fell open again before she clamped it shut, her jaw clenched. "It's important," she said between her teeth.

"I'm sorry. Is this— What am I missing here? Did this house belong to your family or something?"

"No." She immediately grabbed the coffee and began drinking it again.

"Then why do you care?"

"Because it's..." She closed her mouth, opened it, and closed it again. The lines between her eyebrows lessened, and she tucked a stray curl behind her ear with way too much force. "This is not the kind of house a flipper should have."

Now he was intrigued. "Oh really?"

She nodded, indignant. "I can see it now. You'll have builder beige and shiplap everywhere."

"I'm not going to use shiplap."

"But you will have beige or greige walls in every room and, I don't know, probably farmhouse-style ceiling fans and those god-awful barn doors."

He shrugged.

She looked appalled. "You can't," she basically pleaded.

He had to chuckle because this whole conversation confused him. "Why are you so offended? Are you with the historical registry or something?" More importantly, why did he care? He'd always gone about his business with no interest in anyone's opinion except the paying customer's.

"Historical registry? No, I just...I'm a concerned citizen. And neighbor." She added the last part with a nod, like that gave her viewpoint merit.

"You want some Oreos?" he asked, getting up to find his cooler.

"What?" She blinked.

Good, now she was confused too. He stepped out on the back porch again and grabbed the new pack from the cooler. They were best served cold.

"I figured if I'm getting scolded, I might as well have a snack. You want some?"

Cece dipped her chin as he put the pack of cookies on the table and opened them. "I'm not scolding you."

"You aren't? Kind of feels like it. But I'm grown; I can take it. Goodness knows I've gotten a lot worse. Please, continue." He grabbed two Oreos and popped one in his mouth, motioning that the floor was hers.

Cece took a deep breath and looked out the window by the table. She sat silently for a moment, as if gathering herself. "I'm sorry," she said eventually.

"It's okay, really. I was kind of enjoying your speech." Dustin popped the second cookie in his mouth.

She hid her smile at his comment, or maybe at his mouth full of cookie, and reached for an Oreo.

"They're really good with coffee." He grabbed another.

"I just . . . I have a lot of feelings about this house," she said, as if that weren't already obvious. "Since I live near here, I walk by a lot and . . . I've always admired it. I guess I want to make sure someone treats the house properly. I care."

"I promise I'm going to do my best, if that helps?"

She nodded and nibbled at her cookie.

"Have you always lived around here?" he asked. "I'm guessing so, since you're so passionate."

"Born and raised. My sisters and I own the Orchard Inn just down the road and around the bend. What about you? Where are you from?"

Wasn't that the million-dollar question?

The story of his childhood didn't make for a fun ice-breaker. That topic wasn't brought up in small talk, or really any of his talks.

Dustin kept it simple and vague. "I was born near here, actually."

Her eyes brightened as she tried to place him. She wouldn't be successful.

"But I wasn't raised here. I moved a few times and mostly grew up in Michigan." Nowhere near the full story, but enough to satisfy most people. "Cold, long-wintered Michigan. Decided I want to be somewhere a lot warmer, so I came here for a bit."

"We're definitely warmer than Michigan." She smiled.

Her smile alone was warmer than anything in Michigan.

Dustin had known Cece for less than twenty minutes, and she'd already gone through more emotions than he normally experienced in a week. Embarrassed, suspicious, friendly, frustrated, and now back to friendly. Each emotion was so big and fully expressed.

When she smiled, her entire face changed. A dimple graced each cheek, her eyes somehow grew lighter and more golden. When she got mad, her scowl was fierce, crinkling her eyes and forehead. She was one of those people who didn't have an angel and devil on each shoulder. They lived within her, and she wore their expressions on her face.

"We hardly ever get snow," she continued. "I think once when I was little and again when I was a teenager, but it wasn't even an inch. We get storms." She indicated the weather outside, where the thunder was down to a rumble, gaining distance every minute.

"That's the vibe I'm going for." Even farther south though, where cold weather was a rarity and snow unheard of.

"So." She grabbed another Oreo and took a sip of coffee. "If you aren't going to do shiplap and beige for decor, what are you planning to do?"

Dustin grabbed another cookie too, and sat up a little straighter, like he was at a job interview. In his defense, that was the mood she created.

"Other than general repairs to the flooring and bringing certain things up to code, I'm thinking I'll update the kitchen and bath. If the structure can take it, I thought about plumbing a half bath for the upstairs bedroom, but I don't know. Might not want to put that much money into it."

"Yeah, you wouldn't want to put too much money into this place," she snarked. "What kind of updates to the kitchen and bath?"

She was back on the offensive. Something about updating the house set her off, but the house needed to be brought into this decade.

"Modern appliances, modernized bathroom," he explained. "Maybe a walk-in shower since—"

"A walk-in shower?" She all but came up out of her chair. "You can't put a walk-in shower in a Craftsman home. There's a claw-foot tub in there now, and no, it's not in great shape, but you could get another one to replace the original."

"Who takes baths anymore?" he argued. "People want showers. Walk-in showers with bench seats all in tile. And how do you know what kind of tub is in there?"

"Oh my gosh!" Cece raised her voice, and Bruce looked at him like *he'd* done something wrong.

"You're going to tile that bathroom in all gray and white, aren't you?" She angrily finished off her cookie. "There won't be an ounce of warmth left in this place. All the wood framing and accents, gone. Do you know how much original red pine is in here? You'll have it all mismatched with shiny silver appliances. Or worse yet, you're going to pull it out. Ashy gray laminate floors, chrome and white all over, and it will look like every other house that was built within the last ten years."

"I'm not going to tear out the hardwood floors. I'm not crazy."

"But you're not going to take the time to research all this house needs to return it to its former glory. You don't care enough. Not like you should."

He blinked.

"Because I know that these floors are special. It cost the original designer and builder a lot of money, especially around here, to have pine floors and molding. They got the lumber from a local pine forest and put it down themselves. This was a custom build, and you should know things like that. I know that the appliances should remain white, even though that's not popular now. At worst, maybe brushed nickel so they blend with the woodwork. And no walls should be gray or anything too far into the cool palette. Creams, candlelight ivory, maybe the lightest sage green in a bedroom. Nothing that takes away from the natural elements of the framework, wood accents, and open gables. A place like this should feel lived-in, warm and welcoming."

Something in her tone struck his heart. She *loved* this house.

He'd been growing more and more annoyed at her prodding and know-it-all attitude and was just about to tell her to mind her own business, but now he understood. He recognized the ache in her voice. A longing so deep that it'd become a vision. Cece wanted to call this place her own.

How had he not realized until now? "You wanted to buy this place."

Cece recoiled. "No I didn't," she answered way too fast.

His chest warmed as he studied her. Her arms crossed,

refusing to meet his gaze. She was a terrible liar. "You wanted this to be your home."

It wasn't a question because he knew the truth.

Her gaze met his, and he saw how badly she wanted to hide her feelings from him. He knew that look. He wore it every time people asked him about his parents, or his childhood, or his past. The truth wasn't one he wanted to share. He wanted to protect himself from what they might see and think.

"Why didn't you tell me straightaway?" he asked gently. "I wouldn't have gone on and on about my plans. I'm sorry I didn't know."

"Do not pity me." She bristled. "It's patronizing."

"Sorry, I wasn't—"

"You don't have to apologize; I'm just saying. I don't like it when people try to be all sympathetic and like, *oh, you poor thing.* You said you were a grown man and you could take it? Well, so am I. Not a man but..." She pushed her hair back again, flustered. "I'm a grown woman, I mean."

"Okay, but for the record, I don't pity you. I bought this house fair and square, and I won't apologize for that, but I wouldn't have gushed about it if I'd known you were interested."

"Well, that's polite of you, but still. I'm worried you don't know what you're doing when it comes to restoration of this particular kind of house, and that bothers me. That's all."

"I've been doing remodels for almost ten years."

"On Craftsman bungalows that are a hundred years old?"

"No, but—"

"There is a huge difference. Homes like this are part of

a huge architectural revival, and the fact that you can't see that tells me everything I need to know." She stood like she was leaving.

Reviving old homes wasn't the center of his wheel-house. He wanted to do a remodel. What was wrong with a plain old remodel?

Bruce barked at Dustin as if urging him to do something as Cece walked toward the front door.

"You can't just leave like this. We're in the middle of a conversation, and it's still storming."

"Barely. It's let up. I'll be fine."

"Wow."

"What?"

"You're just… You're a lot."

"I know."

"Like the weather today. All nice, and you think, *oh it's going to be a nice, pretty day*, and then boom, black skies and torrential winds. You come into my house, bluster at me for the last half hour or so, and now you're going to leave. You'd rather walk out in that rain than listen to my side when I listened to yours."

"I've heard your side, thank you very much." She marched toward the front door.

"You're welcome." He followed, and Bruce barked at both of them. "You're going to get soaking wet again if you walk home."

"I'll be fine."

"You want to go, go, but I think this is a dumb idea."

She cocked her head before marching toward the door. "Then it's a good thing me and my dumb self are leaving." She yanked open the door and stomped across the porch and down the stairs.

Bruce followed her out and stopped at the edge of the porch.

"I didn't call you dumb!" Dustin yelled after her. "But *this* is dumb."

He slammed the door closed, and immediately, his soul filled with concern.

The wind wasn't completely gone, and though the lightning seemed to be done, the storm hadn't totally died down. Plus, Bruce was still out on the porch.

Dustin opened the front door and watched Cece tromp through the rain, imagining he could see steam rising off her hot head.

"You've got to be kidding me," he grumbled, and stepped off the porch, Bruce right beside him.

He stayed half a football field length's back, but he followed her down the lane and turned where she went through some trees.

"Can you believe she's got us out here?" he asked Bruce.

For his part, Bruce looked delighted to be tromping through puddles.

Cece walked away with all the righteous anger of a woman furious about how he'd paint the walls of a house she didn't own.

He wanted to remain annoyed and angry at her, but she was just so righteous and indignant, like she was president of some imaginary HOA that had a right to tell him what to do with his own property.

She turned again, into the thickest part of the woods. Dustin followed where he thought she'd turned, trying to keep one eye on Bruce—habitual critter chaser—and one eye on Cece. She turned again, almost like she knew he was back there and she was deliberately trying to lose him.

He thought he caught a glimpse of her to his left, and he followed. After another minute of walking, he realized he wasn't following Cece in the name of her safety. He was wandering around in the rain.

He glanced down at Bruce, tongue out and tail wagging.

"What are we doing out here?"

Bruce wagged his tail faster.

"I don't think we need to worry about her, boy. We need to worry about finding our way back. C'mon."

Dustin turned, tracing his steps back to the road.

Cece might've had a point about his lack of experience with a century-old house. But he wasn't trying to adhere to some revival of this home's original state. Even if he decided to go that route, he could figure it out. He had the internet, his experience, and his gut.

"I could figure it out," he told Bruce as if trying to convince them both.

Bruce glanced up at him like he wasn't so sure.

"Thanks for the vote of confidence, buddy." Dustin found the road, and they made their way back to the cabin, his shirt soaked from the rain still dripping off the trees.

One thing was certain, if he ran into a situation where he wanted some input or the opinion of someone who knew the house, he sure couldn't ask her.

Oh, she would just love it if he went to her, wanting any kind of feedback or even recommendations for local vendors. And did he know anyone else in the area to ask?

No.

But he could find someone. Go to the hardware store

and strike up a conversation with some old guys. He'd done it before. Sure, none of them would be pretty like Cece, or even as knowledgeable when it came to all that historical hoo-ha, but they wouldn't give him nearly as much grief either.

Or sit there and eat Oreos with him, polishing off half a row between them without even trying. They wouldn't smile and laugh one minute, then look ready to throttle him a moment later.

"Dang it," he said as he stepped up on the porch.

He wasn't sure if he wanted to see her first thing tomorrow or never again.

Chapter 3

The rain all but sizzled on her skin as she slipped down the narrow trail, between trees.

The absolute nerve of that man. Dustin.

The gall.

Cece let out a little growl under her breath. She was heated, all right. Spitfire mad, as her momma would say.

He was going to ruin her cottage. Ruin it, then sell it, for some price she could never afford, and even if she could, she wouldn't want it after he was done because it'd be a shell of what it should be.

Cece paused and turned to glare at the path behind her.

No one was there, but she felt like glaring all the same. He'd followed her down the lane, probably out of guilt, but then he'd even gone into the forest after her. Maybe he'd thought she couldn't be trusted to make it home in a storm. She ground her teeth at the notion.

But no, more than likely he was trying to chase her down to tell her she was being mighty possessive about a home she didn't own.

If she were a millionaire, she'd buy the cottage from Dustin right now. That was all he cared about anyway.

Money. She'd buy it for whatever top dollar he was hoping to get after the remodel, and then still have plenty of money left over to renovate the house properly. She'd roll up with a big, fat checkbook and whip out one of those fancy pens, say something like *name your price, mister!* Then she'd sign with a flourish and leave dramatically, probably donning sunglasses or sweeping a stole or cape, though she owned neither.

Cece grumbled. But she wasn't a millionaire, and the only thing she had from that entire scenario was sunglasses.

The sky dripped water on her, but the worst of the storm had passed. The storm outside anyway. The one inside her was gaining momentum.

Sure, for a moment, the afternoon wasn't terrible. They'd laughed, shared a few get-to-know-me tidbits. But then. Then the truth had come out.

Dustin had no clue how to refurbish that house, and regardless, he would finish the job, sell off what should've been her home, and then head off to wherever. After destroying her dream.

Cece finally reached the edge of Orchard Inn's property, soaking wet again, and made her way toward the house. Her real home. Maybe the only home she'd ever have. She certainly wasn't going to get married, get a house, and live under the thumb of some man.

Not that Sawyer or Jude were overlords, but some men were, even more so when it came to her. Men and women both acted differently toward her. Most folks around Fredericksburg knew about her struggles growing up. They could tell the gait of her walk wasn't quite "normal," and they knew the story of her emergency birth.

As a result, people always worried over her. They'd

babied her even when she was no longer a baby, and even now, people infantilized her when it came to hard work or doing much of anything alone.

She hated it.

They'd fuss and fret if she did anything remotely strenuous, and not unlike her sisters, they'd freak out about her hiking alone or, God forbid, getting on a ladder.

Ridiculous and so condescending, no matter how well-intentioned.

Nowadays, her frustration when those around her made a fuss had mostly tempered into a stony resolve, but back in the day, and sometimes even now, she lost her cool. She summed it up as most people not knowing any better, and her sisters and future brothers-in-law had improved immensely in the last year or so, but even they backslid.

At the top of the last rolling hill, closest to the house, Cece laid eyes on the inn.

This would likely be her home forever, and that was okay.

She'd never longed to move far away, like Aurora. Cece had only wanted a little something of her own. Some independence. The house on Hollyhock had come to represent that, but she'd find a way without it.

Orchard Inn could still offer an oasis. Maybe she'd even build a place at the edge of the property. The plan would take work and a lot of research, but it wouldn't be altogether terrible. Besides, Orchard Inn had been there for her, and her sisters, in more ways than one. A home as they grew up, the center of so many childhood memories, then a business when they got the wild idea to open an inn, and now it'd be the site of Beth's wedding.

Why would she ever want to leave?

"No!" The word escaped Cece's chest like she'd been punched in the gut. "Beth! Aurora!" She hurried toward the back of the inn, crying out for her sisters.

The beautiful red oak that sat nearest the house had split almost in two, half of it laid across the back quarter of the inn's roof. Their living quarters were back there. Her sisters would've been downstairs during the storm.

"Beth!" she shouted again.

"Cece?" Aurora's voice came from beyond the back entrance. "Cece, where were you? We're over here."

Aurora and Beth huddled together with Sawyer under a big umbrella, steps away from the inn.

Cece ran to them, unshed tears burning her eyes. "Are you okay? What happened?"

"We're fine." Beth hugged her. "All things considered."

Sawyer stepped away, a phone pressed to his ear, giving Cece a reassuring smile.

"I think fear took a few years off our lives, but otherwise, we're okay." Aurora pulled her in to join them under the umbrella.

"What happened?" Cece asked again.

"We think it was the wind. It was a dry summer, and then all that rain at once and the wind. The oak split, and we've got water in those guest rooms." She pointed to the back corner of the inn.

"What about the guests?"

"They were all out for the day." Beth checked the screen of her phone. "Sawyer is calling them now. I've got to call our insurance company and some of our connections in town and see if any of the other hotels have availability so we can move our guests."

"What can I do?" Cece asked.

"Stay here with Beth. I'm going to find another umbrella." Aurora headed toward her car.

Guilt crept into Cece's bones. She should've been here when this happened. Not that she could've done anything to prevent it, but still.

"When did this happen? Where—"

"We were standing in the kitchen, about ten, fifteen minutes ago, talking about the wedding and your cottage, worrying about you being out in this storm, and suddenly, crack! Boom! We heard this huge crash outside."

"I'm so sorry." Cece shook her head, the tears forming fully now, one getting loose and sliding down her cheek. "I shouldn't have run off."

"No, no." Beth squeezed her. "Honey. Stop. You were upset, and you're safe. We're all okay, that's all that matters."

Aurora returned with an umbrella. "I need to call Sloane, check on the restaurant and see if she can cover for me while we deal with things here."

"Definitely. Cece and I will start making calls."

Cece joined her sister and future brother-in-law in their calling efforts, and they spent the next hour on their phones, pacing the yard, dealing with the triage of storm damage.

As they called, waited on hold forever, and eventually got through to a claims manager, every storm cloud in the sky blew away. The late afternoon sun cast a golden glow across the destruction.

Jude arrived as they were wrapping up their calls, peeling into the inn's parking on two wheels. He jumped out of his truck, and Cece wondered if he'd remembered to even put it in park.

"Are you okay?" he yelled as he ran up. "Are you all okay?"

"We're okay. How long have you been worried? You should've called."

"A tree fell across the road about a mile up, and I had to help some folks cut it up and get it out of the road. I've been trying to call for the last hour, but my service is garbage. Oh my god, I started thinking the worst, and then I get here and I see that tree and—"

"Breathe," Aurora told him, taking his hand.

"I guess the network is all messed up because of the storm," he continued. "I was starting to freak out when I couldn't get through." He wrapped his arms around Aurora.

Cece cleared her throat, glancing away from the concern and support both Jude and Sawyer showed for her sisters.

Jude let go of Aurora a little. "You were all inside when this happened?"

"All of us but Cece," Beth answered. "Scared us, and goodness knows the extent of the damages, but we're okay."

"Where were you?" Jude asked Cece.

"I'd gone for a walk?" She sounded ridiculous saying it out loud.

"You were *outside* in this storm?"

"Not exactly."

All four of them looked at her.

"I was on someone's porch."

"Whose porch?" Sawyer asked.

"Did you get in touch with any places that can put up our guests for the next few days?" Cece deliberately ignored his question. "The Grove has three rooms and Blanchard's has four," she kept talking. "That should cover us, since we had a couple of rooms check out today. I also started calling our check-ins for next week to let them know we'll be closed, but I still have several left on the list."

"That's a great start. I'll finish off the list." Beth nodded, deep in thought as she began to pace again. "The insurance company is sending someone out today, but it may be their second stop. Sounds like they've gotten a lot of calls. In the meantime, they said we could call a tree company, and that if we have a contractor, to let them know."

"We can call Lyle," Cece suggested.

"Good idea."

Aurora held up her phone. "I just got a text from the power company. Power won't be restored until tomorrow, at the earliest."

"We better cut the breakers to that part of the house until we can assess the damage," Sawyer said.

"Definitely," Jude agreed. "I'll go with you."

"I'll show you upstairs. It's a mess."

Once they were both gone, and Aurora was done texting on her phone, both of her sisters looked at Cece.

"Don't think we forgot about you being on someone's porch, sis." Aurora arched an eyebrow.

"Did you make it all the way to your cottage?" Beth asked.

"*The* cottage," Cece corrected. "It isn't mine anymore. I guess it never was, but yes. I made it there right as the sky opened up."

"You had to be freaking out. That wind got up to like fifty miles per hour at one point."

"I was inside by then."

Both of her sisters' mouths fell open.

"Inside?" Aurora asked. "Did you break in?"

"No, I did not break in." Cece shoved her arm. "Someone was there. The buyer. He's already moved in. Kind of."

"What do you mean 'kind of'?" Beth asked.

"He?" Aurora chimed in.

"The house needs a lot of work, so that will come first, and then he'll turn around and sell it?"

"*What?*" they said in unison.

"No, that's supposed to be your cottage," Aurora insisted.

"I know, I know. But there's no way I'll ever be able to afford it now."

"Well, I despise this guy on your behalf." She crossed her arms.

"You do not despise him." Beth forcefully uncrossed Aurora's arms.

"Well, I don't like him. He took Cece's place."

"Don't worry, I let my feelings be known about that very fact." Cece frowned. "Pretty sure he hates me now."

"Good." Aurora huffed.

Beth sighed as she tied her long hair back with a ponytail holder she had stashed who knows where. "No, not good. What did you say?"

"I just told him he had no clue how to remodel that house."

"You got on your soapbox, didn't you?" Beth shook her head as Aurora snickered.

"No. I didn't exactly get on my soapbox." Except that was exactly what she'd done.

This time, Beth crossed her arms, clearly not buying Cece's claim. "I know what that house means to you. I imagine there was some level of soapbox involved. You are a Shipley, after all, but you can't be mad at him for buying that place. He's going to be our neighbor..."

"Didn't you hear what she said?" Aurora came to her defense. "He isn't going to be our neighbor. He'll be gone as soon as the place is fixed up."

Beth shook her head. "So? That's his right. I know the dream was for Cece to have the house, but we can't hold a grudge because we don't get what we want."

Beth wasn't wrong on any of her points. She rarely was.

Dustin had been nice to her, had allowed her to come in, had even made it comfortable. Hospitable. And in return, she'd given him marching orders about how the bungalow *he owned* should be refurbished.

But...Cece sighed. But it was only because she cared so much. When she cared, she got a little emotional.

Beth moved closer, rubbing Cece's arm, her gaze deep with understanding.

Cece recognized that look. Beth wore it when she had valid and very good points, and she knew it.

"Do you think maybe you should apologize?"

Cece let her head fall back. "I knew you were going to say that."

"I'm only asking. You know what you said, not me. Was the soapbox high enough to warrant an olive branch?"

She fought the grumble in the back of her throat. "I mean, it was pretty high."

"Neighbors are supposed to help one another, not fuss. We've got enough going on here with the inn a wreck, and we'll lose business over the next month or two. The last thing we need is grief with a new neighbor, no matter how temporary."

"Fine. I know. I was out of line. I just...I was still in shock and mourning about losing the place, and I don't know. I didn't expect to have to ever face the owner."

She intentionally left out the part about Dustin being exceedingly handsome, tall, seemingly capable, even if he didn't know historic home refurbs, and probably single.

Chapter 4

We can't wait two weeks for someone to become available." Beth folded her arms and laid her head on the kitchen table.

Cece and Sawyer had spent the entire night and the next morning calling contractors while Beth and Aurora dealt with moving guests to other accommodations.

Turned out, Lyle, their mother's boyfriend, was out of town working on a project. He gave them several names of reputable contractors in town, all of whom were already booked a week out, or more, because of the storm.

The insurance adjuster had come and gone. Someone had come out to professionally tarp off the roof, and he'd approved them for repairs up to a limit that ought to more than cover all costs, but it didn't do much good when they had no one to do said repairs.

Cece looked at Sawyer. "You know everyone in town. Isn't there someone else we could call?"

"You think I'd still have a half-built house if I had the inside track on a bunch of contractors?"

Beth tensed.

"Sorry, I know it's a sore subject, but it's true." Sawyer

placed a hand on Beth's back. "We'll find someone to work on the inn."

"We need to start now."

"I know."

"And our wedding. It's only two months away. Less, if you don't count this week."

For the first time in weeks, Beth showed something other than absolute calm and fortitude when it came to her wedding date. The vulnerability twisted Cece's heart.

"Try not to worry about the wedding right now," Sawyer urged her. "I'd marry you in the middle of a field if we needed to."

Beth sat up, the lack of sleep showing in the smudges beneath her eyes. "I don't want to get married in the middle of a field. I want to get married here, at Orchard Inn."

With Beth's words about neighborly support and apologies ringing in her ears, Cece thought about Dustin. He was a contractor. Guaranteed no one had booked him up yet because no one in town even knew he existed, except Cece.

Cece held back a grumble of discontent. The very last thing she wanted to do was go back to Dustin and not only apologize but ask him for help.

He would just love that, and she was not built for groveling. Bullish pride? Sure. Blind determination? All day. Going back to someone who'd wronged her with hat in hand, saying how wrong she was, even though she wasn't wrong about everything, and would he please oh please, pretty please, help them?

No thank you.

"Maybe we should postpone the wedding," Beth wondered aloud.

Sawyer pulled one of her hands to his lips and kissed the back of it. "We are not going to postpone. We'll figure something out. I promise."

With the biggest internal groan of her life, Cece made her decision. "I might…I might know someone who can help."

"Really?" Beth's face lit up.

"*Maybe*. Can help doesn't mean he will help. It's a long shot, but I can see if he's available and willing. I can guarantee he'll charge full price." And then some.

"Who?" Aurora cocked an eyebrow.

"The guy who bought my cottage."

Aurora shifted in her seat and leaned forward. "Wait, that guy is a contractor?"

Sawyer looked back and forth between them. "Who and what are you talking about?"

"When Cece went for a walk yesterday right before the storm, she got stuck out in the worst of it, and this *guy* let her stay there until the storm was over."

Sawyer shook his head. "Who did what now?"

"Do you want me to see if he's available for contract work or not?"

"Yes," Aurora answered, right as Sawyer said no.

"We don't know if he's reputable or anything about him," he argued. "Trust me, all contractors aren't good contractors. I've been down this road before."

Beth placed her hand on his arm. "I know, but we can ask to see his credentials and proof of his work. Maybe talk to former clients or something, anything. But right now, we need to book him before someone else scoops him up. If he says yes, then you can ask all the questions and do all the investigative work you like, okay?"

Sawyer scowled, but they all knew he would give in. When it came to Beth, Sawyer rarely—if ever—said no.

Beth turned to Cece. "See if your guy can do it."

"Okay, first and foremost, he is not *my* guy." Cece slowly slid out of her chair. "But I will see what I can do." She did not want to do this, but Beth would do it for her. Beth *had* done it for her. Her big sister had made sacrifice after sacrifice to take care of her and Aurora and to make this inn the kind of place that could support them all, financially and emotionally, and she'd continue to do so, for as long as she lived.

The least Cece could do was swallow her stupid pride and go apologize to the man who bought her home and didn't have the good sense to know it should have been hers.

"I can give you a lift out there." Sawyer rose to his feet.

"Oh no, mister." Beth waved him back down. "You're not fooling anyone. You'll scare him off before we can even get a maybe. We're going to stay put."

Cece smiled as she shook her head. "I'll be fine. I can walk." While other people's fretting rankled, Sawyer's big brother habits were different. Endearing.

He didn't fuss over her because he thought she was less than in any way; he fussed over her because he didn't know any other way to act. Sawyer big-brothered everyone, but he was particularly protective over her.

And he was as hotheaded and stubborn as Cece, so they understood each other.

Sawyer grumbled his displeasure but nodded.

Cece put on a different pair of walking shoes, as her favorites were still damp from yesterday, and headed out the back, retracing her steps.

The tree removal service had already begun working, and the sound of chainsaws and a giant wood chipper drowned out any birds or beautiful nature noises that might make her walk a little more bearable.

She reached the pasture and slowed her steps.

The cows were out, grazing and staring at her as she passed. In the distance, she could barely make out some chickens kicking up a fuss. After dodging a few puddles and muddy spots, she reached the road and neared Hollyhock Lane.

Perhaps she should've rehearsed what she was going to say.

"Hey, sorry about telling you how to run your business? Do forgive me for being a nosy know-it-all, who happens to be right. Apologies you aren't more deserving of this humble abode."

"No." She giggled to herself. "That probably won't work."

Maybe just, "I'm sorry. For everything." Keep it simple and unspecific.

"Yeah." She nodded to herself. "Sorry for what? Take your pick."

At least she'd get to see the dog again. Bruce? He was sweet.

Cece startled as she realized she'd reached the front porch. "Get this over with," she mumbled, then remembered she had to convince this man to be their contractor. She needed him. A lot was riding on her ability to be charming and convincingly pleading.

"We might be screwed." She climbed the stairs and knocked on the front door.

Inside, Bruce barked, and she could hear him tap dancing excitedly.

Dustin opened the door, barely managing to hold him back. "Hey." He blinked with eyes wide. "I...huh." He made the noise of confusion to himself, but Cece heard it anyway. "I have to say, I did not expect to see you again."

She cringed. "Yeah...I know." She hadn't expected to be here either. Maybe this would be easier if she just spat it out quickly.

"I'm glad," he said. "To see you again, I mean."

His words pulled her up short. She blinked back at him. "You are?"

Bruce calmed down enough to sniff her and then continue his tap dance around her and then around the porch.

"This might be hard to believe." Dustin opened the front door a little more. "But I'm not the sort who likes to upset someone and then have her run away, into a storm, just to flee my presence."

"I wasn't fleeing your presence."

He tilted his head. "I don't know; it looked an awful lot like fleeing."

Cece bit back a laugh. "I was...hastily leaving. And the storm was mostly over."

"Mm-hmm. Regardless, I'm glad I get to see you again. I didn't like leaving things like that."

Cece studied his expression. Even after all her lecturing, he seemed to want to smooth things over.

Dustin stepped out onto the porch, petting Bruce and calming him further.

This time, Cece studied him. Had she noticed yesterday that he was built like a brick house and handsome as hell? Of course. Had this fact made her anger a little harder to hold on to? Maybe. Would she ever give him the satisfaction of knowing any of this? Never.

"I wanted to come back today to say I'm sorry for being so..." Finish the sentence. You can do it. "So opinionated and for not being a better guest. In your home, which it is, and I know that, but I was upset because, like you realized, I had kind of wanted to buy this place, so I'm a little bitter. That is all, and I apologize."

The corners of Dustin's mouth crept up. "Did you practice that on the way over or—"

"No." Cece returned his smile. "I just rambled off whatever came into my brain right in the moment. Was it obvious?"

"A little." He shrugged one shoulder. "But apology accepted, and I am sorry for whatever I said, or did, or whatever it was that set you off and made you think you had to run."

Cece bent to pet Bruce and avoided meeting Dustin's gaze.

He didn't owe her an apology. He didn't owe her anything. Perhaps—wonder of wonders—he was just a decent guy?

"I wish you'd said something early on about what this place meant to you." Dustin wiggled the porch's banister, no doubt checking for sturdiness and stability, and leaned against it, crossing his arms.

Cece caught herself staring and glanced away.

"Not so I could take pity on you," he added quickly with a hand out in defense, "but then I would've understood why I got the inquisition."

"I think 'inquisition' is a stretch."

"Is it?" He tilted his head again.

Cece thought back on some of what she'd said. "Maybe not."

Dustin smiled a little. "Doesn't matter. All is forgiven."

As easy as that. "Good." Now for the next part.

"I'm . . . happy to hear you say that. I had some time last night to cool off and think clearly," Cece explained. "This house wasn't meant to be my future home, but another place will be, and that's okay. Right now, the priority is my current home. Orchard Inn."

His expression shifted, growing suddenly serious. Had something in her tone been that obvious?

"What happened?" he asked, no longer leaning. "Was it the storm?"

How did he guess? "One of our old oaks fell on the back corner of the inn."

He inhaled between his teeth. "Not good. Is everyone okay? You get it tarped yet?"

"Yes, we're all fine. Someone came out last night and did that."

"Good, that's good." Dustin scratched at his jaw. "I was thinking there might be a lot of damage with those winds. I hate that. Has insurance come out yet? You got a claim filed and everything?"

"An adjuster came out today, and he said we were approved to fix the damage. Problem is, we need a licensed contractor, and the ones on their list are already booked out two weeks."

She pinched her lips together and let her last sentence hang there, hoping the rest was obvious enough she wouldn't have to ask.

Several beats of silence went by, until she couldn't avoid looking him in the eyes any longer. Her gaze met his, and he stood there, not intimidating but unwavering. He wasn't going to make this easy for her.

Fine. She'd ask.

"I know this is a long shot, but is there any chance at all you'd be available for additional contract work? Like, outside of this house? Maybe two weeks of work? Maybe? Please say yes."

Dustin studied her this time, his face stony and unreadable. "You've tried other contractors?"

"A dozen, at least."

"Should I be offended I wasn't your first choice?" He smirked.

She opened her mouth to respond, but he stopped her.

"I'm kidding. I just wanted to make sure you've tried other options. I'd like to help, but I have a lot of work to do here."

Cece's heart sank into her stomach.

"I know what it's like to be in a jam though."

Then it soared with hope.

Dustin pet Bruce and was quiet for a moment. "I can take a look at the damage and see. But even if I can do it, I can't make your inn repairs my only priority," he said finally. "With this place needing such a detailed reno, I'd need to balance the two."

"Of course. We'd totally understand."

"I could start before two weeks though, unlike the other guys. Maybe even tomorrow."

If he could start right away, they were in no position to look a gift horse in the mouth. "That would be fine. Great. I'm sure my sisters will have some questions, but if you could come out tomorrow and meet with us, that would be great."

"Do you have a tree service yet?"

"They were there when I left. Said they'd finish up by lunch today."

Dustin scratched at the top of Bruce's head, deep in thought. "That's good. Okay. Then let's say I come out tomorrow before lunch, look around, and answer your questions. I can give you an estimate and see where we go from there. The inn is yours and your sister's, right?"

"Yes, both of my sisters. There's three of us," Cece answered, trying not to be a little impressed he'd remembered.

"It's best if all three of you are there then, so everyone can agree on a plan. I've learned the hard way to have all the decision makers in one spot when it's time to decide."

"We can do that."

"Okay, then." He patted Bruce's side. "I'm not one to say no to a paying gig as long as you're okay with me splitting my time."

She nodded, her hopes climbing ever higher.

"And I do feel like I owe you some consideration, seeing as how I bought your dream house and all."

"You don't…really, you don't owe me anything. I'm very aware I can be a little much when I'm all in my feelings."

"Well, I wouldn't even be considering this job if it weren't for us meeting yesterday and you being in your feelings, and you wouldn't know about me if you hadn't rolled up on my front porch, so maybe some things just happen for a reason."

She hadn't thought about their situation quite like that.

"Maybe."

"Okay, then." He slapped his hands on his jean-clad thighs and straightened. "I will come by tomorrow, and unless it's too big of a job for me, I'll take it."

She resisted clapping her hands together and merely said, "Sounds great. Thank you."

"On one condition though."

Uh-oh. Here it came. The other shoe she'd been waiting to drop.

"Okay..." She drew the word out.

"I want you to help me with something."

She scrunched her nose, trying to discern his meaning. "Help you with something," she repeated.

"Don't look so suspicious. I think you might actually be interested in this offer."

Cece side-eyed him with intent. She didn't know where he was going, but she didn't follow.

"I'd like your input, or maybe more like feedback, on some of the reno work I'm going to do to this place. Call it, I don't know, consultant work."

Her jaw fell to the porch. She managed to close her mouth only for it to fall open again. "You're joking."

"I am not, though I may come to wish I was. See, I got to thinking, you may have a valid point about preserving some of the historical relevance of this place. Not my area of expertise but I know people pay big money for historic renovations."

Wait. He wanted her help? Same as she'd come here searching for his? Except he was getting paid for his, so...

"Will this be a paying gig? Because I—"

"Obviously. I mean, I can't pay you a ton of money because I don't have it. I'm a one-man show here, but I think we can come up with an agreeable rate and then a bonus when the place sells?"

Cece stood there flabbergasted as Bruce bumped his big head against her thigh, apparently reaching his limit of one whole minute without attention.

She would have input and some level of say in what

happened to 4 Hollyhock Lane? And she would be paid for bringing this bungalow back from the dead?

"Uh-huh." She nodded, still processing. "And you'll really listen to what I have to say? No arguing."

"I can't guarantee no arguing. Remember, I had a conversation with you yesterday, so I'm pretty sure there's going to be arguing somewhere in there over the next few weeks. But yes, I will listen to your advice and take it into consideration."

Cece's gaze went to the front yard and beyond, down the lane. "You know I'll be unbearable about silly things like...like the continuity of doorknobs and switch plates."

He genuinely laughed this time, the sound so rich and round that a curious energy danced across her skin.

"That is *why* I want you involved," he explained. "As much as I hate to admit it, you were right when you said I don't know about the updates this house needs if I want them to be historically accurate. Turns out, old houses brought back to their original forms, with stealthy modernizations, go for crazy high asking prices."

Cece nodded, because she knew. She'd once found a renovated Midcentury Modern ranch she'd loved...until she'd looked at the cost.

"I'm not hiring you out of the goodness of my heart. Having a consultant makes good business sense, and we could both walk away with a nice check."

"I don't know." Cece imagined putting a nice check into her savings, all for doing something she'd dreamed of anyway. Fixing up Hollyhock was a task she'd do for free, so it should be a no-brainer to do it for pay.

But she could see it now. He'd insist on that stupid walk-in shower, she'd flip her lid, and that'd be the end of this paying gig.

"Are you sure we won't butt heads too much? I can't have you getting mad at me and quitting on Orchard Inn."

Dustin shook his head with a warm smile. "I've dealt with some guys, bigger than me, ready to kick my a—tail over a job because it rained for a week straight and we were off schedule. I'm not going to quit on you if you get mad at me. People get mad at me all the time. Comes with the job."

"I would really like to do this," she admitted with a smile. She imagined the front porch tilting beneath her feet, feeling something important shift in her life. This was something different, a new task to call her own. "You know, I don't just have ideas and knowledge. I sew and do interior design."

"Then you should do it. It doesn't need to be fully decorated or anything, but a bit of staging never hurts. You care more about this house than I've seen anyone care about anything in a while. So, I'm guessing the reason it isn't already yours is money?"

Her face fell.

"You don't have to answer because it's not my business. I'm just saying, if that's true, it sucks, but I get it. I've been there for many, many years. Sometimes, I'm still there. This isn't pity or being patronizing. I'm just saying I understand the need to have a paying gig. Maybe this way, we can help each other out."

Cece gave in and petted Bruce while still watching Dustin.

"It's a good deal," he said. "I need your skills and talent. You want a little more time with this place. You spend your time and energy here, and you could make a decent bit of cash when we're done. You add to your house savings, all while making sure I don't mess up Hollyhock. It's a win, win, win."

He was right on all counts. Plus, even if they did argue here and there, working with him wouldn't exactly be a hardship. Turned out, he was decent at communicating, a pretty good listener, and more than fair. And yes, he was big and strong and good-looking, blah, blah, blah.

The point was . . . She caught herself staring at his arms again. What was the point again?

Hollyhock.

Cece stopped staring at Dustin and stopped petting Bruce. She stuck out her hand. "I think we have ourselves a deal."

Chapter 5

Dustin climbed in his truck and put his travel mug of coffee in the cupholder.

He didn't have a ton of stuff in the house, but he'd brought the necessities with plans to hit a thrift store for temporary furniture later. Right now, he had an air mattress, a folding table with chairs, and a shower curtain for the rusty old tub.

He'd have to break down and get an easy chair soon. Maybe a sofa. At the end of a long day, he only needed three things. A shower, food, and somewhere comfortable to sit. And Bruce, but that went without saying.

He sat next to Dustin in the truck, tongue out as he panted happily.

Dustin had three different protocols when it came to Bruce and jobsites.

If a customer requested, Bruce stayed outside, in the shade, with his food and water. He got plenty of visits and pats, and in exchange, he worked as foreman and oversaw all activity on the project. If the customers were dog people, he lay nearby in the house and watched Dustin work. If a customer was anti-dog, Bruce stayed home.

This third protocol took a lot of consolation work on Dustin's part and extra dog treats.

He reached over and gave Bruce a chin scritch. Cece had assured him her sisters were dog people, and only family remained at the inn now. All guests had been relocated.

Morning dew still clung to the grass along the roadside, but Dustin wanted to get started early on the long day.

The tree removal service had finished up yesterday, and Cece had texted him as they were grinding down the stump. Today, he'd go in, assess the inside, and write up an estimate for Cece and her sisters to send to their claims adjuster.

Once Dustin was done at Orchard Inn, he'd get back to his place and work until dark.

Dual tracking these two jobs would mean long days every day, but the payday would be worth every minute. Paydays were good, especially when he'd sunk most of his savings into buying that house.

He wasn't one to gamble with his money or his security, but he knew Hollyhock was the right investment. Once he made his money off the place, he'd be in business. An actual business. For too long, he'd lived job to job, moving around to follow the paychecks. Now that he'd saved up enough that his money could make him some money, he could buy into a construction company.

Construction work was plentiful in Florida, and Richie, the former client, was already down there. Sure, the work was mostly third-party apartments and condos and no passion projects, but it paid well. All he needed was the money to get his foot in the door.

Hollyhock had good bones. Great bones. Houses now didn't come close to the craftsmanship put into old homes. If he got the right buyer for Hollyhock, they'd willingly pay top price, and he'd be set. No more worrying about the future, no more anxiety keeping him awake. He'd have a decent nest egg and financial security for the first time in his life.

He leaned over and kissed the top of Bruce's head. "We can get ourselves a real home, buddy, a yard, maybe a fenced-in one at that. Heck, maybe we'll find a little starter neighborhood where we can walk."

Bruce licked his chin, happy with this plan. "We won't know what to do with ourselves, will we? Living that high on the hog."

As they made the short drive to Orchard Inn, Dustin took in the sights around him. He'd only been here a few days with no time to look around. The stretch of barely two miles between Hollyhock and Orchard Inn was all rolling hills and grassy fields. Cece had walked to Hollyhock both times. He could only guess why she wouldn't just drive. With her, who knew? Maybe she just loved walking. Maybe she'd lost her license for driving like a bat out of hell when she got mad at someone.

He huffed a laugh to himself. "Wouldn't put it past her," he said to Bruce.

Cece.

He couldn't believe he'd asked for her help with the house. When she'd left during the storm, after their bickering the other night, he'd regretted his words immediately. She seemed like a nice girl—woman—who probably, normally, was quite pleasant with people she didn't think stole her dream home.

She was also undeniably pretty. Drenched on his front porch and mad as a wet cat, she'd still been cute. All wild curls and freckles on her scrunched little nose. In the plain light of day yesterday, he could accept what he'd denied the day of the storm. She was gorgeous.

Gorgeous and headstrong, and that was precisely why he was attracted to her.

Not an issue though. Work was work, and he could admire from a distance with never a word or flirtation uttered. He would never endanger a job with potential drama.

He was here for a short time, and her help was going to be invaluable.

Once her preaching had sunk in, he'd known she was right. While he was a pro at all there was to know about carpentry, plumbing, and some electrical work, he wasn't an expert on historically accurate renos and upfits.

Cece knew all of that crap.

Stuff, he corrected himself.

The house would be part of an architectural revival. Dustin couldn't get her words out of his head, or the way her damp blond hair had curled around her face as it dried. Her eyes warm and golden in the lantern light, right before they flamed hot with her temper.

Bruce nudged him as if to tell him to keep his mind on the road.

"Yeah, yeah. This is the turn coming up." He took the turn for the inn's driveway.

The inn was surrounded by trees. He wasn't a tree guy, but he guessed it was a fruit orchard, given the name. The yard in front of the inn was well-kept, with groomed grass, pruned bushes, and planters out front.

"I bet she's going to have thoughts on what to do with that yard too," he told Bruce. "And that god-awful vine growing up the side. Do people like those? I know people like all those flowers but not in the state they're in now."

The yard was an overgrown mess, but fixed up? Real estate agents would be salivating.

Dustin would have more than enough to get a place near the Gulf, maybe even a fishing boat someday. Salt water, sunsets, and no winter.

He neared the inn, and the place was perfect—other than the tarp.

A two-story white home with a porch and balcony that ran the full length of the front. Slender columns divided both into fifths. There was a big brick staircase down the front, and a huge gazebo connected off the left of the porch.

White rocking chairs and planted ferns lined the porch and balcony, and even though no guests were staying at the moment, he'd be willing to bet both were recently swept and tidied.

If Cece's sisters had even half her eye for detail, he imagined the inside of Orchard Inn was equally immaculate.

Except the rooms with storm damage, of course.

"Come on, fella." He parked his truck and clicked Bruce's leash to his harness. "Let's not keep the sisters waiting. They're going to want this place put back together as soon as possible."

Dustin led Bruce around to the back of the house, like Cece had told him, and checked out the tarp job. "Not bad," he said as he texted to let her know they'd arrived.

Moments later, Cece opened the back door. She looked like the break of day in yellow shorts and a white T-shirt, her hair tumbling loose around her shoulders.

He reminded himself that this was a business call and waved a greeting as another sister—he'd guess Beth, given Cece's descriptions before she left Hollyhock yesterday—joined them.

"Thank you for getting started on this so quickly. I'm Beth." She stuck out her hand.

He introduced himself, and the other sister, Aurora, joined them.

Cece was right: they were all dog people and took to Bruce just fine.

"Why don't I take a look at the upstairs rooms that are affected?" Dustin suggested. "You're welcome to walk me through them if you prefer. Then I'll get the contact info for your claims adjuster, and we can touch base with them."

As they entered what appeared to be the living quarters for the sisters, Bruce immediately started pulling for the kitchen.

The scent of bacon filled the entire area.

"Uh-oh. Bruce's favorite distraction." Dustin made him heel.

"I'm making breakfast," Aurora explained.

"I didn't mention this, but Aurora is a chef," Cece added proudly. "She has her own restaurant a few miles away."

Dustin made a noise of affirmation to cover for the sudden growl in his stomach.

"I can let y'all know when it's ready if you want some," Aurora said. "And Bruce is welcome to stay down here while you look around. Kind of looks like he'd prefer it."

"He definitely would, if you don't mind?"

"Not at all."

Dustin handed over the leash. He'd rather stay with the bacon, too, if he had the option. "Behave," he told Bruce, knowing full well he would.

Beth and Cece led him toward the front of the inn and up a wide staircase.

The inn was traditional and the right amount of formal, but light and airy feeling. The art on the walls had been chosen by someone with a good eye. Not overly cluttered or stuffy, the furniture downstairs in the entryway and living room was classic, timeless. The result was comfortable luxury. Nothing too frilly or fussy.

He would stay here if he ever stayed at inns.

"This is all guest space?" he asked as they walked the hall of the second floor.

"Yes," Cece answered. "Our living space is downstairs, along with the kitchen for the guests, the dining room, and the living room."

"This place is very nice."

"Thank you. Took years of work," Beth said. "Our parents got it for a song before we were born. Our maternal grandmother helped them out. It's taken decades to get it to where it is now. Back in the '80s when they bought it, the market had bottomed out, and even though it was in rough shape, our folks saw the potential."

"And wanted all this space and land for raising a family," Cece added.

Beth nodded. "Yeah, I think they originally wanted more than the three of us, but then they realized three girls were more than enough."

He couldn't imagine it. A big family, taking on a renovation job like this, working together and having each other, always. The only family he had was Manny, and they'd found each other as kids. They had made each other family because there was no one else.

"Here's the first room that was damaged," Beth pointed out. "It has the least. The next one has a little more, and the last one in the corner has the most."

Dustin went into the first guest room and looked around. Some cracking in the drywall but nothing extensive.

"What do you think?" Beth popped in to ask after maybe ten minutes.

He hid his smile. She wouldn't be the first concerned homeowner he'd encountered.

"This room isn't too bad, but I can give you a fuller report once I'm done."

She held a hand up. "I'll leave you to it, then. At least, I'll *try* to leave you to it."

The next two rooms had damage in the ceiling where water and some tree limbs had gone through the attic far enough to reach the next floor. He took almost an hour to thoroughly assess everything while Cece and Beth worked in the hall and other guest rooms. Once done, he found Cece at the far end of the hall, cleaning.

"We have to do something to stay busy," she explained.

"I know the feeling."

"Well?" Beth joined them.

"I want to check the attic, though the roofing company will take care of most of that. You're looking at mostly water damage on the ceilings, some cracks in the drywall, but I don't think it goes deeper. I'd get a foundation expert out here, just for your own peace of mind. Never hurts. You need some flooring and wall repair, and the furniture in those last two rooms is probably toast, but you already know that."

"Yeah, the insurance company said the claim would include replacing those." Beth nodded.

"All in all, you could say you're lucky, for having a tree fall on your house. The roof and tall attic took the brunt of it."

"So?" Cece arched an eyebrow.

"I can do this job. Probably take a couple of weeks. Three at the most if I need to wait on any stock because of all the local repairs."

"Oh, thank goodness." Beth all but buckled at the knees as she clapped her hands together.

"Beth's wedding is at the end of next month. We want to have the wedding party and some family stay here, so we need all the rooms," Cece explained.

"And the wedding and reception will be here," Beth added.

"Got it. That's a motivating deadline. I'll do my best to keep it near two weeks so everything is done and I'm out of your hair with plenty of time to spare."

"That is wonderful news." Cece's smile made the room a little brighter.

Aurora joined them. "What's the verdict? Can you do it?"

"I can." Dustin grinned at her blunt nature.

The three sisters together made quite the combination. Cece was headstrong and passionate, while Beth seemed professional and polished, and Aurora was bold, no-nonsense, like she ran her whole life the way she probably ran her kitchen.

"Great. Breakfast is ready if y'all are hungry," she offered.

He was hungry now that she'd mentioned breakfast, but he really ought to get started.

"You should eat something really quick, before you get to work," Cece suggested, reading his mind.

"You don't have to invite me twice when it comes to food." He was pretty much always hungry. His line of work plus a guy his size working long hours? And a chef making the food to boot? Who was he to say no?

They all went downstairs. Aurora had fixed a spread in the kitchen.

There were these little egg bite things, a plate full of bacon, English muffins, sliced tomato and avocado, fresh fruit, juice, and mini muffins in what looked like blueberry and chocolate chip.

Bruce sat obediently, and proudly, by the table like he'd prepared the entire meal himself.

Dustin needed to eat fast, but he didn't want to rush the ceremony that was this breakfast buffet. He filled his plate with some of everything, then put it all—except the muffins and juice—between a sliced English muffin to form a giant breakfast sandwich.

"That actually looks pretty good," Aurora commented.

They moved to a breakfast nook area, and Dustin worked very hard not to shove it all into his mouth at once.

"Once I'm finished, I'll get what I need from the truck and get started," he told Cece. "Work until around four or five, if that sounds good."

"We'll be here all day, so whatever is good for you."

"Cece tells us you bought the Hollyhock house." Beth politely ate her eggs one small bite at a time.

"I did." He shared a knowing look with Cece.

"I told them about my reaction. It's okay. They know how I can be. They can be that way too."

"Looks like you survived though." Aurora shrugged.

"It was a close one, but yes. I made it."

"Smells like Aurora fixed breakfast." A man's voice bounced down the hall from the sisters' living area.

"Hey." A man appeared, only slightly smaller than Dustin with hair so dark it was almost black.

"Hey, honey." Beth popped up and greeted him with kiss on the cheek. "This is Dustin. Our contractor."

Dustin stood as the man stuck out his hand.

"Sawyer," he said. He had to be the fiancé.

"Nice to meet you."

"Fix yourself a plate," Beth told him. "We were just talking about how Cece found us a contractor."

"You hired the contractor?" Sawyer asked her, lines of concern forming in his forehead.

He didn't look delighted about the decision, but Dustin wasn't getting paid to make friends with Beth's fiancé. He finished off the last bite of his breakfast sandwich. "I should get started."

"Wait." Cece stopped him with a hand on his arm. "You have to try the muffins. Aurora claims she's not a baker, but her desserts beg to differ. Here." Cece piled two of each on his plate.

"She's right," Sawyer insisted, his tone a little lighter now. He sat with an overflowing plate of food, making Dustin's look meager in comparison. "Beth told me you plan to fix up Hollyhock and resell?"

Cece shot Dustin a quick look, one he didn't comprehend, before answering for him. "He is. But he can balance both jobs, and the timing will work out since he can get started today."

Sawyer nodded with his mouth full. "Mmmm."

"Yeah," Dustin added. "And with Cece—"

"With me, you know, explaining the situation to him about the wedding coming up and everything, he knows all about our timetable. Well." She turned to Dustin. "We won't keep you since you need to get started."

Dustin stared at her as he finished chewing. He didn't

know what he was missing, but he was missing something. She didn't want him mentioning her working on Hollyhock with him. That much was clear. What he didn't understand was why.

With families, it was anybody's guess, and the last thing Dustin wanted to do was get in the middle of family stuff.

"Come on, Bruce." Dustin popped the last bite of chocolate chip muffin in his mouth and took a blueberry one to go, for Bruce. "Let's get our stuff and get started. Thank you for the breakfast, everyone."

He quickly excused himself and went to his truck, Bruce only following due to the promise of a muffin.

Dustin had already hauled in his ladder, tarps, and several tools when Cece joined him at the back of his truck.

"Thank you for not going into detail about our arrangement." She followed him around to the passenger side where he grabbed his coffee and water. "I didn't tell them everything because they tend to get overprotective about me doing too much."

"Why?"

She stared out at the peach trees in the orchard beyond the house. "Um...I don't really know."

Cece was a lot of things but a good liar clearly wasn't one of them. She knew exactly why, but she didn't want to say.

"I won't say anything if you don't want me to," he promised. "But they're going to notice you're gone a lot."

She stroked the top of Bruce's head, and he leaned into her leg. "I don't know. Everyone was pretty preoccupied already with the wedding, and now this?" She indicated the roof. "But I'll tell them in a couple of days, y'know, once we're already started. Oh, and just a heads-up. Sawyer is probably going to quiz you on contractor stuff and invite you to lunch one day, or for coffee or a beer. It's part due diligence, part southern hospitality, but also, we're a nosy bunch, and I think—"

"He's protective of his fiancé and her sisters and suspicious of me," Dustin finished for her.

"I don't know that he's suspicious."

"I would be if I were him. I'm going to be here for at least two weeks. I'm new in town, and he doesn't know me. I get it. And listen, you guys keep giving me free food, and so far, we're working well together, so I'll take him up on lunch."

Cece's laugh warmed his skin more than the morning sun. "We do tend to use food as an expression of pretty much everything. As a welcome, a segue to be nosy, consolation for bereavement, help, celebration, because we're bored."

Dustin smiled as they walked back toward the house. "What does boredom food entail?"

"Boredom food is the best," she exclaimed. "Salty, crunchy snacks and sweet treats you can pick at. We're talking chips and crackers and then your brownie and cookie family of desserts."

"Peanuts and sunflower seeds?"

"Sunflower seeds reign supreme for boredom snacks. And pistachios."

"Because you have to work to eat them," he offered.

"Exactly."

"Dustin." Sawyer approached them as they stood at the bottom of the staircase.

Cece kept walking until she stood behind Sawyer, grinning over his shoulder.

"I wanted to see if I could grab lunch with you one day this week since Cece said you're new in town and you're going to be their neighbor, at least temporarily."

"Sounds good to me." Dustin nodded as Cece mimicked his nod behind Sawyer.

He fought not to laugh.

Regardless of how Hollyhock and the inn turned out, one thing was certain. The next few weeks would be an adventure.

Chapter 6

Cece pulled up at the cottage right as Dustin got out of his truck. All six foot and however many inches of him. He was dirty and sweaty from working at the inn all day, and there was just so much of him.

She couldn't look away.

He waved at her and tilted his head, and if he knew what she was thinking, he'd probably ask her if she was done drooling.

"I was wondering where you were," he said, Bruce bounding over to her as she got out of the car. "I looked for you when I left the inn."

"I'd gone into town to get something from the fabric shop."

Dustin had worked at the inn the last few days, and while he was there, she'd mostly stayed out of his way. Afterward, she'd come over to Hollyhock, and they'd work on the house. Most of her first day they'd spent in an awkward silence, taking notes and discussing plans for the house.

"Did you get something for Beth's dress?" he asked, having already learned of her anxiety around refashioning a wedding gown for her sister. Dustin had made good progress on the repairs and even more progress in learning all about the Shipley sisters' dynamics. A person didn't have to be nosy to hear all about Beth's upcoming wedding, Aurora's restaurant woes, and Cece's attempts to help them both while also trying to have a life of her own.

"I went to get some ideas." Cece opened the back door to grab the Tupperware container of Aurora's cookies. "Found some lace I loved, but I'm still not sure."

"Did you find the cabinet handles you wanted in town?"

She grabbed the bag from the backseat, too, and shook it in response. "Found exactly what we need."

"What else have you got there?" Dustin asked as she approached with the container, Bruce sniffing with great interest.

"Aurora made a bunch of snickerdoodle cookies this afternoon. Stress baking. She told me to get rid of them so she didn't eat them all."

"Did you tell her you were coming here to get rid of them?"

It'd been an ongoing discussion, Cece's hesitancy to share her work at Hollyhock with her family, and Dustin's encouragement that she be transparent. But she knew how her sisters, and even Sawyer, would react. They'd have dozens of questions, they'd worry about her overextending herself, and then they'd want to monitor everything.

She'd tell them in the next couple of days, but for now, she liked coming to Hollyhock every late afternoon, working for a few hours, and having something all her own.

"No, but I'll tell them tomorrow."

"Mm-hmm." Dustin took the offered container, and Bruce followed. "Come on in. I was thinking we could keep working in the dining room today."

The dining room, one of two rooms in the front of the house, had proven to need the smallest number of repairs. There were some wiring issues, and the floors would need to be sanded and stained with the rest of the first floor, but Dustin had found everything else was in good shape.

Cece had explained to him that some Craftsman homes had built-in cabinets or shelves in the dining room. Hollyhock didn't, but the addition of a cabinet and a small countertop, set into the wall separating the living room and dining room, was the perfect kind of update that added value to the home without taking away from its original allure.

Dustin found some pine that complemented the floors and began crafting beautiful cabinetry.

"Sounds good to me." She followed him inside and almost fell over at the sight before her. "When did...*How*?"

The cabinet was set into the wall already. There were no doors yet, but the cabinet itself was in place.

"How did you do this?" she asked again, more coherently.

"Did I mention I don't sleep?"

"No."

"Mmm." He crossed his arms as he studied his handiwork. "I don't sleep much, but especially not on an air mattress. So, I got restless last night and..." He held his arms out toward the built-in. "This is what I did to settle."

"This is..." Cece ran her fingers over the freshly finished wood, the levels and corners perfection. "This is amazing." They only needed to add the doors, stain it, and add fixtures to finish up the project.

"It was your idea," he told her.

"Yeah, but…" She held her arms out toward the built-in. "I didn't know you could do *that*. I can just imagine recessed lighting, oh! And even glass inset doors along the top."

This kind of job was top quality. Dustin wasn't just a contractor; he was an artist.

"I don't know what to say. I'm impressed."

He beamed, obviously and understandably proud of his work. He held up his hand for a high five, and Cece obliged. "Say you'll help me get started on these doors."

She settled onto the tarp he'd laid out on the floor, speechless. Bruce settled down beside her, his gaze fixed on the Tupperware container of cookies that'd been placed on the floor.

"I'm not sure how to—"

"Don't worry, I'll show you," he said. "It's not hard."

Dustin showed her how to sand each side of the doors down to silky smoothness while he drilled holes for the handles she'd found in town.

Every day, he'd let her do whatever work she wanted. She'd quizzed him on sanding and restaining the home's coveted pine floors, and he'd promised to not only show her but let her operate the sander if she wanted.

She'd gone into the crawl space with him to check out the floor joists and insulation, and when he'd needed small hands to help with the plumbing in the bathroom, he'd let her lie under the sink to assist.

"So, tell me, what do you plan to do after Hollyhock?" she probed, baffled by how anyone could let go of a home like this.

"Well." He got up to hang a door on the hinges he'd drilled into the cabinet. "A guy I know started his own construction business in Florida, and it's been good for him. Very good. He's looking for a partner, and there's a lot of new construction down there."

Cece worked not to wrinkle her nose like she'd caught whiff of a bad smell. "I've heard. And that's what you really want to do?"

Dustin shrugged as he worked on the door, and she tried to ignore the way his T-shirt stretched across his shoulders. "That's the plan. It's work, good paying work, and lots of it. That's all that matters."

He stood back, studying his work after attaching the first cabinet door. "I think this is going to make this whole room look even better. Don't you?"

"My gosh, yes. And with lights in the upper cabinets with the glass doors, I can just imagine some family's Blue Danube or Carlyle pattern china displayed in here. Oh, or Desert Rose would be gorgeous with the warm wood tones." She looked up to find him staring.

"I don't understand a word you just said beside 'cabinet' and 'glass doors.'"

Cece laughed. "China patterns. You know, fancy dishes that people have just to look at but not eat off?"

He huffed a laugh. "I eat off my plates, but I'll take your word for it. So..." He strong-armed a screwdriver, his bicep straining against his shirt while Cece tried not to notice. "How's it going with the wedding dress in general? Any decisions yet?"

"Ha! From Beth? Not a chance. She still insists I'll make it perfect. I did find some lace I like, but I don't know. I'm hoping an idea comes to me tonight when I see it with the dress itself."

"Then what, you sew stuff on top of the dress?"

"Yep. Lace, beading, you name it. A lot of it by hand if a machine won't work for the job."

Dustin shook his head as he eyed his finished job with one of the doors. "I don't know how you do it. Bunch of little beads and tiny thread. I'd lose my mind."

"Me too." She laughed. "I've had a meltdown or twelve before. Making the curtains that hang in the living room of the inn? The fabric was too thick for the needle on my machine, but I thought I could make it work. I ended up going through several needles, cussing up a storm, and throwing the fabric in a pile near the fireplace."

Dustin laughed. "I bet you threatened to burn the whole pile."

"I did!" Cece exclaimed, undeniably pleased at his guess. "Exactly that, in fact. It was one of my top ten meltdowns for sure. But I took a break for a few days, then went back to it later, and I was fine. I finished the sewing, and now we have great drapes in that room."

"Isn't that always the way?" He started on the other door. "Something is so frustrating, and you swear it can't be done. Two days later, it's a cinch, even though you're going about everything the exact same way."

Cece nodded, their casual conversation and parallel work easing every earlier tension she'd had over Beth's dress.

That was how it'd been every day. She came over to Hollyhock, they worked—hard, dirty work—and talked about all kinds of things. Everything from food to movies, job experiences to family anecdotes.

Except the family anecdotes were always hers. He knew all kinds of stuff about the Shipleys in just a few days, but he'd yet to say a word about his family.

"Aurora can have bigger meltdowns than me." Cece cast her fishing line by staying on the topic of families. "Actually, Beth can have the grandest meltdowns, but they're so rare, you forget how powerful they can be. I think she's only had two that I ever witnessed."

Dustin nodded.

A fishing line wouldn't do. She'd have to cast a net. "So. What about your family?"

He stopped working on the cabinet door but didn't look up. "My family?" he repeated.

"Yeah. Do you have any brothers or sisters?"

"My family," he said again. "That's a ... hmm."

"I mean, we don't have to talk about it if you don't want to." She fidgeted with the door in her hands. She'd somehow managed to make things awkward again, and that was exactly the opposite of the effect she'd been going for. "It's just ... I realized we've talked a lot about my family, and I've never asked about yours. Kind of rude of me not to ask, actually. Sorry about that."

"No need to apologize. I ..." Dustin lowered the cabinet door and finally met her gaze. "I don't talk about them because ... well, because I don't know them. Not my biological family anyway."

Cece's stomach sank. "Oh ... uh." Her and her big, stupid mouth. Of course there was a reason he hadn't talked about family. She wanted to stick this door in her mouth and swallow it whole.

She knew how it felt to have people ask you dumb questions or pry into things that didn't involve them, and now she'd gone and done the same to Dustin.

"I'm sorry, I didn't mean be in your business."

"It's okay, really. You've shared a lot about yourself.

You've got every reason to be curious. Fair warning though, it's not a great origin story. Let's see, I was orphaned before I was two, raised in foster care most of my life. Bounced around a lot to some real garbage humans for years until I was about ten. Then I wound up with a decent couple who fostered a few kids around my age. I guess in that way, I finally got lucky. I have a brother from foster care. Not blood related, obviously, but he's younger than me. Came to the home when he was about seven and I was thirteen. He was a mess, same as me when I first got there, and...I don't know. We bonded. Now he's my family."

She stared, silent, clueless about what to say next.

Dustin smiled, and she felt like she could breathe again. "I'm glad you asked."

"I...you..." She stammered through a response. "I'm sorry. Are you sure?" She frowned. "I feel like I made it weird. Sometimes I do that."

His laugh was light and low, like soft wind. "We've been talking about your family and all kinds of stuff for the last couple of days. I know I've been tight-lipped about my family and background, but that's only because there isn't much to say. Other than Manny, it's not a great story with funny memories to share like with you and your sisters."

Cece turned to face him better. "What about Manny? How old is he?"

"He's twenty. He thinks he's grown, but he's not. Now that you mention it, I need to call him. I haven't heard from him in a few weeks, which isn't like him."

"So, when he came to foster care, you were in middle school?"

"Yeah, and he was starting elementary school because he'd been held back—or really, I guess he was truant because no one took him to school."

"Wow."

"Pretty typical, actually. That's how CPS ends up taking a lot of kids. They're never in school, so the school eventually lets someone know, *hey, this kid has stopped showing up*, and someone investigates. Anyway, it was a big turning point for me, Manny coming to live with us. He was a cute kid, but man, was he full of spitfire and vinegar." Dustin laughed, his face lighting up at the thought. "You grow up hard in foster care, and he was mean and defensive. Probably felt like he had to be. I wasn't having it though. I guess I saw so much of me in him, how I felt at that age. I took him under my wing and made sure he knew someone had his back." Dustin cleared his throat. "No one had mine at his age, and I didn't want that for him."

She'd known Dustin for a few days now, but for the first time, Cece felt like she really *knew* him. It was the most he'd ever shared with her about something deeper than renovations and favorite midnight snacks. This was something real, and the fondness in his voice, the tenderness with which he spoke about his nontraditional family, melted her heart.

"Don't look at me like that." Dustin grinned at her.

"Like what?" Cece swallowed the giant knot in her throat.

"Like you're about start crying."

"I'm not—"

"You know how you said you didn't want my pity for getting this house? Well, I don't want pity for my past. It is what it is, and I turned out okay, I think."

She nodded. "I know, it's just…"

"We have a 'no pity' rule here at Hollyhock. Agreed?"

Cece nodded again. "Agreed." This was a rule she could appreciate, especially because it meant Dustin let her do the things she wanted without fussing over her. True, he didn't know everything about her past either, but maybe she'd tell him eventually, with a "no pity" rule in place.

"Sorry if it seemed like I was stonewalling you when you've told me so much about your sisters. I'm just not much of a sharer, unless prompted. You know?"

"Yeah."

"Seriously though, I'm glad you asked. Maybe I should talk about it more." This time when he smiled, his hazel eyes warmed, crinkling at the edges.

Cece caught herself staring again, her whole body feeling weird and tingly. She returned her focus to her cabinet door and handles, her insides doing a frantic tap dance.

"Should we break for cookies in a minute?" Dustin asked, and Bruce popped up from where he'd been fast asleep. "I think that's a yes vote from Bruce."

"A break sounds good," Cece agreed, her heart thumping while he sweet-talked Bruce with such affection.

Really knowing Dustin might really be a problem.

Cece returned to Orchard Inn at almost midnight. Luckily, no one else was home. After a quick shower, she jumped on the project of Beth's dress.

Inspiration had struck as she'd looked at the almost-finished cabinetry project. Hers and Dustin's hard work turned out beautifully, the perfect complement to Hollyhock's dining room.

Beth, much like a 1920s Craftsman bungalow, was a classic beauty. Clean lines, structured, unfussy, yet *very* glamorous.

While Aurora was more boho and earthy and Cece was more whimsical and colorful, only a timeless, tried-and-true style would do for Beth. Beth was their Grace Kelly, and as Princess Grace's wedding gown was iconic, Cece had immediately called the fabric shop and left a voicemail to order Brussels lace instead of what she'd chosen today.

Cece leaned over the kitchen table of their living area, determined to make some progress while inspired. Plus, dress work would keep her mind off Dustin.

Dustin and his broad-shouldered, soulful-eyed sincerity. Dustin who, when asked, was so honest and genuine it made her rethink every notion she had about dating and men in general.

Dustin who, as he walked her to her car tonight, had said he'd fix dinner for them when she came over to work tomorrow evening.

Was it a date?

He hadn't presented the offer as such. More of a *why not have something to eat while working*–type situation.

Still. *He'd* offered to cook for *her*. That had never happened before in her entire life.

Maybe all men didn't suck? Maybe she'd only come across the ones who did, and now that she'd met one who didn't, she'd have to recalibrate her thought process, at least as it concerned Dustin.

Cece shook off her thoughts. The point was to *not* think about him.

"Wedding dress," she said to herself, studying the top

of her grandmother's gown and a classic bodice pattern laid out before her.

"You in here talking to yourself?" A tall, dark-haired woman stepped out of the kitchen, a cup of hot tea in her hand, with Aurora right behind her.

It was Sloane, Aurora's sous chef and best friend.

Cece stuck out a stiff arm. "No food or drink near the dress."

Sloane took a cautious step back. "It's almost midnight. Aren't you exhausted? We are."

"I couldn't sleep right now, even if I wanted to," Cece answered.

"Is this *the* dress?" Sloane asked.

"Yes, and I know what I'm going to do now. Inspiration struck, finally."

Aurora walked around the table. "Did Beth approve it?"

"Not yet, but she's going to love it."

Aurora shared a look with Sloane.

"Excuse you." Cece caught the look. "Do I doubt your cooking skills?"

Aurora pinched her lips together. "No, you don't. I'm not doubting you, and I'm definitely not trying to offend, but Beth doesn't wear my cooking on her body."

"To be immortalized in photos on her biggest day ever," Sloane added.

"Exactly." Aurora pointed at her. "This is Beth we're talking about. I'd get her to commit to it before I did anything permanent."

"Ha!" Cece scoffed. "Commit? I've tried to get her to commit for weeks. I've already left an order for the lace, and I *know* she's going to love this idea."

The last few days had taught her she had good instincts.

She'd doubted herself or second-guessed herself most of her life. Now it was time to try something different.

"I know what I'm doing," she insisted.

Sloane peered over at the pattern on the table and studied Cece's set expression. "I believe you. If you say she'll love it, she's going to love it."

Aurora nodded. "Me too. But it's your funeral if she doesn't."

Sloane sipped her tea and set the mug down on the counter. "Where'd you go earlier anyway?"

Cece tried ignoring the question and focused on pinning the dress.

"I had to run up here to grab something for Aurora around nine or so, during closing. Noticed you were gone."

"Running errands." Cece didn't meet their gaze.

"At nine o'clock at night?" Aurora asked.

Cece merely nodded and kept pinning.

There was at least a minute of silence before Sloane broke. "You think you are so slick." She laughed. "We know you've been gone every night this week."

Cece looked up at them, both grinning from ear to ear. "What?"

"Ever since I moved here from Cali, you've been a homebody." Sloane pulled out a chair and sat. "Now, all of a sudden, you're gone every night. I told Aurora that her sister either has a side hustle or a fella, but we didn't want to say anything at first. So, which is it? You seeing someone?"

"No," she answered way too sharply. There'd be no way they bought it.

"Bull crap. I told you!" Sloane looked at Aurora. "I told you, I bet she has a man."

"I do not have a man." Not exactly. Though, if she

fessed up to what she'd been doing, maybe they could tell her if dinner tomorrow was a date or just dinner.

Sloane quirked her lips. "Then what is it? Side hustle sewing gig? Cult meeting? Sewing cult meeting?"

"I might have a side hustle, but it doesn't involve making clothes or cults."

"Darn, I was hoping it was a guy. I need some romance in my life, even secondhand."

"You have a side job?" Aurora's tone shifted into something far too serious, given the current mood of the conversation.

Cece put down her pins, preparing to be over-mothered. "I have a little side project that pays. Yes."

"Since when? Where?"

"Dang, Aurora." Sloane's gaze jerked toward her friend. "She's not twelve."

"See, even Sloane sees how you get. This is why I didn't tell you sooner."

"I'm not..." Aurora took a breath. "I'm just curious. I didn't know you were working somewhere else."

"Everyone else has real work. Why shouldn't I?" Better to just spit it out and get this over with. "I'm helping Dustin renovate Hollyhock."

"Who is Dustin?" Sloane asked as Aurora blurted over her.

"Renovating a house?"

"Wait." Sloane put up her hands. "Who cares about a house? *Who* is Dustin?"

"He's the guy repairing our upstairs," Aurora answered.

"Ohhhh." Recognition dawned as Sloane had been by the inn one day earlier this week. She grinned. "You're working with *him*? *Okay.*"

"He bought the bungalow I wanted," Cece added. "I know more about the historical aspects of the home than he does, so he hired me to consult and help. We added built-in cabinets today. They're gorgeous."

"You're doing like...heavy labor?" Aurora's eyes were wide as saucers.

"I'm not on the roof laying shingles, okay?" Cece raised her voice a notch. "I'm fine."

"I think we're missing the point here, 'Ro." Sloan called Aurora by the nickname only she used. "Cece is working with Dustin. I mean, I wouldn't worry about her having to do any of the heavy labor. Pretty sure that man has it covered. More importantly, how is he as a coworker?" Sloane's face lit up, playfully. "Is there a personality to go with the brawn? Has he flirted with you at all? Please tell me you get to watch him drill things."

"I wanted to talk to y'all about that, actually."

Sloane clapped her hands together with glee, making Cece laugh.

"I'm serious. I need y'all's opinion. That's why I even told you about this in the first place."

Sloane made another noise of excitement and sat up straighter. "Yes, talk, talk. Ask us anything. What's going on?"

"Sloane." Aurora shook her head but sat down too.

"What? All I do lately is work in a kitchen and sleep. I need to get my social life and fun via other people. Shush it. Now, Cece. Talk."

Cece settled herself before spilling the story of her day. "Then, before I left, he offered to fix dinner when I'm over there working tomorrow. So, is that just dinner or is it a date?"

"You have a date." Sloane leaned forward, her expression certain.

"But we'll be working too."

"I don't care. It might be work first, but it's a dinner date at the end."

"And he's cooking for you," Aurora added, her tone finally relaxed again. "Can he cook?"

"I don't know." Cece shrugged. "I guess I'll find out."

"Do you feel like you know him well enough for this step? Like, are you ready?" Aurora asked.

"Don't be Beth right now." Cece scowled.

"Ugh. Bite your tongue! I'm not being Beth right now, I'm just…"

Sloan and Cece shared a look.

"Fine, I'm not *trying* to be Beth; I just want to know. But not in a micromanagey way—in a curious, what's-going-on-with-this-guy kinda way."

Sloane patted Aurora's shoulder good-naturedly. "Nice save."

"You guys are a tough crowd."

"I am so excited for you, Cece." Sloane beamed. "A date, and he's a yummy drink of water. Not a sip, a whole drink."

"What are you going to wear?" Aurora asked.

"Like the kind of guy who could pick you up and put you places. You know what I mean?" Sloane kept talking. "Just put you where he wants you."

Heat rushed to Cece's face. "I don't know," she managed.

"See, Cece knows what I mean."

Aurora shook head, but she was smiling. "You're embarrassing her."

"I'm not embarrassing her. She's a grown woman. She's blushing because she knows I'm right and she's thought about it too." Sloane laughed loudly at Cece's smile. "See?"

"And you like him?" Aurora asked.

"I think I do. He's nice and good-looking, and he trusts me to know what I'm doing." She stared at her sister with intent. "He doesn't hover because he knows I'm capable."

"Look at you." Sloane clapped her hands together again. "Got the guy paying you *and* cooking dinner for you. I swear, it's always the quiet ones who've got it going on. Good for you."

Cece laughed and shook her head. "I think it might just be work though."

"So?" Sloane leaned forward. "You were glowing just talking about him. Who cares what it is? Just enjoy it. You love doing the work, and he's hot. Lean into it. Like we say in the kitchen, you only get out of a dish what you put into it."

Cece looked to Aurora.

Her sister hesitated a moment, then nodded. "We do say that. If you're happy and having fun, enjoy yourself. Just, you know, be careful, but...yeah. You deserve to have fun too."

Chapter 7

Dustin had never hung out with a cowboy, nor did he fully understand exactly what it meant to be one, but Sawyer was not what he'd have imagined.

He'd always pictured cowboys as wearing the hat 24-7, possibly a big belt buckle, and that they'd be slightly more bowlegged. Sawyer wore jeans and a T-shirt, and if Dustin didn't know he was a horse guy, he wouldn't have guessed by looks alone.

"Beer okay?" Sawyer asked, sitting back in the booth, one arm stretched out as he sized Dustin up.

As Cece predicted, Sawyer had insisted they grab lunch together, outside of working at the inn. Today had ended early because he'd restained the floors in both guest rooms, and they'd need to sit, untouched, until later tomorrow.

For lunch, Sawyer had recommended a place called the Pizza Parlor because he swore they had the best pizza in town, great pool tables, and sometimes live music.

"Beer works for me."

"They have a really good lager on tap. Bring us a pitcher of the Altstadt lager," Sawyer told their waiter. "Thanks."

While they waited for their pitcher, they picked out an open pool table and set up shop.

Of course, Dustin wasn't an idiot. He knew the real reason for this confab was so Sawyer could do some investigative work. A little background check on the who, what, and where of Dustin Long.

And he was fine with that. In fact, Dustin had a few questions of his own.

"What exactly does it mean to work with horses?" he asked first, truly baffled by the idea of working with animals that weighed more than four Bruces put together. "What's an average day like?"

Sawyer laughed and picked out a pool cue. "Running a horse ranch means never having an average or normal day."

Dustin could relate.

"One day, I might be training or working with the horses, next day it might be the same—but with people. One day, you're buying or selling or making contracts on a horse that isn't even born yet, and another day you're birthing a colt."

"Get out of town." Dustin forgot about the lunch's purpose of casual interrogation, fascinated by the idea of baby horses. "So, you're with them like—?" He held his hands out like someone was hiking him a football.

"Basically." Sawyer smiled. "If all goes well and there's no trouble, then I'm mostly on standby, trying not to get in the way. If there's trouble, then I'm more involved. Big trouble means our vet is there, heck, maybe even my uncle, and a nosy neighbor. It can get a little crowded."

"Hmm." He couldn't imagine being a part of something like that. The nervous energy and worry, and then the satisfaction when a horse was born. "That's probably pretty cool, huh? When it all goes well."

Sawyer smiled, joy filling his eyes as though he was remembering something. "It's very cool. Some are more special than others too." He racked the balls on the table as Dustin picked a cue.

"You any good at pool?"

"I'm okay." Dustin kept it humble. "You?"

"Same."

A couple of minutes into playing, it became clear they were both being humble. Sawyer was as excellent a player as Dustin.

"Just okay, huh?" Sawyer chuckled.

"All things relative. Most folks would barely be okay against you."

"I'd say you're a sight better than okay."

"There isn't much to do when you're poor and it's winter in Michigan. Lots of pool and foosball tables at the youth center in town. I got really good at both."

"Oh man, I love foosball. I think they have an old-school table in the back. We should play that sometime."

Their waiter showed up a few moments later with the beer, and they ordered a couple of pizzas. One supreme with all the meats and veggies and one called the Buffa-Whoa that promised piles of buffalo-sauced chicken and blue cheese. Sounded like delicious heartburn, so why not?

"You live in Michigan your whole life?" Sawyer asked.

Here it was. The real reason for the pizza and pool. Normally, he didn't talk about himself. He wasn't a small-talk guy or an info-dumper. Unless he really knew someone, it seemed pointless to open up about his life.

There was no casual way to talk about being orphaned as a baby and growing up in foster care, so he just didn't talk about it.

But after talking to Cece yesterday, he'd felt...lighter? He hadn't told anyone his story in years. Had he ever really told it? He'd always figured that keeping it in, not rehashing his life, would help him forget.

That was not the case.

He had questions, resentment. None of that had gone away over the years. Telling Cece his story had made the past feel less heavy, and Dustin wasn't against sharing his story with her family. They'd been nothing but nice to him since day one. Well, except when Cece jumped on his case the moment they met, but now he could only think about that night fondly.

"I lived most of my life in Michigan, yeah. All that I remember, anyway, but I was born in Texas."

"Yeah?"

"Around here, actually. I think Hays County."

"No kidding."

He hadn't even told Cece this. Maybe he should tonight. "That's what originally brought me here to look for an investment property. I thought, *why not find something around my birthplace* and, I don't know..."

But he did know, kind of. Part of him wanted to look for details, information about his last name, his birth parents. All he knew was what he'd once seen, accidentally, on his release forms. Part of him wanted to bury that part of his life down deep and never think about it again.

He hit the solid two into the corner pocket. "Anyway, I found the perfect fixer-upper here. I plan to do the work myself and sell it, then take the equity and start my own business. Something more stable than following one-off jobs around my whole life."

Sawyer took his shot after Dustin missed one. "Fredericksburg what you're looking for long-term?"

"Not exactly. I know a guy who is doing well in Florida. Lots of people moving that way equals lots of construction work. Warmer and near the water too. No winter or snow, and lots of fishing."

"We don't get snow here either, and it's rarely freezing."

"Yeah, from what I've seen, this place is great."

"No ocean though," Sawyer added.

They finished their first game, with Dustin winning by only a few balls. Sawyer racked again. "I guess Cece fessed up to working with you on the Hollyhock house last night."

Dustin stood a little straighter. "She finally told you?"

"Oh no, not me. She told Aurora. Then Aurora told Beth, and Beth told me."

He had to smile. Big families operated like games of telephone.

"I think Beth and Aurora are worried she'll get hurt, but I think she'll be fine. Plus, Aurora said she seemed really happy about the work."

"Why would she get hurt? I'm a careful contractor. I don't tolerate risk on my sites."

"No, no. Sorry, I didn't mean she'd get hurt as a result of your work. I meant…" Sawyer clamped his mouth shut. "You know, construction can be dangerous in general, and she's never done that kind of work before."

Dustin stared as Sawyer broke and took his turn on the solids.

He was covering for something, and he was not a good

liar. Dustin preferred bad liars, and he let it go. Sawyer seemed to approve of him, and the fact that Cece was working on the house with him. She'd been so worried. Why?

Sawyer was protective, naturally, when it came to all the Shipley sisters, so Dustin didn't take it personally. He struck Dustin as the sort who took the role of big brother very seriously. Nothing wrong with that, and Dustin took no offense. He was equally protective of Manny.

Speaking of. Dustin reached for his phone and shot off a quick text to Manny.

He'd texted him yesterday and never gotten a reply. Manny was young and independent, but it wouldn't kill the guy to check in every now and then.

"How are things going with Hollyhock anyway?" Sawyer asked.

"Great so far. I'm cautiously optimistic, but with renos, you never know what might pop up that you'll have to deal with."

Sawyer missed a shot, and it was Dustin's turn. He stood there watching Dustin and apparently just couldn't help himself. "Cece is headstrong and a hell of a strong worker, and she means a lot to us. All of us."

Dustin stopped lining up and stood. "I'm going to level with you, Sawyer, because if the roles were reversed, I'd feel the same as you. Cece won't get hurt working with me. I know to you, I'm some guy who showed up, in and out of town to flip a house. I won't be here long, and you don't know me. You've got no reason to trust me. I get it. But I have experience, and I'm responsible. I want to really fix that house up right, which is why I hired Cece. I know someone with a good eye, skill, and a strong work ethic when I see one. The last thing I'd ever do is endanger her. I've got a younger brother myself. I pretty much raised him, and he means the world to me. I'd do anything for him, because he's the only family I've got, and right now, he's really pissing me off because he won't text me back." Dustin glared at his phone sitting on the edge of the pool table.

Sawyer studied him a moment and then rounded the table to clap him on the shoulder good-naturedly. "It is really nice to talk to someone who shoots straight."

Dustin accepted the compliment, a little stunned.

"I know it sounds like I'm questioning your—I don't know—abilities. Motivations? But I'm not. And sure, I worry about Cece because I care, but she can take of herself. I'm only around for backup, in case I'm ever needed."

He didn't need to tell Dustin how capable Cece was of standing her ground.

"I just…Her sisters worry, but after meeting you, I've got zero concerns. I appreciate your candor. I really do."

Sawyer laid down his pool stick. "Our pizza is here." And with that, the conversation was over.

They washed up and ate the pizza, sweating through the buffalo sauce, and talked about everything from horses to football, to best pizzas and pool hall memories.

He'd gotten Sawyer's approval, but Sawyer would no doubt remain close as "backup," if needed, and Dustin would be the same way.

He checked his phone for any word from Manny. Nothing. But the time had grown later than he'd realized. He needed to get ready for his dinner with Cece.

"I hate to eat and run, but I need to get some stuff done at Hollyhock," he said.

"Totally understand. Got a client coming by at five myself. I enjoyed this. We'll have to do it again sometime."

Dustin found he wouldn't mind having lunch with Sawyer again. "Just let me know when and where."

They wrapped up, and Dustin wished Sawyer well with a firm handshake before making his exit.

First, he went by the Vine Market. He'd heard Aurora raving about their produce selection in the inn's kitchen the other day. He found a huge deli with a variety of meats and cheeses, a great selection of fresh produce, and his biggest score, a section for fresh pasta.

Dustin put rigatoni noodles and the ingredients for his sauce in his cart. Pasta was simple, filling, fed a lot of people, and was usually affordable, which made it popular in foster care. Plus, over the years, he'd perfected the best sauce in the world. He made a spicy rigatoni that'd become a hit with his foster family. A vodka sauce that satisfied all the cheese lovers as well as the tomato sauce fans, some basil, and enough red pepper flakes to give it some heat.

Once he'd found everything he needed for the main course, he considered dessert and wine.

He knew Cece was a dessert person, but was she a wine drinker? Having wine on hand, even if they didn't drink it, would send the message this was a dinner *date*, not just a dinner.

Would she be upset if the dinner felt too much like a date? Did he *want* it to be a date?

When he'd asked her, he'd definitely had a date on his mind.

After sharing so much about his past with her, walking her to her car, and her looking disheveled but beautiful from working on their inset, he hadn't been able to resist. He'd had no intention of going down this path with Cece. They were going to work together, and that was it.

Except, she insisted on being irresistible. So much caring and kindness rested beneath all that passionate energy. In a moment of weakness, he'd given in to his attraction. He wanted to know her as more than just a coworker, spend time with her outside of the renovations.

Now though, he hesitated. His time here was temporary, and Cece deserved the kind of guy who could give her everything she wanted, one who had his life together, who was steady and stable—a man with roots. He wasn't sure he deserved a date with her, but she'd agreed to his suggestion.

Dustin suddenly realized he'd been standing there, staring blindly at the shelves of red wine like he was trying to read Latin. He shook off his thoughts and tried to pick a red, even though he had no clue what he was doing.

"Do you need some help, hon?" An older woman leaned into his peripheral.

"Yes please. I do. What's a nice wine to go with a heavier pasta dish?"

"Are we talking tomato or cream based?" She stared at him from over the top of her glasses.

"Tomato. Well, vodka sauce actually, leaning more toward the tomato side of the scale."

"Meat?"

"Sausage."

"Right." She stretched out the word as she studied the shelves with all the precision of a surgeon. "Okay. Is this just for you or do we want to go a little nicer for a guest?"

"Nicer for a guest."

"Got it." She reached for a bottle with a cream label and whole bunch of Italian he couldn't pronounce. "I had this at a friend's house over the summer. Her grandmother is Italian, and she swore by it. It's delicious and smooth. Room temperature or slightly chilled, it'll offset the richness of your pasta dish. You could also get the tiramisu they make here if you really want to impress a guest. Over in the bakery section. It's to die for."

Dustin turned the bottle in his hand. "Thank you."

The lady disappeared down the aisle with a wink.

He glanced around, wondering if the entire exchange had really happened. No one offered help unsolicited in the stores outside of Detroit. You were lucky if you could find someone to answer a question, including the people who worked there.

Dustin followed the lady's advice and went to the bakery section. He put a tiramisu in his cart and threw in some fancy dog treats on his way to check out. A consolation prize for leaving Bruce most of the day.

By the time he got home, Bruce had missed him enough to welcome him by trying to tackle him in the doorway, nosing into the bag with the sausage.

"Not for you. I got you something else though. Come on outside. We have to work on your manners." Dustin let him run out in the yard to take care of nature's business. "We have company coming tonight!" he yelled after him. "You've got to behave!"

Casual company, he tried telling himself. The kind of casual company who he'd just spent quite a bit of money on because he wanted to impress her.

Cece was a coworker, and they deserved this. She was a beautiful, funny, fiery coworker who made every day a little better with only her presence and a few simple words. She was coming by to discuss work plans over a meal and friendly conversation, but this wasn't a date.

Unless, of course, she wanted it to be one. Would she want it to be a date?

He was the worst person in the world for gauging things like this.

Obviously, they liked each other. They got along well, worked great as a team, and had naturally flowing conversation. But there was liking each other and then there was *liking* each other.

Dustin shook his head at himself.

Who was he kidding? The latter *liking* had gained ground daily, and now he needed to admit it. He was into her. He *liked* her. The way she talked to him, so open and welcoming when it came to her family, her thoughts, and her opinions. There were no hidden meanings with Cece. What you saw was what you got. No game playing or holding back. A thought entered her mind, she said it. She might regret it zero-point-five seconds later, but she said exactly what she thought.

Liking her made dinner tricky though. He couldn't be overly flirtatious or put any moves on her, because if she felt differently, it would blow up in his face. However, if she was moving toward *liking* him too, he couldn't sit back and not act.

If he didn't show interest when she was interested in him, then that could also blow up in his face.

Bruce trotted back inside, all tongue and open-mouthed panting.

"I could always ask her outright."

He was straightforward, but that might be a little too

straightforward. Surely making a woman dinner was a clear indication he was interested.

But, knowing his time here was temporary, how would she feel about that? He already knew with certainty that Cece wasn't the type to do short-term or casual. Maybe she'd make an exception.

"I don't know what I'm doing," he confessed to Bruce.

Bruce had no response, still nosing into the grocery bags.

"But I want to do this for her, even if she only sees me as some guy she's working with temporarily. I like her. I'll regret it if I don't try."

Still no reaction from Bruce. He was being ignored in favor of dog treats.

"Fine. Take your treat." Dustin pulled out the peanut butter dog cookies and gave Bruce one. "You're no help at all."

He'd have to see how she reacted to dinner tonight. Let the evening play out and follow where she led. Luckily, Cece wasn't the type to hesitate to take the lead.

Chapter 8

Cece fisted her hands on her hips and stared her sister down. "What do you mean, this weekend may not work for you? We've had this planned for weeks. *I've* had this planned for weeks."

Aurora stirred a giant pot of something that smelled divine and garlicky. "Look around you. Does it look like I can leave Lavender for two days?"

Cece scanned the kitchen of her sister's restaurant—her sister's dream come true.

She understood the responsibility and knew the restaurant was Aurora's baby, but this was Beth's weekend. They never did anything fun and relaxing, just the girls, anymore. Her bachelorette trip was important.

"I made reservations in San Antonio. Beth isn't a party girl, so I arranged to do things she'd like. The River Walk in the afternoon, then go to a winery for a nice tasting and dinner. The next day, wake up and do a whole spa day. The works. Massages, facials, hydrotherapy, mud masks, even mud baths if we want them."

Sloane wiped a smear of pesto from a dish and nodded to a server, sending it out of the kitchen. "The kind of mud baths where you get to, like, lay around in it like a giant mud monster?"

"I think so, yeah."

"I miss all the fun."

Cece frowned. "There's no way you could come too?"

"Cece, I don't even know if I can go." Aurora huffed. "We have a huge party that's reserved the patio that weekend, and we're already short-staffed. How could Sloane and I both leave the restaurant all weekend?"

Sloane frowned. "If I'm missing mud baths, then you have to go, 'Ro. This will be my chance to shine at Lavender. But FYI, we're going back sometime. We can do it on a Monday. Say it's employee appreciation or something."

Sloane was best friend first, coworker second. She'd moved from California, lured by Aurora's dream and a change of scenery, and she saved Aurora's skin on a regular basis. If Cece couldn't talk sense into her sister, maybe Sloane could.

"It's barely even two full days. We could come back early Sunday morning."

"I'll miss two of our busiest dinner services on Friday and Saturday. We haven't been around long enough for me to up and leave for a weekend."

"Again, I'll be here," Sloane piped up. "I could take the lead for two nights."

Cece mouthed a *thank you* to her ally.

"That's a lot to dump on you," Aurora argued.

"You're not dumping on me if I'm offering. I'm ready. I can do it. This is Beth's bachelorette. You have to go."

Aurora stirred without responding. "Does Beth know we'll be gone all weekend? Have you checked with her?"

"Why don't you trust me to handle anything?" Cece

raised her voice. "I'm not taking our sister on a booze cruise with a bunch of strippers. I know what I'm doing. I have a nice weekend planned. I told her my ideas, and she loved them. If she trusts me to do this, why can't you? What is your problem?"

That got Aurora to quit stirring. "What is yours?"

"Ladies." Sloane motioned for them to lower their voices. "I'm sure this will all work out once you discuss it, but there's no need to have a family spat in the middle of the kitchen."

Cece and Aurora glared at each other.

"Listen." Sloane reached over and took the spoon from Aurora. "You're both stressed out. Between you both working a lot, and the inn getting damaged and being out of commission, and Beth's wedding around the corner, it's a lot. Everyone just needs to take a deep breath. A weekend getaway would be nice. Some fun to break up the daily grind."

They stopped glaring at each other momentarily.

"Doing something other than work might be nice," Aurora admitted. "I feel like we haven't just hung out and laughed in a while."

"And this is Beth we're talking about," Cece tried, growing more frustrated. "She'd do anything for us." She had done so much for them. What was Aurora thinking, even hesitating a moment? They never did trips like this anymore. This was special.

"I need to see what I can arrange before I commit for sure."

Something in her sister's tone set Cece's teeth on edge. She'd been looking forward to this time with her sisters for so long, and now, of all the self-centered, inconsiderate—

"Could you do that, please?" she snapped. "It would be so nice if you could fit your sisters into your busy life. Do us the honor of celebrating Beth's future marriage and enjoying a weekend I've worked my butt off to plan. But do just let us know if that works for *you*."

"I didn't mean it like that."

Cece turned on her heel, done with listening. She loved her sister, but sometimes she wanted to throttle her.

"Cece," Aurora called after her as she stormed out the back of the kitchen.

Was she a little harsh there at the end? Maybe. But Aurora deserved it. She could get so focused on her own goals and ambition, that she didn't stop to think how those around her felt. She didn't pause to consider how she sounded.

Beth was getting married, for crying out loud. This was it. It wouldn't just be the three of them anymore, officially. And this was going to be her big weekend. Big weekend for big sister Beth. You know, the big sister who helped raised them?

Their mom did the best she could once she was a single parent, left by their father with a scandal and big house they struggled to keep up. But Beth had stepped in and helped, without complaint or question. As the eldest, she'd taken on the role of emotional support system for both Cece and Aurora.

If their mom had kept a roof over their heads, Beth had kept the home fires burning—as the saying goes.

Beth was the one who read Cece stories at bedtime. Beth was the one who stood outside the bathroom when she first got her period, walking her through what to do and how to always be prepared. Beth taught them how to study for algebra, told them about boys and sex, and explained how to identify a toxic friendship *and* get out of it with as little drama as possible.

Sure, sometimes she'd driven Cece and Aurora crazy, but they'd survived. They'd made it, and they were all still close, thanks largely to their oldest sister. So what was Aurora's problem?

Restaurants were demanding, but this wasn't some random girls' weekend. It mattered.

Their time together mattered.

"We'll just go without her," Cece said to herself, slamming her car door shut. She started her car and headed toward Hollyhock.

Not having Aurora there would put a damper on the whole experience. Shelby, Beth's best friend, and Cece couldn't make up for the fact that one whole sister was missing from the equation. Aurora was the outgoing one, the glue that held all the conversations together. Plus, they'd done enough of life without her already.

Until last year, Aurora had been out of their daily lives, living in Los Angeles, pursuing what she'd thought was her dream of being head chef at a big California restaurant. But when Orchard Inn needed a chef to rescue them, Aurora hadn't hesitated. In saving their inn, she'd found a better dream and reconnected with her high school sweetheart.

Now, Aurora was home for good, but they had a lot of lost time to make up.

"I don't get it." Cece shrugged.

Her sisters were everything to her. She can't imagine wanting to move away or missing out on a girls' weekend with them. Talk about FOMO.

She barely registered the drive to the cottage, talking

to herself off and on the whole way. Before she knew it, she'd pulled onto the long driveway to Hollyhock.

The house glowed in the early evening dusk.

The yard was still an overgrown mess, but the hollyhocks were wonderfully tall. A rainbow of frilly florals.

"Crap." Cece realized she hadn't stopped to change for dinner. She still had on what she'd worked in all day. A floral top as busy as the sea of hollyhocks along the driveway, a ratty old pair of jeans, and Birkenstocks.

She'd meant to change into... something. Something better than this. If she turned back now though, she'd be late.

"I wanted to look cute." She debated with herself.

"Are you locked in the car?" Dustin's deep boom of a voice made her jump. Bruce was already running to the driver's side.

Cece opened the door to be greeted with his excited wiggle dance. "No," she yelled back to Dustin. "Just caught up in my thoughts."

"Bruce, that's enough. Let her get into the house at least."

She got out and followed Bruce to the porch, thinking she should've brought something to contribute to dinner. Wine, cheese, something. She'd been so caught up in the renovations lately and planning Beth's weekend, it'd skipped her mind to bring a host gift.

"Hey!" Dustin waved her inside with a cheery smile, a whiff of something buttery and warm slipping by him to fill the porch.

"What smells so delicio— Oh!" Cece stopped midsentence and midway to the kitchen, grinning at the sight before her. "Look at you!" How had she not noticed as soon as she saw him?

Dustin had on an apron, covered in different sizes and

colors of cupcakes. It had a ruffled edge and barely came to his thighs.

"I'm a messy cook, and this is all they had in the store. You like?" He took a step back to model. "I mean, who doesn't like cupcakes?"

"You make a very valid point." Cece stepped into the kitchen, and the scent of garlic and tomatoes wound through the buttery notes. "So, you really cook. Like, with ingredients and everything."

"You thought I was bluffing? Yes, I cook. Look at this." He showed her the pot of sauce, the noodles boiling, and the bread toasting in the oven. Cece held out her hand to give him a high five.

"I don't cook a lot of things," he said. "But I can make a few things very well."

"I'm just surprised, I guess." She definitely should've changed. He was cooking real food, and somehow pulling off sexy and adorable with the apron, and—

"I'm no chef like your sister, but I had to learn so I could feed myself. It was either that or eat out all the time. I love a good burger, but not every day."

"I should've changed before I came over." She blurted out what was bothering her. "And brought something to contribute. I feel bad."

He turned to her, big mixing spoon in midair, confusion all over his face. "Changed?"

"Clothes. I meant to, and then I went by Aurora's restaurant and—"

"Why would you change? You look great exactly like that."

Cece bit the inside of her lip and quickly glanced away. He thought she looked great?

"Nonsense about contributing something too. I invited you. This is my treat. But if you want to help, you can finish the salads while I work on the sauce." He pulled a bowl out of the fridge he'd brought in the other day.

There was still a lot of work to do on the kitchen cabinets, namely sanding and staining, but now there was a fridge, the stove worked, and he'd set up a folding table and chairs in the small dining room.

He had the lettuce ready in a plastic bowl but no toppings. Cece washed her hands and got started chopping a cucumber and carrot.

"By the way, tonight we are eating on Chinet." Dustin held one of the plates up in presentation. "I was fresh out of Desert Flowers and Blue... what was it?" he teased her.

"Desert Rose and Blue Danube."

"Right, right. Those. I don't have any of those, but the store had White Chinet." He waved the ladle at the plate in a flourish.

Cece laughed, covering her mouth. This was already the best... date? she'd ever been on.

"Also." He stopped stirring and hovered near the far counter. "I don't know if you drink, but I got wine. Here's the catch though, I didn't think about it until I got back here, so I only have plastic cups." His smile made her insides go all gooey. "So, obviously it's high-class all the way tonight. Sorry about that, but it's good wine. At least, that's what the lady at the Vine place said."

"You went to Vine Market? *Fancy.*" She smiled as he nodded. "Wine would be lovely."

Dustin wiped his hands on his apron before reaching for the bottle. "It's a red she said would go with the pasta. Savi... no, Savo-ge-something?"

"Sangiovese." Cece pronounced it perfectly.

Both of Dustin's eyebrows crept up. "I'm sorry, *who* is fancy?"

She laughed as he opened the bottle. "Aurora serves it at her restaurant." Her smile melted into a frown. Stupid Aurora.

"What's the matter? You don't like Sangiovese?" He mimicked her exact pronunciation.

"What? No, no. I like it. All of this is perfect. You did..." She didn't even have the words. No one had ever done anything like this for her, except maybe her sisters, and they didn't count. "This is really nice. Thank you for doing all this."

"My pleasure. But why were you scowling?"

"Because of my sister." She scowled again.

"Uh-oh. Beth?" Dustin poured the wine into two little, clear plastic cups.

"No, Aurora."

He handed her a cup and clinked his against hers. "Cheers. Do tell."

She took a sip. "Oh my gosh, this is good."

He sipped too, making a humming noise after he swallowed. "Honestly? I don't know jack about wines, but this random lady said to get this one, and she knew what she was talking about."

Cece tilted her head, her nerves smoothing out at the sight before her. Big, burly Dustin, fixing dinner in a cupcake apron, secure in who he was, and not the least bit self-conscious.

How could she not feel fondly for someone like him? Even if he only ever saw her as the bossy neighbor turned coworker, he still made her feel all warm and wonderful inside.

"So? Tell me what happened with Aurora."

She took another sip and stared at the scuffed kitchen floor. "You don't want to hear about girl drama."

"Are you kidding me?" He checked on a boiling pot. "I want to hear *all* about it. Growing up in a home with a bunch of kids, I loved hearing about any drama that wasn't mine. My drama was school suspension and the threat of expulsion. I loved it when the girls had boyfriend drama or fake fights in the grocery store parking lot. Took the focus off me."

She flinched. "You got expelled from school?"

"Threatened. Never happened. The threat of throwing me out was enough to scare me into shape."

Cece closed her mouth, realizing it was hanging open.

"Listen, I was a very angry twelve-year-old, okay? Imagine whatever you were like at twelve, think of the exact opposite, and that was me. I was ready to fight anyone who looked at me wrong, and I pretty much did. Later though, I realized I wanted to graduate high school so I could get out and get on with life. Then, Manny came along, and I don't know, I knew I needed to do better. Be better. For him."

Dustin was Manny's Beth. A younger sibling had needed support and guidance, and Dustin had stepped in.

"Now," he encouraged. "Back to being mad at Aurora."

Cece laid it all out for him: her plans for the weekend in San Antonio, how the sisters never had time to do anything fun lately, Beth being their pseudo-parent because their dad had left, and Aurora's objection that she might not have time to celebrate their oldest sister.

Dustin listened intently through their first glass of wine as she fixed their salad bowls and he prepared their pasta on the fine Chinet and as they sat at the little folding table to share a meal.

"You think she meant it as harshly as it came across?" he asked. "Because I've met Aurora, and she doesn't seem like someone who'd be mean or harsh intentionally."

"No, she's not. And no, I don't... Maybe she didn't know how selfish she sounded."

Dustin nodded. "Most of us don't know how we sound or come across when we're stressed. It's not exactly our best foot forward, you know?"

"She just— She's so absorbed in the restaurant right now, and I get it, but she's got blinders on regarding everything else. I know it will be tough, but this is one weekend. A special event for our big sister. It's not some random trip for no reason. How could she not want to go?"

Dustin made a noise of understanding as he chewed.

Cece took the opportunity to come up for air and try his pasta dish. She'd been drooling since the moment she caught a whiff.

"Oh my god," she managed to say, her mouth full. "This is *so* good."

"Isn't it?" He took another bite. "I know I made it, but I love this dish. Took years to get it just right."

Cece nodded as she kept eating.

"I'll be honest with you," Dustin finally said. "To me, I think it sounds like Aurora wants to go. Like you said, how could she not? But she's also afraid to leave. She might be scared if something bad goes down at the restaurant, it'll be all her fault because she left. It's still a fairly new business. Most restaurants fail within the first year, and she takes full responsibility for the place. I do too, when it comes to my jobs. Good or bad, the whole thing ends with me."

She considered his insight as she studied him. He made a good point. As much as Cece had worked with her sisters at the inn, she'd never been the boss of anything. She'd never felt like everything depended on her. Orchard Inn was a group effort, and if anyone took on the lion's share of responsibility, it was Beth. Aurora loved a good time; she was the outgoing one, the life of the party. Lately, she'd had to be all business, serious and work, work, work. Of course, she'd *want* to go away for a girls' weekend.

"You might be right," Cece admitted.

Dustin jerked back in his chair in jest. "I might?"

"Yes." She smiled as she rolled her eyes. "My feelings were hurt because I've put a lot of time and care into planning this weekend, and I couldn't see past Aurora...I don't know, wronging me by be anything other than super excited to go and participate."

"I get that your feelings were hurt too though. You worked hard to make the trip perfect. Naturally you were upset. Just talk to Aurora. Listen to her side and explain yours. I bet if you help her with her worry, maybe get some extra help on hand at the restaurant for while she's gone, she'll be really excited to go."

He was full of good points, and when she got over her anger, the bottom line was Aurora needed to go with them to San Antonio, and that was what mattered most. "I'll talk to her when she gets home tonight. See if we can figure out a way to make her okay with leaving."

Dustin poured them both another glass of wine and toasted hers again. "Good plan."

They finished the meal with light conversation about other favorite Italian dishes and restaurants, moving on to best produce markets, and from there, to flowers, land-scaping, and yards.

"I'm sure you've noticed the yard here." Dustin chuckled.

She crossed her arms. "I have. It needs some work."

"Agreed. Obviously, the hollyhocks should stay, but they need weeding. The rest...out front, I can't tell the weeds from the flowers."

"You definitely need to keep the wisteria that's grow-ing on the pergola, but it's got some other junk vines mixed in that need to go. We'd have to really get into the flower beds to see what's worth keeping."

"There's a ton of underbrush that needs clearing out too. The yard needs to be shipshape before the house is on the market."

Cece tilted her head to the side. "Are you asking for my help with yard work?"

"Maybe." He smiled.

"It'll cost you."

"I'm accepting all bids. For now, all I have to offer is dessert. Interested?"

"Always. What are we having?"

"Tiramisu, courtesy of Vine Market. You want to have it outside? Take a look at the yard? I think it's cooled off enough, and I put bulbs in the porch lights."

"Sure." Cece helped him with two servings of tiramisu and carried her plate outside.

The sun had set, and the air was less humid with a slight breeze. Dustin followed her with his serving of des-sert, Bruce, keenly interested, right behind him.

Cece waited until Dustin was beside her on the porch to take a bite. Creamy and smooth, sweet with the sharp taste of espresso and cocoa. "Whoa. This tastes homemade."

"Mmm," he agreed, taking a second bite. "I'll be getting this again. They may get tired of seeing me at Vine Market."

They finished their desserts quickly, neither of them speaking again until they were done.

"You know something is good when there are no words." He wiped his mouth with his napkin.

"I'm going to have to roll home after this dinner."

Dustin nodded. "Everything was delicious."

"C'mon, we can walk it off looking around the yard." Dustin started down the steps.

She followed him into the yard, and they surveyed the general layout. Flower beds, once properly tended, were still recognizable in the landscaping.

"I can get someone out here to mow all the grass down, maybe stake off the beds so they aren't cut. I'd sod it if I wanted to sink that kind of money in, but I don't really want to spend that much."

Cece stepped back to take in the front of the house, the beds, the pergola, and the porch, and crossed her arms again. "Mmm."

"What?" Dustin perked up.

"I don't think a full grass yard, and definitely not sod, is the answer."

"I should just leave it as is?"

"No, but..." She walked around, imagining some of what she'd seen online put into this yard. Longer grasses, stonework, native plants that required little to no upkeep. Greens in various shades, purples and pinks to complement the stone and wood that flowed naturally with the forest.

"I've been reading a lot about native grasses and sedges for yards, instead of non-native or even invasive species that you have to fight to keep alive. You get ground cover naturally found in whatever zone you're in: plant grasses, wildflowers, mosses, and the like. The result is a healthy ecosystem for insects and birds."

"Won't it look like an overgrown mess?"

"Not at all. I'll show you some pictures and videos of finished results people have. The yards look natural and beautiful. Plus, if you're going to live in the country, it should look like you live in the country. Lots of nature and wildlife, nothing overly manicured and golf-coursey."

"Golf-coursey," he repeated with a smile.

"You could preserve some of the hedgerows down the sides, and then it's just a matter of weeding, edging, and hoping for the best come spring."

They circled the house, studying the ornamental bushes that could be shaped into topiaries if someone wanted to put in the time. There was a significant amount of underbrush and weed growth, but nothing that a couple of days of hard work wouldn't tame into shape. The back and side yards were sizable, as the house sat on several acres at the end of the lane, not another home in sight due to the surrounding trees.

"There are tons of options with this backyard," Dustin observed. "Patio space, even an in-ground pool if someone wanted."

The new homeowner could easily build a detached garage, greenhouse, or vegetable garden. The possibilities were endless, and all ones she'd daydreamed about, in detail. That old longing knotted in her gut, thinking about what might've been if this had been really *her* bungalow.

She had to remind herself that there were other houses she could call home one day, but not Hollyhock. This was all bonus time, giving her the chance to fulfill some of those daydreams, and meeting Dustin was just the icing on the cake.

The stranger she'd once demonized was now a... friend? A friend with flirtatious benefits? Whatever he was, she liked it. She might not have the house, but she had something all her own, and that was what she'd really been after. She wanted a life and experiences for just herself. Work she could be proud of, and the independence to prove she existed outside of Orchard Inn.

Dustin, and the work they were doing together, were hers and no one else's.

They reached the bottom of the front porch steps, and Cece turned to him. "Thank you again for tonight. This was very nice. I was half expecting pizza delivery after we finished replacing flooring or something."

He laughed. "Flooring happens in a couple of days. But I thought we'd earned a real dinner, without the work. I don't know if you've noticed or not, but we make a good team. We've already made good progress, and I... I wanted to do something nice for you." His gaze softened as he took her in.

Cece felt herself leaning, pulled into that look. "You did?"

"Yeah." Dustin moved in closer. "I did."

Her heart did a backflip. He was so near, and that look in his eyes was *not* how her friends looked at her. Maybe her instincts were right. Maybe he saw in her what she saw in him. "I...I'm glad. I mean, I appreciate it," she managed. "When you said dinner, I wasn't sure what..."

"What it meant?"

She nodded.

"What would you like it to mean?"

"I don't know."

He smiled. "You don't?"

The front yard spun in slow motion. Yes, she knew what she wanted it to mean, but she was afraid to hope he wanted it to mean something similar.

Cece hesitated, her old fears creeping in, telling her to play it safe. But she'd promised herself that was the old Cece. Her sisters had lived boldly in the last year, and she'd seen what that meant for them. There was no reason she couldn't do the same. She was no less than anyone, and sometimes there was nothing to do except to just say it.

"I was hoping you meant this as a date," she blurted.

His widening smile was all the reassurance she needed. "I was hoping it was a date too. I mean, I got wine I can't even pronounce and tiramisu. That's my ham-handed attempt to impress you."

She broke into a smile, her heart soaring.

"I like you, Cece," he said plainly. "You're funny and smart, you're gorgeous, not afraid of hard work, and you keep me on my toes because I never know what you might say or do."

Cece glanced down, her cheeks on fire, but she didn't want him to stop talking.

"I know we're working together, and if this muddies things, I'll back off, but—"

"No." She cut him off. "No, you don't need to back off. I…I like you too. It's okay if this muddies things."

Dustin took her hand, tugging her that little bit closer

to close the gap between them. "Literally and figuratively if we work on this yard?"

She laughed, and he caught her chin. His eyes were dark in the evening light, but she imagined fire in them. He wanted to kiss her; she could feel it in her bones.

More importantly, she wanted him to. If this was their first date, she wanted it to end with a kiss.

He lowered his lips to hers, but Cece closed the gap.

She was tired of being patient, tired of watching everyone else fall in love and have great adventures, done with waiting for someone to see her—really see her—and want what they saw.

Dustin was her someone, and she didn't want to waste a second playing coy.

His lips met hers in a crush a of heat and need.

She wasn't sure what she'd expected. Sincere and polite? Like the man himself? But no. Dustin's kiss was passionate, needy yet so, so giving.

He put his arms around her, and it was a good thing since her knees decided to turn to molasses. She molded her body into his, and the guttural sound that came from deep in his throat sent sparks up her spine.

Dustin whispered her name as he pulled back slightly.

She blinked up at him, stunned at their chemistry. But she shouldn't be. The last few days had shown her how well they mixed and meshed. Why shouldn't they be electric at this too?

"I'm so glad you invited me over," she said. "And kissed me."

"Me too." His soft laugh returned. "In fact…" He pulled her in and kissed her again.

Cece wrapped her arms around his broad shoulders,

her nerve endings singing. How long had it been since she'd felt this alive? Had she ever felt like this?

Yes, eventually, Dustin would leave Fredericksburg. Out of her life in a matter of weeks, but right now that didn't matter. She wasn't going to let something like reason or fear stop her from enjoying something she wanted so much.

She deserved to relish this, like Sloane said. The future would happen, good or bad, but right now, she was in Dustin's arms, his strong arms, and he was kissing her like she was the air he breathed.

Chapter 9

She all but floated home, still feeling Dustin's lips on her, his arms around her shoulders, his hands on her waist.

Cece giggled. What was she doing? She hadn't felt like a giddy schoolgirl since...well, since she'd been a giddy schoolgirl.

As soon as she walked in the back door of Orchard Inn, the scent hit her. The thick sweetness of sugar, the sharp tickle of cinnamon. She followed her nose across the living room and into the kitchen like she was a cartoon character.

"That has to be cinnamon rolls." Nothing else smelled that good.

Aurora turned from the oven, her eyes wide and pleading. "They are. They're *I'm sorry* cinnamon rolls."

Beth stood next to her with three plates stacked in her hands. "I helped even though I don't know what she's sorry about."

Cece was already so happy that she couldn't hold on to her anger at Aurora. Now she'd gone and made cinnamon rolls to add to the apology. Cece smiled and took the plates from Beth. "I'm sorry too, Aurora. And I forgive you."

"I was a big ole butthead." Aurora opened the oven. "They need two more minutes."

"Yeah, but I was too," Cece admitted. "Once I cooled off and had time to think, I could see that I was way too harsh."

"Are y'all going to tell me what you're apologizing about?" Beth asked.

"No," they answered in unison.

"Fine." Beth plopped down at the counter. "But I still get cinnamon rolls."

"I was so focused on the wedding, and the restaurant, and the expectations and pressure," Aurora explained. "You were right. I had on blinders."

"That's understandable though. You have a lot on you, and trusting others is scary."

Her sister sighed with relief. "Exactly."

"What if we got Jude and his sisters to be on standby to help out?" Cece suggested.

"I thought the same thing." Her sister took her hands "I asked them today, and they'd be happy to help."

Beth leaned forward, elbows on the counter. "Okay, someone better tell me what's going on here, because you're having an entire conversation in code."

"Uh..." Aurora hesitated.

Cece jumped in. "There was just a bit of a scheduling conflict with the restaurant, but we've found a solution."

"Conflict? Wait. Were you not going to be able to go to my bachelorette party?"

"No. Well, yes, but not now. Not anymore." Aurora tried to defend herself. "I was just hesitant."

"She was scared to leave Lavender when it hasn't been open for very long and there's a huge party coming in."

"But I've thought about it, I talked to Jude and he had some great ideas for backup support, and it's all good now. And remember, I made cinnamon rolls, *at night*. For both of you." Aurora hugged Beth.

"You may need to make a second batch. Out of principle."

"I will, I will. I'm sorry. I'm human!"

"I think we should forgive her." Cece floated over to her sisters, still riding high after leaving Hollyhock, and hugged them both. "I have an amazing weekend planned, like the best Beth party ever, and we're going to have an amazing time."

Beth turned in her chair. "Tell me everything."

"Wait." Aurora held out her hands. "Cinnamon rolls." She ran back to the stove.

"Yes, and then tell me everything."

Aurora served up Sawyer's recipe that had become their special treat, and they gathered around the counter to hear Cece's itinerary.

"So, I know the typical bachelorette party thing isn't your style. Instead, I've made reservations at the Mokara Hotel & Spa in San Antonio."

Beth clapped her hands together with a delighted squeak.

"And, and, we'll have lunch on the River Walk Friday afternoon, followed by walking around and shopping. We have a seated wine tasting with dinner at a local vineyard that evening. And Saturday, we have reservations at the resort spa for a day of facials, massages, soaks—the works. Then they have a whole pool, hydrotherapy, and a rainforest shower room, all of it for after."

Beth clapped again, hugging Cece so hard she lost her breath. "That sounds perfect! I love it!"

"And I booked a double, but I told the hotel about the occasion, and they upgraded us!"

"No way!" Beth exclaimed.

"It's concierge level, so the three of us and Shelby can all stay in one room and be up late talking and stuff but still have plenty of room to make it really nice and special."

"You've outdone yourself planning all of this," Aurora agreed.

"I cannot wait." Beth glowed with excitement as she cut into her cinnamon roll.

"You don't have to wait long. Just a few more days until Friday." Cece just stared at her cinnamon roll. She was stuffed from dinner, and there was no room for even a bite of this roll.

Her sisters talked excitedly about what spa treatments they'd choose. Aurora was leaning toward deep-tissue massage for her chronically knotted-up chef's neck and shoulders. Beth wanted a facial and a full-body scrub. They were both giddy about the rooftop pool and concierge service.

A tingle of pride filled Cece as she listened. A couple of years ago, maybe just a year, she would not have been in charge of organizing and planning such an important moment. Now, not only did her sisters believe in her enough to hand over some responsibility, but Cece had also knocked the planning out of the park.

Beth's weekend would be amazing, and maybe she was proving this to herself as much as she was proving it to them.

"Hey." Beth paused to finish chewing. "You aren't eating."

"I'm...I had a big dinner."

"Where?"

Aurora's eyes widened comically. "Was tonight the—?"

Cece nodded.

"The what?" Beth looked back and forth between them. "What did I miss?"

"Well..." Cece paused for effect. "I had a date, with Dustin."

Her sisters responded with giddy questions and noises, none of which she could really distinguish.

"What are y'all asking?" She giggled.

"Sloane is going to be so mad she missed this conversation. You'll have to retell her."

"*After* you tell us everything," Beth insisted. "I didn't know you had a date. How did I not know this?"

"You've got a little bit going on right now, sis," Aurora teased her. "I can't keep you updated on everything you miss."

"Well?" Beth looked at Cece. "How was it? Where did you go? I need details."

Cece laughed again as Aurora poked her in the ribs. "It was really nice. He cooked dinner at Hollyhock, and it was delicious. We had some wine, walked around the yard, and he kissed me."

Her sisters squealed in delight again.

"Was it a good kiss?" Aurora asked when she came up for air.

Cece nodded.

"Do you like him?" Beth asked.

"I do."

"That's so great. Good for you," Aurora praised.

"Yes, good for you. I thought there might be some

chemistry there after you came back from meeting him the first time when you blessed him out."

Cece sighed. "I didn't bless him out, exactly."

"You did, but it happens." Beth waved her off. "Do you remember when Sawyer first came around here, acting like he was going to tell me how to plan Shelby's wedding? My best friend's wedding, just because she was marrying his brother. Ha! We butted heads from the start. Now look at us."

Cece didn't have the heart to point out that she and Dustin wouldn't have the happily ever after Beth did with Sawyer. Theirs was more enjoying the moment, rather than spending forever together.

Better to let her sisters just be happy for her right now.

"Jude and I butted heads too," Aurora agreed. "I mean, I came back here thinking *geez, I hope I don't run into that guy.* He basically ripped my heart out the first time around. I never want to see him again." She took a dramatic bite of her roll. "But I did, and now here we are."

Her sisters had wound down the roads that led them to their partners. The loves of their lives.

But this thing with Dustin wasn't that.

Yes, she was over the moon about the date, and kissing him was all she'd thought it could be and then some, but he wasn't here for Cece. He hadn't come to town looking for forever. He was here on his way to a life he had planned. She was just part of the stop along the way, and that was . . . that was okay.

They were going to enjoy the present, the right now. And after years of thinking she'd never enjoy any romance, this time with Dustin was exactly what she wanted. She was going to absorb it all, happily, and when the time came for him to go, she would gracefully watch him leave.

Chapter 10

The roof repair was complete at Orchard Inn, and Dustin had completely torn out and replaced the damaged upstairs walls. He'd worked at the inn every day for almost two weeks, and only some painting and trim work remained. The paint he needed for the guest rooms was on special order though, so he had a free day that he could completely dedicate to Hollyhock.

Hollyhock needed its own floor repair in the kitchen, and he'd ordered knotty pine to match the original just like Cece wanted.

"Um, I can see the ground." Cece stared at the hole near the middle of the room.

"Yeah, I'm thinking someone hack-jobbed a dishwasher install at some point, and it slowly leaked. Once I started pulling up the flooring, I found water damage all the way through the subfloor. If you're going to fix it—"

"—you've got to fix it right," she finished.

Dustin held out his hand, and she high-fived him without even looking. She just knew it was there.

She walked around the hole in the floor, Bruce following her, a perfect mimic of her studying the hole, with a few added sniffs and a low woof.

"The rest of the kitchen is in good shape though. Same for the rest of the house. I should only need to replace this part of the floor, then sand and stain it all to a shiny finish."

Her face glowed as she looked around, no doubt imagining this house in its original form. Someone's pride and joy.

"Thought that might make you happy," he said.

"You can't imagine." Her smile warmed his chest, making him stand a little taller.

"You want to hang out here while I work on this? I can show you a few tricks of the trade."

"Really? I'd love to."

"Of course. You can give me a hand."

Dustin went about laying the subfloor and flooring, while showing her every step along the way. Cece listened and watched with sharp-eyed attentiveness, asking questions and clarifying details.

She was better than any newbie he'd ever hired, and way more interested in carpentry and contracting than Manny had ever been.

Manny, who had finally sent him a one-sentence text reply yesterday.

Good, bro. Just busy.

True that texts couldn't emote, but anyone would be irritated at such a clipped response. Dustin had tried to call this morning, but he'd been sent to voicemail.

He shook off the thoughts with a grumble as Cece rose to her feet. She stretched out her legs from where she'd been sitting so long, and again, Bruce followed suit but in a perfect downward dog.

"If it's okay with you, I'm going to go work on the fixtures in the bathroom," she said. "I need to move around a bit."

"Yeah, sure. I'm just going to repeat what I've already shown you until it's all nailed down."

She nodded and walked away. In an interesting development, Bruce followed her instead of staying right at Dustin's side, and Dustin noticed a little hitch in Cece's step, like her leg had fallen asleep.

He thought nothing else of it and finished the job in the kitchen in silence. He'd just stood to stretch out his lower back when Cece called to him from down the hall.

"Are you done?" she yelled.

"Yeah."

"Come here and tell me what you think of something."

He made his way down the hall to the bathroom, where Bruce lay stretched out on his side just outside the door.

"Hard at work, I see." Dustin stopped to give him a quick belly scratch.

Cece stood in front of the sink, facing the tub, her features set like she was studying artwork. "I know we shared, uh, words about this bathroom, but what do you think about trying to get a modernized claw-foot tub? You could still install something like a rainforest showerhead or whatever people like nowadays, but the look of it would still be authentic to the house."

He looked at the space, imagining her suggestion. "I like it. I'll have to order one though. I don't usually see those sitting around in the stores."

"I could probably sweet-talk this distributor out of Dallas into a good price too. We used them for some of the bathroom stuff at the inn."

"If you can get what we need without it costing an arm and a leg, I'm down."

"Good." She turned to him with a smile.

Dustin's chest grew warm at the sight of that smile. He wanted to scoop her up and kiss her again, like he had the night before last, but kisses like that were not conducive to getting work done. Kisses like theirs weren't conducive to getting anything done except more kissing, and then likely a beeline to making out.

He cleared his throat and tried to focus on the work she'd done on the fixtures. A new antique toilet paper holder matched the cabinet knobs and doorknobs and complemented the light fixtures. "These look great."

"Thanks. I got them from the hardware store in town. I forgot to mention, they're friends with Sawyer's family, so we can get a discount."

"Does Sawyer and his family know everyone in town? I get the feeling he's connected."

"Just about. His family has been here for generations, always in ranching."

"Mmm." Dustin nodded. "I like Sawyer. He's easy to talk to, even when he's doing a background check on me."

Cece's pop of laughter bounced off the bathroom walls. "Background check. I warned you it'd be an inquisitive lunch."

"I know." Dustin wiggled one of the light sconces by the mirror to make sure it wasn't loose. "I don't mind though. I'd check up on me too. But I passed muster."

"Whew!"

"Does he know about…" He pointed back and forth between them.

"Oh, I'm *sure* he knows. I told Beth and Aurora about our date, and Beth tells Sawyer everything."

Dustin had to laugh. They were one close-knit family. "I hope you didn't go into details."

Cece shrugged with a grin. "You'll probably get asked out for lunch again."

"Uh-oh. Follow-up check-in?"

"Yep." She tilted her head to one side, waves of blond falling over her shoulder, the sunlight coming in the bathroom window surrounding her like a halo.

Dustin took her hand, pulled her into his arms, and placed a quick kiss on her lips, then one on her cheek. He found her lips again, deepening the kiss.

"We're supposed to be working," she whispered.

"I know," he said against her skin. "But if I'm going through another inquisition, might as well make it worth the time."

Cece laughed, the sound sending sparks across his skin as she pulled him down for another kiss.

"Hello?" a voice called from the front door, along with the sound of knocking. "Anybody home?"

Bruce's bark of warning was enough to scare off anyone who meant them harm. Cece and Dustin jerked away from the kiss but remained in each other's arms.

"Who is that?" he mouthed to her.

"I don't know," she mouthed back.

"Cece? It's Shelby and Garrett."

Cece straightened up and smoothed back her hair. "That's Beth's best friend and Sawyer's brother."

"The ones you guys were saying got married at the inn." She nodded.

Dustin grabbed Bruce's collar in one hand and a screwdriver that'd been lying on the floor in the other. A crease formed between Cece's eyebrows.

"I don't know." He shrugged. "To make it look like we were in here hard at work."

Her mouth formed the perfect little *O*, and she gave him a thumbs-up. She turned to go out into the hall, and all he wanted to do was kiss her again. When she insisted on being cute like that, how else was he supposed to feel?

"Shelby?" Cece's accent deepened to an even thicker drawl as she reached the living room and saw the couple at the door. "Hey. What on earth are you doing out here?"

"Hey!" A brunette in a perfectly ironed blouse and slacks hugged Cece, while the man behind her—a younger, less rugged version of Sawyer—stuck out his hand to greet Dustin.

"I'm Garrett Silva, Sawyer's brother."

Dustin put down the screwdriver and joined in the greetings. He introduced Bruce and let him have a sniff of their guests. As soon as Bruce saw how Cece acted around the new-to-him people, he immediately relaxed, all wagging tail and open-mouthed smile.

Dustin invited the couple in.

"Y'all want something to drink or…" Cece glanced toward the kitchen. "We've got some water, maybe some lemonade and Gatorades."

"No, no. We didn't come out here to be a bother," Shelby explained. "But Beth told me you two were fixing up this house, and I told Garrett we had to see this place. It's sat here empty for years, and I just know it's going to end up gorgeous."

Dustin's gears started turning. Shelby thought it had potential; Shelby was married to Garrett; Garrett and his family had ranching money; Garrett probably gave Shelby whatever she wanted. And even if these two weren't potential buyers, if they knew everyone in town, they'd likely know a potential buyer out there somewhere.

"You guys want a tour?" Dustin offered. "We're nowhere near finished, but you can see what we've done so far."

Shelby looked at Garrett, and he nodded. "I'd love a look around, if we're not interrupting."

"Nonsense." Cece took Shelby by the arm. "I'm so proud of what we've done. Come see."

First, they showed them the repaired fireplace and hearth in the living room, then the freshly laid floors in the kitchen. "Dustin ordered this fridge that looks vintage but has all the modern bells and whistles." Then they showed them the dining room.

Shelby's jaw dropped at the inset cabinetry. "Did y'all do this?" She gently touched the glass doors along the top, the sensor turning on the recessed lighting. "Oh my gosh, Garrett, look! It's beautiful."

"We finished that just a day or two ago," Dustin told them.

"Wow." Garrett ogled the craftsmanship.

"Come see the bathroom." Cece led the couple down the hall, and Dustin brought up the rear, observing their reactions while letting Cece take the spotlight.

As expected, she was a natural at bragging on the house. Every little detail and the thought process behind it, she put on display.

They saved the upstairs bedroom for last. "This could be the primary suite and the one downstairs for guest or kids, or vice versa. This one is roomier, but some families might want the kids up here with room to play and their own bathroom."

"You know, for a smaller bungalow, it feels roomy." Shelby led the way back downstairs.

"All the natural light and flow of the floor plan," Cece explained. "That's how they designed homes back then. Every bit of architecture had a reason and function, along with the artistry of how it was built."

"Thank you so much for letting us look around."

"Yes, thank you," Garrett echoed. "This is impressive. Sawyer ought to hire you two to finish his place."

Shelby rolled her eyes and shook her head.

"Sawyer has a place to finish?" Dustin asked, always perking up at the sound of potential work.

"No, he has the shell of a house," Garrett answered.

"Why does he have a shell?" Dustin asked Cece.

"At this point, we don't know for sure because he doesn't talk about it." Shelby pursed her lips and shook her head. "Beth doesn't talk about it either. Sore subject. You know he had someone start on it right after we got married and they got engaged. Took forever just to get the foundation laid and then go vertical. Well, by the time they got a roof on it, Sawyer had to fire the contractor and the whole team—and there it sits. We haven't heard any updates about it since."

"Been like that for a couple of months," Garrett added. "He told me he can't find the right people. It's down near the end of the property, past the main house."

"Does Beth ever say anything to you?" Shelby asked Cece.

"No, and we don't ask. She's got enough on her plate at the moment."

Garrett nodded. "And there's plenty of room for them to live at the main house until theirs is finished. Finally."

"Well, this place is perfect." Shelby held out her arms and hugged Cece. "Y'all are the dream team. You could always rent it or sell it to Sawyer if he can't get his place together."

Cece forced a chuckle.

Dustin and Cece walked the couple out to their SUV and waved as they pulled down the lane.

"Don't worry." He nudged Cece. "I'm not going to let your sister have your house either."

She hid her snort of laughter behind her hand. "Was I that obvious?"

"To me. I don't think they noticed that look on your face."

"I know, I panicked a second, not because I don't want Beth to have whatever she wants, but because I know how jealous I'd be. I want to be a better person than that, but—"

"You're already a good person, Cece. I think jealousy is a normal human emotion."

"Maybe, but then I remembered, this place is not hers or Sawyer's style, at all."

"No?"

"No. Sawyer needs wide-open space—a big, ranch-style home with high ceilings and big ceiling fans. It's how he grew up out here. I guarantee you, the floor plan of this half-built house he's never mentioned is the junior version of his father's home. Same as Garrett's. The Silvas know what they like, and it isn't change."

"Shelby and Garrett were impressed though," he pointed out.

"As they should be. We're the dream team after all."

Dustin returned her smile of pride as Bruce started whining inside the screen door. "Guess it's time to go out. Come on, boy." Dustin opened the door, and they let Bruce run out into the front yard.

At first, all was fine. A normal afternoon outside

break. Bruce sniffed around the yard, looking for the perfect spots to bless, while Cece wandered toward the hollyhocks, literally taking the time to stop and smell the flowers.

Cece's face lit up as she turned back toward the house and something in the overgrowth caught her eye.

"Aw, a bunny." The words seem to come out long and slow, like a film that'd been slowed down. As soon as her words registered with Dustin, Bruce caught sight of the wild hare.

Then, *he* got a wild hair. And still in slow motion, all hell broke loose.

"No!" Dustin yelled, just as Bruce took off like a shot, going straight for the bunny.

Cece screamed, tossing aside the hollyhocks she'd deadheaded.

Dustin ran after Bruce, who ran after the rabbit, Cece following after all three of them.

Around the house they went, the rabbit outmaneuvering Bruce at every turn. They dove under bushes, through bushes, and into brambles. They made it all the way back to the front of the house, and the rabbit hightailed it toward some thick underbrush by the side of the porch.

Dustin followed the pair at full speed, and as Bruce dove headfirst into the brush, Dustin caught a tree root with the toe of his shoe. He pitched forward, windmilling to catch himself.

It was hopeless. Momentum and gravity won out, and he also went headfirst into the brush, falling onto Bruce.

"Dammit," Dustin yelled.

Offended instead of injured, Bruce jumped to the side, tail tucked as he skittered out of the way.

Dustin hit the ground, but his collision with Bruce had softened the fall.

Behind him, gasping for air, Cece called to him. "Are you all right?"

Dustin rolled over and lay prone on his back, nothing hurt but his pride, arms and legs out like a starfish. "I think? How do I look? I look all right?"

Cece collapsed into hysterical giggles, crumpling to the ground beside him.

"What the hell just happened?" he asked her, his body shaking with mirth.

She swiped at the tears of laughter on her cheeks. "I don't know, it...it all happened so fast, but also slow? I saw a bunny, then I saw Bruce, then you, then y'all were all in the bushes."

Dustin sighed and pushed himself to sit up. "I didn't want him to get the bunny."

"Me neither."

"I think we succeeded." He started laughing again.

Cece leaned against him, giggling into his shoulder. "You're sure you're all right?"

"I think so."

Bruce crept over, head down as he sought forgiveness with a gentle nudge.

"Oh, now you want to make up, huh?" Dustin teased him, rubbing his side as they did exactly that. "You're an agent of chaos."

"Has he ever seen a rabbit before?" Cece asked.

"Not that I know of. Just squirrels and birds and cats."

"Come here, boy." Cece held out her hands, and Bruce went to her, plopping himself between her legs to welcome her doting and consoling. "He can't help that he was curious."

"Shameless." Dustin shook his head at Bruce's wide-mouthed smile.

Cece rested her chin on the top of his hard head, joyful tears drying on her pink cheeks, her breath still high from chasing them, her hair tousled from the excitement, and it hit him.

He'd never met anyone like Cece Shipley. The way she made him feel, simply by existing, set off something warm, welcoming, and glowing inside him. She was leaving tomorrow for Beth's bachelorette trip. He'd use the time to find a thrift store and check on a secondhand sofa, and maybe a bed frame. The air mattress wasn't cutting it anymore. He could also sand the upstairs bedroom floor and the stairs of Hollyhock, but the work wouldn't be the same without her here. Actually, the house wouldn't be the same.

Cece brought the place to life, and it struck him that everything might be a little dimmer without her.

Chapter 11

Beth insisted on driving to San Antonio, even though this was her bachelorette trip and Aurora had offered to let Beth be the passenger princess.

"You can navigate and make sure we don't get lost," Beth insisted. "You're a better navigator than me."

"Better navigator?" Aurora shifted in the passenger seat and studied her sister. "Not because you think I'm a crazy driver?"

"I have heard some stories." Shelby nodded, winking at Cece across the backseat.

"I've lived them." Cece returned her knowing grin.

"That's enough from the back row. Y'all pass the Sour Patch Kids." Aurora held her hand out for the bag of their traditional road trip candy.

It only took a little over an hour to get to San Antonio, but tradition was tradition.

They made it to their destination, all sugared up on sour candies, and went straight to lunch on the River Walk.

"We have reservations at a highly recommended Tex-Mex place with seating on the water," Cece told them as they made their way down the iconic Walk, which had sidewalks along the San Antonio River, footbridges across it, and flotillas providing tours to cruise down the river itself. "I was told their fajitas and margaritas are a must."

"This was such a good idea, Cece." Beth looked around, admiring the various shops and restaurants. "I haven't been here since college."

They found their restaurant, and a hostess showed them their table right next to the water. Their waiter appeared a moment later, and all three of the Shipleys ordered margaritas on the rocks.

"Just soda water for me," Shelby told the waiter. "One of us needs to drive to the winery, and I've heard one margarita here is like two anywhere else."

"Good thinking." Beth smiled over the top of her menu, but Cece and Aurora shared a look.

Shelby wasn't a drinker in general, but on a girls' trip, in San Antonio? Cece had suspicions.

The waiter returned with their drinks, and Aurora held up her glass for a toast. "First, thank you to Cece, who did such an amazing job organizing all of this, and most importantly, to Beth. The best big sister anyone could wish for. Here's to a wonderful weekend, celebrating you and your future."

They clinked their glasses together and had a sip.

"Whoo boy." Aurora smacked her lips together. "That is a stout margarita."

Cece started to laugh. "Do you remember the high school reunion we hosted a couple of years ago?"

Beth's eyes went wide. "Yes!"

"No." Aurora shook her head.

"You were in L.A. at the time. We still had a catering company helping with events."

"Oh my gosh, I remember hearing about this." Shelby's face lit up.

"Well, the food was all right, the drinks were fine, but the folks at this reunion? I think we thought, *eh, it's a bunch of sixty-five-year-old retirees or near-retirees. They'll have a few drinks, listen to their cover band of Steely Dan, and go home by eight thirty.*"

"But they *did not*. It was after midnight." Beth laughed.

"Those seniors partied their patooties off. The theme was Very Texas, so lots of grilled meats, margaritas, palomas, and beers. We ran out of tequila and lime juice!"

"Yes, and one of the bartenders had to run to a store where they knew the owner to beg them to sell us more."

"Luckily, some of the people were staying at the inn and the rest just down the road. They'd hired drivers too, because I guess *they* knew they were going to party like it was 1975, but we did not."

"Do you…" Beth dissolved into giggles. "Do you remember when the cover band played Bad Company?"

Cece set her margarita down with a thud. "Yes! Seventy people singing 'Feel Like Makin' Love' at the top of their lungs."

"We had no food left, the bar was drained, and no one—and I mean no one—came down for breakfast the next morning."

"Is that going to be your wedding reception?" Aurora teased.

Beth sipped her margarita and shook her head. "Hardly."

"I don't know." Cece disputed her claim. "I bet Sawyer's side of the family could throw down. They'd sing some Bad Company if the mood hit them."

Shelby giggled. "I'll admit, I have heard Garrett pull up to the house, blaring some Boston. He's not above a classic rock sing-along."

They shared a laugh at her confession and the imagery of buttoned-up businessman Garrett, performing karaoke in the car.

"Sloane has already said she intends to meet Mr. Right or Mr. Right Now at your wedding." Aurora reached for a tortilla chip from the basket the waiter had dropped off. "She said there'd better be, and I quote, 'a big bunch of cowboys present' or she'll demand a refund."

"A refund on what?" Beth smiled.

"I don't know, but I don't want to find out."

The four of them talked and laughed their way through lunch. They decided on two fajita platters to share and a trio of dips for their chips. By the time they were done eating, Cece's face hurt from smiling so much.

She'd missed this kind of girl time with her sisters. Instead of stressing about work and talking endlessly about everything that needed to be done, they shared funny stories and memories. She heard stories about Sawyer, Jude, and Garrett that she never could have imagined.

"That reminds me." Cece gave the waiter her card and pointed at Beth. "What's going on with Sawyer building that house?"

Aurora's gaze jerked toward Beth. "Yeah, I'd almost forgotten y'all don't have your own house yet."

"I haven't." Beth ate a chip.

"What happened exactly?" Aurora asked. "Y'all were like, halfway done, and then nothing."

Beth sighed and sipped on her margarita. "Well, the plan was to have the house finished by the time—or at least near the time—we were married. He found a floor plan we both liked and hired someone because he got all impatient and excited, but then the contractor got into some shady dealings. Sawyer fired him, and he hasn't found anyone since. And with the ranch being so busy, the whole project has sort of just sat there. The house is in the dry, so the timing has drawn out."

"Dustin could finish the job," Shelby suggested, planting her elbows on the table. "I've seen some of his work, and isn't he almost done with the inn?"

Cece and Beth looked at each other.

Cece spoke first. "I don't know if he'd—"

"I don't know what Sawyer has planned either," Beth finished. "I'll let him know though, that it might be a maybe, and he could talk to Dustin about it."

Cece let go of the breath she'd been holding. "That's a good idea."

She didn't want to go booking jobs for Dustin or imposing him on others or others on him without talking things through with him first. They weren't only workplace associates anymore. Mixing business with pleasure complicated things she'd never considered.

Once they'd paid the bill, the four of them returned to the car and headed to the hotel. Check-in was simple, and after hopping on the beds and oohing and aahing about the plush robes and room service breakfast they planned to order, Shelby offered to drive them all to the winery outside the city limits.

Cece had organized a guided tour, including a ride around the property on a souped-up golf cart. They walked a little, took a boatload of pictures, then returned to one of the winery's cellars for a seated tasting with food accompaniments.

"I love this flatware." Aurora twirled a fork between

her fingers. "Wouldn't mind upgrading to this once Lavender takes off."

Cece studied her fork. "Of course you notice the forks and knives. Meanwhile, we're in a literal cave."

"I know; this is like something from a movie," Beth cooed. "Or Broadway."

"I'm half-expecting the Phantom to appear around that corner."

"I love *The Phantom of the Opera*." Cece clutched her heart. "So romantic and dark."

"We should go see it onstage somewhere," Aurora suggested.

"I would love that."

"If this weekend goes well, maybe I'll be able to get away from the restaurant occasionally, to do things like see a show or a concert. Have a little bit of a life. Maybe," she repeated.

"How are things going at Lavender?" Shelby asked.

"Great, so far." Aurora put down her fork. "Just overwhelming, and good staff is hard to find right now. Jude and his sisters have been a huge help. They step in when we need it, and he's gotten really good at running the front of house so I can focus on the back."

"That's wonderful and sounds promising."

"It is. I just..." Aurora's gaze met Cece's. "I need to be reminded things are going well and the restaurant won't come crumbling down if I take my eyes off it for two days. I worry though. It's easy to get wrapped up in the grind and lose perspective. Chefs do it all the time."

"And what about the wedding menu?" Shelby smiled as a sommelier appeared.

"Good evening, ladies," she said. "Tonight, we're

going to start with a dry Riesling, paired with a pear Gorgonzola salad."

Their food appeared as if by magic via two waiters as the sommelier informed them of the wine, its region, and the details which made it unique. Once everyone had a few ounces in their glass, they were left alone to try it.

This time, Cece toasted the ladies in front of her. "To many more years of adventures and new experiences."

Once they'd toasted, instead of trying her pour, Shelby sat her glass down, her brows knitted together.

"You don't want to try it?" Cece asked, her gut already telling her why.

"Um…" Shelby looked to Beth. "I do, but…"

"Tell them," Beth encouraged.

Shelby still hesitated.

"You can tell us, or I can guess," Cece said.

"I really want to, but I'm pregnant."

"I knew it!" Cece and Aurora clapped and exchanged knowing glances. They all got up to congratulate Shelby on her news.

"I didn't want to say anything because this is Beth's weekend."

"Which I told her was nonsense," Beth argued. "Plus, I knew if she wasn't participating in the tasting, y'all would know something was up."

"When did you know?" Aurora asked Beth.

"She and Garrett came over for steaks the other night at the big house, and she didn't have a glass of Cabernet with me. She always has Cab and chocolate with me on a steak night."

"I thought about not coming because I don't want to take away from Beth's—"

Cece held her hand up. "Just stop talking right now. This is even more reason to celebrate!"

The three sisters toasted again, this time to Shelby's news, before diving into their first course.

Aurora explained to them how the sweetness of the pear and sharpness of the Gorgonzola perfectly complemented the bright acidity of a dry Riesling.

"And to answer your question, the wedding menu is pretty much locked in, though I may take some inspiration from this dinner. We'll see. Beth keeps saying she trusts us, so maybe I'll have a few surprises up my sleeve."

"I love surprises."

Cece stared at Beth. "Since when?"

"Uh...Since I learned some of the best things in life can't be planned for. I never planned for someone like Sawyer. A hardheaded cowboy? Getting in my way and challenging me at every turn? I would've told y'all you were crazy if you'd said he was the man for me. But he is. He was surprising and perfect."

Aurora nodded as the waitstaff cleared their plates, replaced with warm Brie on crostini with crispy prosciutto and small bowls of almonds and olives. The sommelier then poured a smooth Chardonnay, explaining how they should taste the wine alone, then after a bite of each of the accoutrements, to note the complexities brought forth.

Cece reached for an almond after her first sip. "I'm glad we don't have to drive. Thanks, Shelby."

"If you start singing classic rock tunes, we're in trouble." Aurora tried an olive. "What you were saying about Sawyer, Beth—the same is true for me and Jude. All I ever wanted, when I was young, was to get out, get away from my hometown, spread my wings and prove to everyone, and really to myself, that I could make it on my own. I never thought I'd be back in Fredericksburg, putting down roots with my own restaurant, and in love with my high school sweetheart."

"That's me and Garrett." Shelby nibbled on a Brie crostini. "Sure, he's a corporate attorney, and I knew I wanted to marry a professional who was highly driven and had goals, but I didn't think he'd be from a family of cowboys, and I never expected to settle down with someone who is so smart and kind of ... well, he's a bit of a closet geek."

The sisters laughed.

"No, it's true. He loves the geekiest stuff and reads all these fantasy books and tries to talk to me about places that aren't real. I have no idea what he's talking about, but I love it. He's just so happy when he's talking about some world with dragons or in another universe, and it's not exactly my thing, but he loves it, and I love to see him happy. Sure, he'll go play golf because it's expected, but y'all, we have toy figurines in our study, and he'd much rather spend a rainy Sunday afternoon at home, watching *Game of the Rings* or whatever."

Aurora choked on her wine again. "I don't think that's right at all."

"*Game of Thrones*, hon." Beth patted Shelby's hand. "And *Lord of the Rings*."

"Well, whatever it is. He loves it all." She smiled sweetly. "And he loves me."

Cece took in every word these ladies said. Their genuine happiness and deep love for their partners made her happy for them but also a little envious. Dustin said jealousy was a normal human emotion, and while they were technically dating—albeit temporarily—that didn't make her less envious of her sisters' relationships. If anything, the longing grew deeper.

"What's the situation with you and Dustin?" Shelby asked, as if reading her mind. "I detected some... vibes."

"Probably because Beth already told you about our dinner date."

Beth's mouth fell open as she feigned shock and outrage.

"Please." Cece rolled her eyes. "If you two gossip anything like the three of us gossip, I know you would've told her."

"Only a little bit," Shelby confessed. "I don't know the latest."

"Yes." Aurora leaned forward with her Chardonnay. "What is the latest?"

"The latest is we work all the time on Hollyhock, but we enjoy the work and each other and..." She let her sentence drift with a shrug.

"That's wonderful, but working all the time?" Shelby shook her head with a tsking noise. "This won't do. You two need another date."

Beth nodded. "Agreed."

"I know!" Aurora set down her glass. "You should come to Lavender one afternoon during the week. Come when it's slower, and I'll do a couple of special entrees, just for the two of you."

"Seriously?" She'd love the chance for another date—this time knowing it was such from the get-go—with Dustin. Plus, there wasn't a nicer place to have one. Aurora's restaurant sat next to Jude's family's lavender farm. The view from the dining patio was acres and acres of rolling lavender fields. Were you dining in Texas or the middle of France? Some days it was hard to tell.

"Yes, seriously. You're my sister, plus y'all can be my guinea pigs for some new menu items I'm thinking about."

Cece was touched by her sister's consideration. "I think that would be really special. Thank you."

The waitstaff returned to their cellar room to add a mushroom risotto dish and a platter of roasted brussels sprouts with shaved Parmesan and cranberries to their spread. The sommelier poured a beautifully colored Pinot Noir.

"How many more courses are there?" Beth whispered, her words coming out a little slower than normal.

"I think two?"

Aurora snickered into her wineglass. "We better have a caution lap and some water in the mix."

"You are wise beyond your years, sis." Cece reached for her water glass with a snort.

They made it through the remaining two courses of filet mignon with a Cabernet Sauvignon, and for dessert, a chocolate mousse with a rich Syrah.

Once back at the hotel, they got ready for bed, wrapping themselves up in the oversize hotel robes and even putting on the matching slippers. Cece crawled into her bed with Aurora, and they found *The Proposal* playing on a movie channel while Beth and Shelby took part in their much longer nightly facial routines.

With everyone finally in bed, the covers pulled up to her chin, Cece texted Dustin good night with a group picture they'd taken by the river. He hearted her picture, wishing her good night.

They all fell asleep with the television on, Sandra Bullock falling in love in the background.

Chapter 12

Y ou have to behave while we're here, son." Dustin patted Bruce's side with a thump.

Bruce gazed up, mouth open and teeth showing as if he were smiling.

"There are other dogs, or at least one other dog, and I don't know how many horses. Not sure you even know what a horse is, but they're here, and after your performance with the rabbit, we're going to go with the harness to be safe. Your kind has a reputation that precedes you, so we've got to prove them wrong, okay? Show everyone what a good boy you are."

Bruce gave him a sloppy kiss.

"That's right, you are a good boy. Okay, okay. Glad we understand one another."

Since the Shipley sisters and Shelby were all out of town for Beth's bachelorette, he and Bruce had gotten an invite to the Silva Ranch, as predicted. The ranch was basically a compound with hundreds of acres where Sawyer, Garrett and Shelby, and their father and his fiancée lived, along with all the stables, horses, and land needed to call yourself a rancher.

Dustin knew nothing about horses or ranches. Curious

about the whole thing, he'd responded with an eager yes to Sawyer's text. Two could play the inquisition game.

He couldn't imagine a life that included miles of land to call home, horses all over the place, growing up and still having your family right there in your pocket. Cece's family was the same. And Aurora's boyfriend, Jude, and his family, to hear her tell of it, all lived on or near the family's lavender farm and shop.

"Must be something in the water." He shared a glance with Bruce.

Dustin pulled up at Silva Ranch a few minutes later, taking the long driveway through tall, what Cece would undoubtedly call *native*, grasses. He picked out the house Garrett described as Sawyer's.

"Yep. That is a half-built house," he told Bruce. "But it has a roof, so that's a good start."

Bruce sat up in anticipation, his nub tail wagging wildly.

"Like I said, we've got to put on your harness and leash for this outing. I can see it now. You head off through a pasture after a deer, and I don't see you for two days."

Bruce was too excited to notice him putting on the harness or leash.

Sawyer walked down the steps of his not-quite-finished front porch to meet them as they got out of the truck.

"Bruce is a big boy," he said as they approached.

"Scares some people at first, but he's a teddy bear," Dustin told him.

Sawyer held his hand down at his side, but out a little, palm down, and let Bruce smell him. "We always had big dogs until Garrett got a terrier."

"A terror?" Dustin smiled.

"Exactly. Dodger has settled down some, but let there be a squirrel in the yard, and it's full-tilt chaos."

"I'm familiar. Bruce decided to chase a rabbit just the other night. I ended up taking a header into some underbrush to keep him from catching said rabbit."

Sawyer chuckled. "Sounds about right." A true animal person, he remained still while Bruce gave him a thorough search and sniff, even in the nethers.

"So, we're going to be close friends? Okay." Sawyer laughed as he stepped away. "As you can see"—he indicated his house—"still some work to be done on this place."

"Yeah, Garrett was telling me about some of your issues getting it built. You got it in the dry though."

Sawyer went back up the stairs, and Dustin and Bruce followed. "My original contractor was a disaster. Turned out to be pretty disreputable."

"Not unheard of in my line of work." Dustin had finished more than a few jobs after a contractor ran off or got fired. The industry was littered with people looking to skim money off the top and sides, but there were decent, hardworking folks too. The cheats only made it harder for those trying to make an honest living.

"Right, and I knew that, but…I got in a hurry. I know better though. I should've gotten more recommendations and been patient on getting started. Waited until one of the best was available. But I'm not known for my patience, know what I mean? So, I fired the guy, and Lyle—have you met Lyle?"

Dustin shook his head.

"Beth's mom's fella—good man—he's helped me out when and where he can. He went over what the guy did before and fixed a few things, but he stays booked up. He won't let me pay him either, and I'm not going to have anyone do this pro bono."

"I hear you. Business gets sticky when you start trading favors or taking on jobs for free and miss out on paying gigs. Better to keep it all on the level and on the books."

"Exactly, thank you. That's what I told Lyle. He's got a calendar full of jobs that are his priority. Meanwhile, Beth and I have half a house." The dissatisfaction in Sawyer's tone was obvious. He wasn't a man accustomed to letting people down, least of all Beth, and he must view the delay on this home as a huge disappointment.

That feeling wouldn't sit well with Dustin, and he imagined it didn't with Sawyer either.

"I know we could stay at the big house, but I don't want to do that long-term," Sawyer continued. "Beth deserves a home of her own. Plus, staying at my uncle's would be like us staying at the inn. I love the place, but there's not a lick of privacy, people coming and going, and everyone in your business."

Dustin had to smile. With big families and lots of friends, it seemed like privacy would be in short supply.

Sawyer walked him around the house. The layout was nice and open, good for a young couple or family. Primary downstairs, two bedrooms upstairs. Nothing over the top, but a very functional space that'd suit them for years to come.

"The house has good bones," Dustin observed.

"Thanks. Lyle inspected everything for me, for peace of mind. He had to fix some of the wiring."

"Plumbed yet?"

"The big stuff, yeah. Had a plumber check it last month. Still needs toilets and sinks, but water heater, overflow, all that is in."

The majority of what was left was interior work, flooring, carpentry, tiling, light plumbing, and a whole bunch of installs. If a contractor had a reliable team of a couple of people, it wouldn't take forever. The hardest parts were done, even if they did require a second person to ensure it was done right.

Dustin circled the living room downstairs that sat off the kitchen. "You won't be in here after the honeymoon, but you might be in by the new year. Maybe Christmas, depending on how many people worked on the job."

"You need any more work?" Sawyer said, laughing like he was half-kidding, half-serious.

It wouldn't be a bad job, but he had to get Hollyhock done if he wanted to get it on the market. Still, Sawyer's job would be another good paycheck.

"I..." Dustin hesitated. "I would, but—"

"I'm kidding, man." Sawyer waved off the topic. "I know you've got your hands full."

Bruce finished his sniff test and sat at Sawyer's feet, leaning his full weight against Sawyer's leg for some ear scratches.

"We're good now?" Sawyer asked Bruce. "I probably smell like all kinds of interesting critters right now. I've got some about five times your size. Want to see them?"

"We'd love to, if you think it's okay to have Bruce around them."

"Yeah, come on. We can take one of the UTVs, and he can ride up front with us. Most dogs love it. I have some horses I wouldn't let him around, not because of him but because they're skittish. They'd be the ones causing chaos. But I have others who are so even-tempered, I can take them anywhere and have them around anyone."

As they walked toward one of the utility vehicles,

another truck, much older and more beat-up, pulled down the drive.

"That's Jude," Sawyer said. "You met him?"

Dustin shook his head.

"Aurora's fella. He runs the lavender farm down the road. The whole family is real salt-of-the-earth folks."

The old truck was parked, and a tall, sandy-blond guy emerged in dirty jeans and a wide-brim hat.

"Jude, this is Dustin. Dustin, Jude." Sawyer made the introductions.

"Nice to meet you. Sorry, I know I look rough," he said. "Been on the farm all day, and I almost forgot Aurora asked me to bring these to y'all."

Dustin finally noticed the platter in the man's hand.

"It's samosas. She wanted me to give them to Lina for feedback, and I forgot about them this morning."

"Lina is my dad's fiancée," Sawyer explained. "Samosas are her specialty."

"Aurora doesn't trust me when I tell her they're delicious," Jude said. "She said it's Lina's recipe, and she must approve them before they're served in the restaurant."

Sawyer took the offered tray. "Can't say I blame her. I'll take them to the big house.

Jude turned toward Dustin after Sawyer left. "The Hollyhock house, right?"

"That's right."

"Aurora told me about that. It'll be nice to see that place all fixed up again. It's been years."

"Renovations are moving along quickly now."

"And Cece is helping out."

Dustin smiled as he nodded. Seemed the word was out all over.

"Okay." Sawyer pulled back up on the UTV. "Food delivered. You want to go see some horses?"

Jude put his hands up. "I'd love to, but we're in the middle of harvesting an acre today, and my sisters will never forgive me if I skip out on work. Enjoy though!"

They all said their goodbyes before Dustin and Bruce loaded up onto Sawyer's off-road vehicle and bounced down a dirt road through some pine trees. They passed one set of stables and a working corral with someone training inside. They passed another set of stables and parked near an empty corral.

"Stay here a sec. I've got someone I want you to meet first."

Around ten minutes passed, but then Sawyer emerged from the stables with the most vibrant burnt-orange-colored horse Sawyer had ever seen. .

The horse let Sawyer lead as they went into the corral, and he walked the horse toward their side of the fence. He waved Dustin and Bruce over. "Come on up to the fence. Let her smell you."

Dustin held on tight to Bruce as they approached. Bruce whined a little but was a lot shyer than Dustin had ever seen him.

"This is Amber." Sawyer stroked the horse's muzzle. "She is Shelby's horse. Beth and I helped whelp her, so she's very special."

Dustin studied her huge, dark eyes as she studied him. She bent low, sniffing toward Bruce. He jumped back when she got close, but Amber didn't flinch at all.

"Don't tell me you're a fraidy-cat now," Dustin teased.

"He's probably thinking *that is the biggest, weirdest-looking dog I've ever seen.*" Sawyer laughed.

Amber remained close, and eventually, Bruce leaned in, allowing them to meet.

"Good boy." Dustin kept his voice low and soothing.

"You want to pet her?" Sawyer offered.

Did he ever. Dustin had never been this close to a horse, let alone touched one. She was so big and powerful, yet gentle, and as curious about Dustin as he was about her.

"It's okay?" he asked.

"Yeah, just hold your hand out, palm up, and let her smell you the way a dog does. Then pet her up here on her muzzle, where she can see what you're doing."

Dustin held out his hand as instructed, and she sniffed and then bobbed her head as if encouraging him to pet her. He gently stroked her muzzle, her eyes easing closed before opening again to watch him.

"That's a good girl," Sawyer praised her. "She's got the best temperament. Best one we've had in years, especially given her age. She's my old soul, aren't ya, girl?" Sawyer patted her shoulder. "I'm trying to convince Shelby to let me show her, with her riding, but we'll see. I taught her to ride, but they told her she can't right now because…" Sawyer clamped his lips shut.

"Because why?"

"Dang it. Uh, I don't know if I'm supposed to say. The announcement rules about this stuff get complicated."

Dustin narrowed his gaze in confusion. Announcement rules? Announcement rules, and she can't ride horses.

Realization dawned. "*Oh*. Is she—?"

"Yes, but *don't* tell anyone I told you. Act surprised when you hear."

"Roger that."

"I don't know why they told me if I'm not supposed to

say anything. I'm no good with secrets. My mouth always gets away from me and I just blah, say things."

Dustin laughed. "Cece mentioned you two have that in common."

"Yes we do. Thought comes in, words come out. We make horrible liars. I tried to keep something from Beth once when we first met, and I failed miserably. Then, when I tried to explain and talk my way out of it, I made it worse. I'm better at using actions than words, but Beth swears I've gotten better at the latter."

"I'm more action than words myself."

"It's easier, right?"

Dustin nodded.

"So, you'll appreciate my problem here. Beth wants us to write our own wedding vows."

Dustin felt woozy just imagining.

"I am not a writer, man. And not only do I have to write the vows and have them perfectly describe how I feel about her, but I've got to read them, *out loud*, in front of other people. I'm going to do it because I love her, but this is my literal nightmare. In front of people, talking—I freeze up."

"The things you do for love."

"No kidding. I'm getting the cold sweats just talking about it. Anyway, I want y'all to meet one more member of the Silva family. Hang on." Sawyer took Amber toward the stables, and not for the first time, Dustin thought how natural it felt hanging out with Sawyer.

His whole life, the only confidant he had was Manny. Manny was his younger brother though, the dynamic totally different than having another guy you could talk to who saw things similarly, someone you could trust. Same with Garrett. He was very different from Sawyer, but it seemed like he was also a stand-up guy.

And obviously, he could talk to Cece. The two of them talked so much. When they got going on a particularly interesting subject, they had to remind each other to get more work done.

He reached for his phone and pulled up the picture she'd sent him. She was a ray of sunshine by the river, her dress covered in green, yellow, and orange flowers.

The last couple of weeks, he'd met and gotten to know more people outside of work than he had all last year. His life, by design, was mostly solitary. He'd had no reason to put down roots when he'd always dreamed of moving on.

Now here he was, meeting the kind of people with family ties and friendships he'd only seen on sitcoms, the kind of connections he'd dreamed of.

"This is Max," Sawyer called out as he emerged from the stables with the biggest horse Dustin had ever seen. "Mad Max."

Dustin's mouth fell open, but he didn't care how he looked. Mad Max was pitch-black, towered over Dustin, and had a thick mane and hair around all four ankles.

"He's my first draft horse, and I love him." Sawyer brought him into the corral. "Is he not the best-looking horse you've ever seen?"

"He doesn't even look real," Dustin commented. Bruce took a step back.

"I won't bring him over as close, as I haven't worked with him since birth like with Amber. Max here is a draft I bought at auction in Dallas."

Max's eyes were as dark as his coat, and he stared at Dustin like he was staring into his soul. Oddly though, the result wasn't ominous. Maybe he was what Sawyer called an old soul too. After studying Dustin, Max moved on to Bruce.

"I don't breed or raise drafts, so you might wonder why I'd spend so much money on a looker like this."

"I guess?" Dustin knew nothing about breeding or raising any kind of horse, but sure.

"Max might be my first movie star."

"Come again?"

Sawyer laughed. "I have a Hollywood horse trainer coming out this winter. Apparently, they like draft horses in movies, mostly for looks, but riders usually go with quarter horses and the like. I've heard how now they do all these films outside of Hollywood, right? They film in New Orleans, Atlanta, on the coast of North and South Carolina. Well, they aren't going to haul horses clear across the country, but New Orleans isn't *that* far from here. Neither is Atlanta, compared to here versus California. Anyway, I'm just going to see how it goes. Always trying to broaden the business."

"Silva's showbiz horses?"

Sawyer nodded. "Yeah, maybe. Something like that. When I saw him at auction, I knew I'd never find a more handsome horse. He's meant for movies, right? If nothing else, I can show him."

Max, or Mad Max as it were, would tower over the people around him. The best word Dustin could think of was...thick. He was dark as ink and massive. He could imagine Max pulling a dark carriage in some spooky historical film, or a horseman with no head riding atop him.

"I can picture him in movies," Dustin admitted.

"Right?"

Sawyer stood back, grinning from ear to ear, as proud as a papa.

Dustin had to smile too, Sawyer's joy was that contagious. "You love what you do, huh?"

"So much, man. It's all I've ever known, and like I told you, living around here? Best place on earth. Yeah, I'm biased, but I said what I said. Come on, Max, you want to get a picture with Dustin?"

Dustin stared at his new buddy Sawyer. "I don't think so."

"Nah, he looks intimidating, but he's a gentle giant. You don't have to get on him, just get closer to the fence."

Dustin kept looking at Sawyer.

"People probably think Bruce is a big meanie too, don't they?" he argued.

Dammit, he had a point. "Yes."

"But he isn't."

Dustin grumbled as he moved closer to the fence. "Okay, but not on him, just near him."

Sawyer handed Dustin the reins across the fence, so he had Max's lead in one hand and Bruce's in the other.

"Okay, everybody smile." Sawyer took out his phone to get the picture. "Next week, we'll have you sitting in his saddle. Say cheese!"

Dustin smiled stiffly.

"Oh man." Sawyer laughed as he took the reins back and texted the picture to Dustin. "Your face is priceless, but I'm telling you, give me a week, and I could have you riding. Maybe not Max but riding nonetheless."

Dustin. On a horse. Manny would get the biggest kick out of that.

Sawyer took Max back to the stables and came out to

ride around the property with Dustin and Bruce. They cruised across pastures, down to a creek, and followed a path through the woods.

"This is one of Cece's favorite trails, now that she knows about it," Sawyer told him. "She loves her walks in the woods."

"Yes, she does."

"Sometimes I'll see her car parked by my house, my half-house, but I won't see her. I know she's out, wandering the grounds. Her sisters worry about her out here, but I don't. I'm never far."

His words reminded Dustin of something he'd said the last time they hung out. "Why do her sisters worry about her so much?" he asked. "I know she's the youngest, and I worry about Manny, but he's hundreds of miles away. Cece is right here with them."

Sawyer glanced over, then back at the path. "Honestly? I think it's because old habits die hard. Especially for Beth. Their dad took off when they were young. I think Cece was barely in grade school. He got in some financial trouble, and Anita, their mom, had to take care of the girls, pay the bills; do all of it on her own. Beth was a teenager, so she took on the surrogate parent role. Plus, with Cece's surgeries and stuff, they always babied her more."

"Surgeries?"

"Ah, crap." Sawyer glanced over again. "Y'all haven't . . . ?" He let the question hang, but Dustin didn't offer a response. "Cece had health issues as a baby. She hates talking about it, and I shouldn't have said anything, but like I said, I just *blah*, and it comes out. You should find a way to ask her if you want to know. Otherwise, she's not likely to bring it up."

He'd told her some about his past, and he wasn't exactly an open book when it came to his childhood, so maybe that made it okay to ask about hers. They'd built up enough trust so it wouldn't come across invasive. Plus, he genuinely cared and wanted to know more about her.

Sawyer pulled up beside his half-house and parked the UTV, Bruce gleefully jumping down, having had the time of his life.

"Thanks for having us out here." Dustin shook Sawyer's hand. "I appreciate the hospitality everyone's shown, and Bruce loves a good field trip."

"Anytime. Got to get you on a horse next time, see how you like it."

Dustin shook his head with a laugh. It'd take a lot more than a next time to get him on a horse. "We'll see about all that. Thanks again though."

They said their goodbyes, and Bruce plopped down, half asleep as soon as he got in the truck. Dustin grabbed his phone and texted Cece the picture of him and Mad Max. He'd just pulled out onto the road when his phone buzzed next to him, startling Bruce. Dustin checked the caller. Cece.

"Please tell me you didn't climb on top of that horse," she said as soon as he answered.

"That's the first time I've ever been close to a horse, so no, I didn't climb on top of any of them."

She chuckled, and the sound, even through the phone, made him smile. "Sawyer will have you on a horse if you keep hanging out with him. That's a whole thing with him."

"I gathered as much."

"It's a great picture though. How was this inquisition? Not too bad, I hope?"

"Actually, he didn't question me at all." Now that

Dustin stopped to think about it, they'd just hung out, no ulterior motives. "I saw the house he doesn't like to talk about, saw the property, saw some horses. Bruce is worn out from all the excitement."

"How bad is it? Doesn't look terrible from the outside, but I've never been in to poke around."

"It's not bad at all really. He said your mom's boyfriend, Lyle, helped get the structure to code. Now it's mostly interior work, installs. I kind of got the feeling..." Dustin didn't finish his thought.

"What?"

He was learning quickly that in small towns and within big families, words and opinions traveled fast, but he trusted Cece. "I think he might've considered me to finish the job, but he knows I'm busy right now."

"Yeah, probably, but his house isn't going anywhere. What about when you finish Hollyhock?"

She asked it so casually, like *wouldn't you take on a paying gig before leaving town?* Did he have a deadline to get down to the gulf? Not really. He could take on Sawyer's place and then go. Why hadn't he thought of that?

"That's actually a good suggestion. Maybe I'll mention it to him. You sure you won't be ready to get rid of me by then?" he asked, teasing. He stopped breathing when her end of the call fell silent.

Part of him was joking, but maybe, subconsciously, he also wanted to know. No matter how much he told himself otherwise, they were growing closer. Their short-term flirtation had some real feelings involved now. If he stayed longer, those feelings would only grow stronger.

"I doubt it," she finally answered, her tone light but sounding forced. "Guess we'll have to wait and see."

Dustin finally took a breath.

"If you're free tomorrow afternoon"—she changed the subject quickly—"Aurora has invited us to lunch at Lavender. Her treat."

Again, he didn't say no to free food. "Sounds good to me."

He wanted to say he couldn't wait to see her, how his day was automatically better just by talking to her. He wanted to ask her about her childhood and tell her how much he missed her, but the words wouldn't come out.

"I'll see you tomorrow then," she said.

"See you then," he managed. Dustin ended the call and pulled up her picture from the river again. The notion of staying in town longer felt good; spending more time with Cece felt right. So why was his stomach suddenly knotted? Why did dread creep in, making him want to run?

But didn't he know why? The same reason he led a mostly solitary life to begin with.

The closer you were to people, the more they could hurt you. People could be selfish and mean, and people left. The more time he spent around Cece, the more likely it was he'd fall in love with her.

No, not likely. Guaranteed. And the people you loved most were the ones who hurt you the most. His whole life, he'd intentionally let one person in: Manny. Now, there was Cece, and in his heart, he wanted to be closer to her. His mind knew better though. He wasn't made to have that kind of connection or even the connections she had with others, the huge family and array of friends.

How did people function, walking around caring about a dozen different loved ones, all entwined in their lives?

He'd gotten close enough to her already, even to her

family, and it terrified him. Maybe it was already too late. If he left now, would his heart survive?

Dustin reached for Bruce, a hand on his rising and falling belly as he snored deeply.

"I don't know what I'm going to do," he whispered, but he knew he wasn't ready to leave yet.

Chapter 13

Cece had been away from Dustin for maybe forty-eight hours, but it felt like ages.

She all but leapt into Dustin's arms when he walked out onto the porch of Hollyhock, delighted to see him. He was the same as the day she left, though she wasn't sure why she'd worried he'd change in two days. Still, the anxiety that she'd return and he'd be somehow different or distant remained.

Until he pulled her close, dropping a kiss on her forehead before pressing his lips to hers.

"It is so good to see you," he whispered.

Cece's heart warmed, delighted he felt the same. "Same here."

"Is that weird to say?" He leaned back. "After only knowing you a couple of weeks, is that too much?"

"No!" She'd said that too fast. "I mean, I don't think so." She'd never missed a guy like she'd missed him.

"Good." He pulled her in close again. "Sounds like you all had fun."

"We had so much fun." Cece burrowed back into his arms. "I can't wait to tell you about it."

Even if this feeling was mildly codependent, she didn't

care. If this was what infatuation and the early stages of dating felt like, she was loving every minute of it. The fresh rush of adrenaline and giddy excitement was addictive, especially because she'd never felt anything like this before.

She'd texted Dustin as soon as they got home, keeping the back-and-forth quick, knowing they would spend the rest of the day together with lunch at Lavender and then a promised tour of Jude's farm.

A whole day off with Dustin. No work or other obligations. Another date, this time an official one, out in public.

Anxious trepidation crept in like a thick fog, enveloping her joy. A girl could get used to this. The acceptance and appreciation, the affection. But then what? What happened when it all got yanked away?

She'd been fine on her own for years now and had even contemplated a life like that, always. Then, Dustin came into her life and made things more... vivid. More fun and exciting. More *more*.

"What time is lunch?" Dustin asked, leaning away.

"We should probably leave now. One o'clock at Aurora's restaurant. Be prepared though."

"For what?"

"Jude's family has been helping out at the restaurant all weekend, which means they'll all still be there. There are *a lot* of Joneses. More of them than there are Shipleys or Silvas."

Dustin laughed.

"And they'll be everywhere. Sisters, parents, maybe a nephew or niece, some cousins. Who knows?"

"Right, and Jude's family—"

"Owns the lavender farm and shop."

"Got it."

Sure enough, when they arrived at the restaurant, half the Jones family was there, either working or eating or both.

"That's Jenna, Jude's oldest sister; his youngest sister, Bonnie, and her girlfriend, Meredith." Cece pointed out the who's who of Joneses as they bustled about the restaurant. "And you remember Sloane." She had barely managed to get the sentence out when Sloane popped out from behind the bar.

"Hey, guys. Aurora told me you were coming for lunch today, so I kept an eye out for you. Follow me."

"Does the whole family work here full-time?" Dustin asked Cece out the side of his mouth.

"They work at the farm, but they help out here as needed, and like you'd suggested, Aurora got them all to fill in this weekend while she was gone. For peace of mind."

"Nice."

"Yeah," Sloane chimed in, overhearing them. "And we had a couple of waitstaff call out this morning. Long couple of days this weekend, and I kind of predicted they'd call out. They'll roll in wanting dinner shift tonight though. Just watch."

"How did things go with Aurora gone? No one called her in a panic, so good, I hope?"

"Good. No catastrophes. Not nearly as bad as I thought it might be, but tougher than I'd like. I learned a few things I'll do differently next time she's out. I'm running on caffeine and anxiety right now though, and I am very much looking forward to the restaurant being closed Monday and Tuesday."

Cece gave Sloane a squeeze. "I bet you did amazing."

"I'll be able to better assess once I've slept longer than two hours. Okay, guys. Back to the kitchen. Just wanted to say hey. Bonnie will be your server. Enjoy."

She left them with their menus at a beautiful table on the patio, a cool autumn breeze in the air.

"Wow, that's some view." Dustin looked out over the lavender fields, the sea of purple swaying in the breeze.

"Isn't it? I love sitting out here. Aurora said she wants to buy heat lamps so they can use this space year-round. It's too pretty out here not to."

"Agreed. I can't imagine sitting inside with this out here." Dustin reached over the corner of the table and took Cece's hand. "So, tell me about your weekend."

"Oh yeah," She put down the menu. "We're not ordering anyway. Aurora is making us a menu to try."

Dustin squeezed her hand and smiled. The way he looked at her lit her up inside. Maybe it made her corny, but she felt tiny fireworks exploding every time he gave her that look. She knew from the warmth of his gaze that Dustin not only cared for her, but he made her feel... wanted. Desired. And it was a wonderful feeling.

"The weekend was amazing," she told him, returning his smile. "Everything went according to plan. We had a little too much wine Friday night, but we ended up having the best talks because of it. We laughed so much my face hurt the next day."

She filled him in on their lunch, the winery, and the news of Shelby's pregnancy.

"Wow, really?" Dustin widened his eyes. "Congratulations. To them, I mean. That's... that is great news."

He was a terrible liar. "You already knew," she said.

"No I didn't?"

She had to laugh at how bad he was at this. "Who spilled the beans? Sawyer?"

"Um."

"He's such a blabbermouth; I know it was him. I can get anything out of that man. Beth? She's like a vault. I don't even ask her if I want the scoop on anything. I just go straight to Sawyer."

Dustin started chuckling.

"Seriously. He'll spill the beans and not even know it. When he broke ground on that house, he and Beth didn't want to say anything, in case people got judgy, thinking it was jumping the gun or whatever. I knew something was up, because they were acting all twitchy one night and hiding something they were looking at in our kitchen. I knew if I asked Beth, she'd wall up and get even more secretive. Instead, one day I rolled the dice and said to Sawyer, 'Beth told me about y'all's plans. I think it's great.'"

"And he bought it?" Dustin reached for his water.

"Yep. He was relieved to talk about it. Told me all about the house plans and what he wanted to do. He didn't even care that I'd set him up to spill. He was too excited to share the news."

Dustin laughed as he shook his head. "I like Sawyer. He's a good guy."

"He's great. He's really mellowed out since being with Beth too, but he was always good to me. Having him as an older brother..." She shrugged. "I don't know, it just feels natural."

"That reminds me." Dustin shifted in his seat and leaned closer. "I wanted to ask you about something."

"Cece! Hey!" Shelby waved as she came over. "Hey, Dustin."

Dustin sat back in his seat but greeted her with a smile.

"I'm sorry to interrupt your lunch, but...well, I saw y'all here when we walked in, and I've been thinking ever since we came to see y'all at the house the other day."

Garrett joined them right as Bonnie came over to take their drink order. "Y'all want to sit together?" she asked.

"No, we're not here to intrude on their meal," Garrett answered.

"But we do want to talk to them," Shelby whispered loudly.

"It can wait, hon."

"Why don't you guys sit for a bit, and we can talk," Dustin offered. "Sounds like something is on your mind."

"It is." Shelby sat down, and Garrett shrugged, giving in. "I can't stop thinking about the work y'all did in that dining room," Shelby said. "The whole house actually, and with our exciting news, we need to make a few adjustments upstairs in our home."

"We need to plan for a nursery," Garrett added. "Right now, one of our spare rooms is a guest room, and one just has a TV and treadmill in there."

"I thought, knowing what you two can do, and Cece, knowing how well you've decorated parts of Orchard Inn and how you helped with our wedding, maybe we could hire you to get our house ready for the baby."

Dustin looked at Cece, his eyes wide.

"Wow." Cece blinked and stared at Dustin. "Uh, we haven't...I mean, we don't really..."

"We haven't discussed taking on other jobs," Dustin finished for her.

"You should," Shelby encouraged. "You guys could be booked solid."

"Honey," Garrett said gently, reading the table. "Maybe they don't want to be booked solid."

"Oh." Shelby smiled sweetly.

"But," Cece offered, "maybe we do. Who knows?" She looked at Dustin. "Why don't we, y'know, why don't you let us talk about this, and then we can get back to you?"

"That would be wonderful," Garrett said. "We appreciate you considering the job."

"Yes." Shelby smiled, her whole face glowing now that the word was out about the newest Silva. "Okay, we're going to leave you two alone. Enjoy your lunch." She gave Cece another hug before they hurried away.

"Nice save," Dustin said as they sat back down.

"Same to you. They caught me so off guard."

"Me too."

Bonnie returned. "You guys want to order anything to drink? I think Aurora is about to start pushing out the plates to your table. I've seen what's coming. I hope you're hungry."

They both ordered half lemonades, half unsweet teas, and the drinks were served as the first round of small plates arrived.

"So." Dustin reached for one of the flatbreads. "What do you..." He hesitated. "What are your thoughts about their request?"

Cece sipped her Arnold Palmer. "I think it's more important to know what you think about their request. I live here. I can do whatever. You're the one who's on a timeline."

"Yeah." He chewed as he thought. "I've been thinking about that, actually."

Her stomach did a backflip as she tried not to grip her glass so hard it cracked.

"I guess it's not a *strict* timeline. I don't have to leave on a particular day, but I hadn't planned to take on a bunch of jobs. Shelby and Garrett's job sounds small though. A lot smaller than Sawyer's."

He was on the right track, but they couldn't do one brother's job and not the other's. Not in this town. "Yes, but if you work on Garrett's house and not Sawyer's..." She gave him a pointed stare.

"Mmm, good point. Probably need to go with all or nothing, huh?"

She nodded, secretly voting for all. Yes, Dustin staying longer would have repercussions, but she couldn't help but want more time with him.

"By the way, I don't know what all is on this pizza thing," he said. "But it's delicious."

"I think it's duck." Cece tried a bite of the meat alone. "Duck and a tart cherry drizzle with some kind of cheese."

"I like it."

Bonnie returned with a bowl of pasta, and Cece decided she'd better change the subject before her nervous system went into overdrive.

"The meals we had this weekend were great too. I'm going to need to walk all week after all this food."

"Tell me all about it. I've never been to San Antonio."

Cece filled him in on their weekend, sparing no detail. The more she could distract her thoughts from the prospect of him taking on other jobs, staying in Fredericksburg longer, the better.

Allowing herself a short fling for a month or so was

one thing. But the longer he remained, the harder and deeper she'd fall. It was inevitable.

He'd given her no reason to believe otherwise. Dustin was fall-worthy. No red flags, no flashing warning signs. Except the fact that he had made it clear he didn't intend to stay. His plan was a life elsewhere, and she had no desire to move far away from her hometown. Aurora, the most independent of them all, had done it and even she'd come back.

If Dustin stayed in town for months, Cece could be in love. Real love. How would she survive such a thing? She'd had no heartbreaks in high school, not a college romance gone bad to prepare her for the roller coaster of a relationship.

She couldn't risk giving Dustin her heart, but the fact was, he already had it. She'd be heartbroken if he left tomorrow. Why shouldn't she make the pain later worth it with more joy right now?

Cece reached for her tea and lemonade and tried to swallow the knot in her throat. "So, um . . ." She needed to let him talk for a while, get her mind off the two of them. "Have you talked to Manny or heard from him?"

"No." Dustin scowled. "Well, kind of. A four-word text, if that counts. He said he's fine, just busy. But . . . I don't know."

"What?"

"My gut tells me something is up. He's never gone this long without us talking. He's not the withdrawn, reserved, or quiet type at all. Actually . . ." Dustin's scowl melted. "He'd fit in great with you guys. He's a talker, extroverted, always wants to stay busy and get in other people's business."

"Maybe you should try calling again? Tomorrow

or something. Give it a day or two. If your instinct says something is up, it probably is."

Dustin looked out at the lavender fields beyond the restaurant, the corners of his eyes creased in thought. "I should. You're right. I can't shake the feeling, and I'd rather know than keep worrying."

"All right, guys." Bonnie showed up at their table. "Last course. Aurora is trying a new dessert. Pear and plum puff pastry with blue cheese."

"Good gosh," Dustin exclaimed at the sight.

Aurora had baked phyllo dough squares with alternating slices of pears and plums drizzled with honey, then another drizzle of honey after baking, and a sprinkling of blue cheese and what looked like thyme.

The yellow and burgundy fruit together mimicked beautiful fall leaves; the scent of warm honey and baked dough smelled like a cozy home on an autumn morning. The dessert was an homage to Jude's farm with the honey and thyme, and to Orchard Inn with the plums. The pears were an inspiration from their weekend in San Antonio.

"You okay?" Dustin asked.

Cece smiled. "Yeah. This dessert is just so...It's so Aurora."

They both tried a bite, the combination of sweet and savory a symphony of taste.

"Wow," was all Dustin could say with every bite.

Aurora had outdone herself, enough to make Cece misty-eyed.

"No one has a right to cook this good." Dustin wiped his mouth.

"I know. Having her own restaurant has really..." Cece shook her head. "I'm so proud of her."

His gaze softened as he gazed into her eyes. "You love your family so much."

It wasn't a question.

"I think that's wonderful." He smiled. "It's really special what you guys have."

Cece reached for Dustin's hand and squeezed it. "Even though I get so mad at her I have to vent to you?"

"That makes it even better. You can fight and get mad, but deep down, you know it's temporary. You're always going to be there for one another, so it's a safe place to be mad. Get angry and yell and scream; let it all out. They'll still catch you when you fall."

She nodded, thinking about all the times she and Beth had bickered, she and Aurora, Aurora and Beth, Aurora and their mom. Over the years, some of the arguments had gotten explosive, with more than few tears, but they were all still together and would always be.

"You want to go for a walk?" she asked Dustin.

His gentle smile turned giddy. "Are you inviting me on your most coveted activity?"

She dipped her head with a laugh. "Yes. We could walk through the lavender fields. Jude won't mind. Customers do it all the time to pick their own lavender."

"I'd love to go for a walk with you."

They left his truck at the restaurant and walked straight from the restaurant to the back of the fields. Even in September, with warm Texas weather, the lavender was a vibrant purple, rolling in waves against the sky.

Only a few minutes into walking, they came upon a man in a wide-brimmed hat, bent over, pulling weeds in the middle of a thicket of rosemary.

"Jude? Is that you?"

"I think." He straightened. "Oh, hey, Cece. Hey, Dustin."

Cece's gaze jerked toward Dustin. "Y'all have met?"

"At Sawyer's." Dustin stuck out his hand to shake Jude's. "Cece wanted to show me the fields after we just stuffed ourselves at Aurora's restaurant."

"Ahh yes." Jude nodded. "Aurora told me what she had planned for y'all. Feel free to do all the walking you need after that. And if that doesn't do the trick, just come on back here and help me weed this herb garden."

"Sure thing, Jude," Cece teased as she led them away.

"Seriously though," he called after them, lightness in his tone. "Anytime. I'll be here. Just come on by."

They walked quietly for several minutes.

"This is like something from a movie," Dustin finally commented. "Sawyer should bring Max out here for his acting resume."

"I take it he told you about his big plans for getting into horsey Hollywood in the southeast?"

"He did. Sounds like he wants to expand the business into something new."

"I guess. It sounds so surreal though. Sawyer and his horses in a movie? Sawyer on a movie set trying to tell, I don't know, Brad Pitt what to do?"

"Why not? Someone has to do it. I imagine there's a ton of red tape to protect the horses, and Sawyer's willing to go through all that because of how much he loves what he does. Most people wouldn't want to jump through those hoops. No pun intended."

Cece laughed anyway. "True. And I don't know that anyone else is doing it large-scale yet. Not like in California." She shrugged. "Maybe he's on to something. Regardless, it makes him happy."

"Yeah." Dustin shook his head.

"What?"

"Nothing." He studied his feet as they walked. "I guess I just can't imagine that."

"Hollywood?"

"No. Taking a chance with work like that, just to be happy. Like, he could be successful, or he could fall on his face. Either way, he'll be okay, and just trying will make him happy." Dustin shook his head. "I can't imagine even having that kind of option. I've always been careful, overly cautious really, when it comes to money. Growing up, it was always a concern. When and where is the money coming in? You had to be sure you had some kind of income, steady was best, and there wasn't even an option to take chances like that, or you'd end up broke and sleeping in your car."

Cece studied his profile, imagining what it must've been like to have no security growing up. Even with her childhood struggles, she'd always had the stability and support of family. When their dad took off was the roughest part, security-wise. She could remember her mom being worried and stressed all the time and Beth taking on the role of guardian.

"I think the only time my family faced something even close was when my dad ran off," she said. "But I was so young, I didn't even know to worry that we might lose everything. I remember Mom saying we had to be frugal, and she would get our clothes secondhand, sew a lot of stuff herself, to save money. Actually..." Something occurred to Cece. "That's why I first got into sewing. Because my mom used to sew. I didn't make the connection that she probably only did it out of necessity."

Dustin took her hand. "I'm glad you were able to make it through that time, you and your family, and keep what's now the inn."

"I know. It was a risk for sure, and if it'd failed, I don't know what we would've done. We would've lost our home, everything. Still, we had a community here that could've helped if we'd needed it. We had families around us, friends. Somehow, we would've gotten back on our feet, but it was scary. A lot of people don't have safety nets."

"I'd say most people don't have safety nets. They can't go out and be brave. They're too busy working three jobs to get by."

She nodded, deep in thought about the past.

"I want to ask you something," Dustin said, pulling her out momentarily. "About why your sisters worry so much about you. I get the feeling it's more than just regular big sister habits. Am I right?"

Cece stopped walking and turned to face him, pulling her hand away to cross her arms. She'd put off letting him into this part of her past, not because she didn't trust him with the truth, but because she didn't like looking back when she could look forward.

"I had some health issues after I was born, and . . . um, my family worried a lot about me the first few, well, years of my life. They didn't even know anything was wrong at first, not until I was old enough to start crawling around and walking." She took a steadying breath, knowing how some people reacted to her diagnosis. If Dustin was one of those people, this could be the end of him letting her work on the house with him. Still, she couldn't lie about who she was. She didn't want to lie to him about anything.

"They noticed I wasn't able to walk, you know, the way I should," she continued. "My mom got scared, and the doctors ran a bunch of tests. They determined I have what's called level one cerebral palsy." Cece stared at the lavender off to the side of Dustin, not wanting to meet his gaze as she finished telling her story. "It's a mild case, and even though it's not something that ever goes away, because we got a diagnosis so quickly, I got into therapy and had a couple of procedures, wore a brace for a while when I was little. By the time I was in elementary school, around eight and nine years old, you could barely tell. Now, when most people meet me, they'd never know, unless—you know—I tell them."

Cece pinched her lips together, done talking, but she didn't meet his gaze.

When seconds went by silently, she knew she had to look up. She found him studying her, his eyes warm and impossibly deep.

"We have a 'no pity' rule," she reminded him, praying she didn't tear up now.

Dustin reached for her crossed arms. "I don't pity you, Cece. I'm amazed by you."

The knot wound tight in her throat again.

"Thank you for telling me your story. I feel like, I don't know...knowing that, I can see the whole picture of who you are. If that makes sense?"

She managed a nod. The same was true for the picture of him. Dustin's background was the reason he was so caring and understanding.

"I think you're even stronger than you realize," he said. "Because I know that wasn't easy to share."

She nodded again, afraid to speak because her voice

would probably shake, but she needed to tell him. "I know it wasn't easy for you to talk about your past either, but I'm glad you did."

His look softened even more as he was able to take her hand and move her close, into his arms. "The truth is"—he spoke into her hair—"I envy the roots all of you have here, with your family, friends, with this town. I wouldn't change my life because I found family in Manny, and my last foster parents were really good to me, but sometimes I wonder how different life would be if I'd grown up like you or Jude or Sawyer."

She shook her head against his chest and pulled away. "But just like me, your life has made you *you*. Your past, what you went through, made you who you are. Tough but empathetic, no-nonsense. You're hardworking but fun, genuine, and kind. And loving. I wouldn't change a single thing about you."

Cece leaned back into him, letting herself melt into the warmth of his embrace.

She'd told him her story, and he hadn't overreacted; he hadn't jumped to the conclusion she was incapable of work or a liability to be lamented over. He'd listened to the past but focused on the here and now and who she'd become.

"You want to go home?" he asked against her hair.

He meant Hollyhock, which wasn't her home, but they'd both slipped up before, using the term. "Yes."

Dustin took her hand, and they walked through the lavender, silent. Cece didn't need words to know something between them had shifted today, and in her heart at least, there'd be no going back to believing this was still merely a flirtation or infatuation.

"Today was... special," Dustin said, as they pulled up at Hollyhock.

"It really was," she agreed.

"I'd forgotten how wonderful a day off could be, especially with you."

"Monday is going to be rough."

"Tomorrow, you mean?"

Cece let her head fall back against the headrest. "That is tomorrow, huh?"

"After every Sunday." He chuckled as he urged her upright and closer. "At least your coworker is awesome."

"He is?" she teased and leaned forward.

Dustin leaned in too. "He is." He brushed a kiss against her lips, and Cece moved in for more. After being away all weekend, then sharing so much of who they were, she wanted more than a little kiss.

Dustin cupped her jaw and cheek, deepening the kiss until static filled her brain.

"Ahem." A deep clearing of a throat made her jump.

Dustin sat back, searching the yard.

A young man had emerged from around the house. He was not as tall as Dustin but broadly built with thick, dark hair that flopped into his eyes.

"Manny?" Dustin exclaimed.

Cece gaped, her heart pounding. "Manny?"

Chapter 14

Good to see you're alive." Dustin wrapped Manny in a bear hug, needing to confirm he was real. "What the hell, man?"

Inside the house, Bruce was barking uncontrollably.

"I know, I know." Manny returned his hug. "I'm the worst. I'm sorry."

Dustin gave him one last clap on the back. "Hang on. Let me let Brucey-boy out, or he's going to start breaking things."

He opened the front door, and Bruce bounded down the stairs, tackling Manny.

"He's like a linebacker." Manny chuckled. "Sheesh. Easy, fella. I missed you too."

Bruce proceeded to kiss his entire face.

"I've texted you for days, and you couldn't pick up the phone?"

"I've had a lot going on. I'm here now though. That's even better, right?"

Dustin swiped a hand across his jaw, trying to grasp the reality that Manny was right here, in the yard with him, and he was okay.

From the corner of his gaze, Cece moved.

"Manny, this is Cece. Cece, Manny, my brother—who forgot how phones work."

"Ha, ha. Nice to meet you, Cece." He shoved himself up from the ground and shook her hand.

"Nice to meet you." Cece studied Manny with a smile, but Dustin's study brought a frown.

Manny was here and clearly safe, but he looked thinner. Too thin. His color was good, and he seemed healthy enough, but perhaps like he wasn't eating enough or well. When Manny got stressed, he didn't eat. Almost like he forgot.

Not good.

"You're too skinny," Dustin stated.

Manny glared up from petting Bruce. "It's good to see you too."

"That's not—" He held back an annoyed sigh. "Of course I'm happy to see you. I've been worried for weeks now. I'm just saying. What's going on? You don't call me back; you show up here and you're at least ten pounds underweight; and I—"

"Why don't we go inside," Cece suggested. "Y'all can sit down and catch up. Manny can see the place."

Dustin's gaze met hers, and he thanked her silently.

He was mucking up this reunion by trying to big-brother his brother, but look at him.

"Yes, let's go inside." Dustin tried a more relaxed approach. "Come on, Bruce. Everyone in the house."

They went into the kitchen and gathered around the sad little card table. Cece suggested coffee.

"Coffee would be great, thank you," Manny said.

At least he'd remembered the manners Dustin had driven home, even if he'd forgotten to feed himself. Or worse, he didn't have the money to eat right.

"Here." Dustin jumped up and got the loaf of bread, mayo, and turkey from the fridge, and a whole new pack of Oreos from the crisper drawer. "You had lunch?" He plopped all the food and a paper plate on the table in front of Manny.

"I mean, I could eat, sure." He grabbed the bread and pulled out two slices. "You still keeping the Oreos cold, I see."

"Best way to have them."

Manny started making himself a sandwich, and Dustin glanced at Cece. She stood by the coffee maker, sharing his concerned expression.

"So, how have you been? What's the latest? Just here to visit or...?"

Manny took a bite of his thick sandwich and nodded with a smile. "Got some time off and thought I'd come see you."

"Good, good," Dustin said, trying to convince himself everything was fine, even as his gut told him the opposite. Something was wrong, and all the forced smiles in the world wouldn't convince him otherwise.

"You know how I've been working in St. Louis for, what, almost two years?" Manny took another huge bite of his sandwich.

"Yeah."

"Yeah, well, that job ended."

"What do you mean it ended? That was a good gig." Dustin turned to Cece again. "Manny was working for a fabrication shop, making aluminum parts for golf carts. Pay was good, benefits. Big business in golf carts these days. What happened?" He directed the question to Manny.

"Layoffs. The owner sold to a bigger company."

"They didn't need staff?"

Manny shook his head, his mouth full. "Just wanted the equipment, customers, and inventory to absorb into their company."

"That's not good."

"After that, I got a job driving for this company. I got my CDL and everything, but that work? Really sucks. Not the driving itself but the hours. You're gone all the time, which gets old after a while, unless you like always being on the road. I got to see the Rocky Mountains though. Bro, incredible. You would die. We've got to go see them sometime."

"What are you doing now?" Dustin ignored his comment about the mountains.

"Like, right now? Nothing."

Dustin dropped his chin, his head feeling like a fifty-pound anvil. He knew it. He'd known something was wrong. "Manny, I've told you: you can't just be unemployed. Don't get in a position where you don't have work. You've got to have a job to get a job. That's just how the world works. It's all about momentum."

"I know, but I couldn't keep driving for days on end." Manny put his sandwich down with more force than necessary. "That's not a life, man. I was getting all depressed. My sleep got jacked up, and the other day I had like, an anxiety attack or something. Me! I don't get stuff like that. Thought I was having a heart attack."

Dustin shook his head. "No, you can't live like that either, but…what are you going to do? What are your plans?"

Manny shrugged and picked his sandwich back up.

"First, I thought I'd come see you. Spend some time with you and catch up. It's been months, bro. Many months."

"Okay. That's good, and I'm so glad you're here and that I know you're safe. But then what?"

Manny scowled as he took a bite.

"Um." Cece set down their coffee mugs and grabbed her own. "Why don't we let Manny finish eating, and then we can show him around the house. Then you can spend some time together and figure out plans after that? I'm sure he's tired after coming all this way. I know you must be exhausted." She looked at Manny intently.

He stopped chewing, his eyes wide. "Uh-huh," he managed through his chewing. "I…" He swallowed. "I am really tired. That's a good idea."

"Good." She nodded and looked at Dustin.

He wasn't sure exactly what that look meant, but he gathered he was to follow her lead in this, and he could ask questions later.

"Is this your house?" Manny finished his second sandwich and reached for the Oreos.

"For now." Dustin shifted in his seat. "I'm fixing it up. Cece is too, and I'll sell it once we're done."

"Still planning to go to the Gulf?"

"Yeah, that's…That is the plan." *At some point*, he thought. But lately, between Cece and the potential job offers, nothing was clear anymore. His intentions had never been to get into something serious with Cece, but today felt like maybe they were already there. She deserved better than someone with no roots and no firm plans in hand. Oh, who was he kidding? Cece deserved the world, and he wanted to give it to her, but he couldn't. Not right now.

He might be wiser to finish out the year in Fredericksburg and head farther south in later winter or early spring. Leaving paying jobs on the table, even to follow his goals, was a foreign concept. His Florida opportunity versus real opportunities right here, right now, or he could do both.

He was selfish for wanting her at all, knowing she could do better than the likes of him.

She'd convinced herself he was wonderful, but he knew she could do so much better if she really knew her worth and got out there and looked. Still, he couldn't stand the idea of letting her go or of her being with anyone else. He wanted to deserve her.

"Are you a contractor too?" Manny asked Cece.

Cece started with a hand to her chest. "Me? Goodness no. No, my family owns the Orchard Inn down the road, and I..."

"Cece specializes in interior work, historical homes, and vintage fixtures." Dustin filled in the blanks. "She knew all about this Craftsman and what it would've looked like in its original form. We're doing the reno as a mix of old and new. Keeping the classics that make this kind of bungalow so popular, with modern upfits that people want for their daily lives."

She tilted her head with a smile and held out her hand. "Nicely put."

"Thanks." He high-fived her.

"So." Manny grabbed a few more Oreos. "How'd you two hook up?"

"Uh..." Cece began, but that's as far as she got.

"She showed up the day I got here, during a storm, and let me know how wrong all my plans were for the place."

Manny laughed. "Wait. You didn't know each other at

all, and you rolled up in here, telling him he was going to do this all wrong?"

Cece grimaced. "Kind of?"

Manny laughed deep and low, slapping his hands together. "Yes! That is the best thing I've heard in months." He laughed even harder.

"It's not that funny," Dustin deadpanned.

"Yeah it is. Someone's got to keep him in line besides just me. I love it."

Dustin shook his head but had to smile. He was right. Manny was the only other person to ever give him what for, until Cece.

Manny reached for more Oreos.

"Listen." Dustin reached for the pack. "After we show you around, would you like some real food? I don't know, like meat, potatoes, and vegetables. You act like you're starving."

Manny nodded. "Sounds good to me. I can always eat, and I was on the road awhile getting down here."

Cece set her coffee cup down and stood. "Let's show you around, and then I'm going to head out."

"Why?" Dustin and Manny asked at the same time.

"You two need some time alone to catch up," she said with a smile. "I'll stay for the tour, but then I'm going to get out of your hair. I'll be back tomorrow."

Dustin didn't argue, but he wished she'd stay. He would undoubtedly put his foot in his mouth again with Manny, and she wouldn't be there to help him not choke on it.

"Come on, you've seen the kitchen. We can show you upstairs."

They gave Manny the ten-cent tour, and he made noises of approval at everything they'd done. Carpentry and construction weren't his thing though, never had been. After he finished high school, Dustin had tried to get Manny to come on jobs with him. The action and manual portion of the work suited Manny fine, but it didn't speak to him the way it did to Dustin.

He was going to have to forge his own path in life, but so far, that path was proving rocky.

They finished the tour in the living room, Bruce right behind them like he knew they were about to go somewhere.

"We can go out and get something to eat," Dustin said. "But I've got to take Bruce. He'll revolt if I leave him again after being gone all day."

"I'd love to have ol' Brucey-boy as a date." Manny scratched his haunches.

"There's a really good diner in town," Cece offered. "Lucky's. It has outdoor seating that's dog friendly. Best pies in town too. My sister, Aurora, is a chef, and even she says Lucky's has some of the best pies around."

As they got ready to go, Dustin walked Cece to her car.

"Try not to lecture him too much and make a fuss," she said, turning to him after she unlocked her door.

"I am trying, but you see him. You're concerned too; I saw it on your face."

"I know, but trust me, I speak from experience. You get too preachy, and he's going to shut down and shut you out. Get him to talk first, let him open up about what's going on and why he's unhappy. Don't dive right into trying to solve it for him."

Dustin shifted on his feet, knowing those were wise words. But knowing and doing were two different things. "I know you're right. It's not easy though. He's unemployed, probably homeless, way too skinny, and I—"

"The important thing is he's here, he's safe, and you're together. You'll both figure something out. Just don't run him off before you have a chance to help him because you got too bossy."

"Me? Bossy?" He smirked.

"I realize that's rich, coming from me, but this isn't about me." She smiled. "You and Manny are different. Being bossy to you doesn't have the same effect."

"Nope. I kinda like it." He pulled her close.

"I've noticed." She rose on her toes and kissed him.

"I'll call you later or text if it's really late."

"Good luck." She kissed him again on the cheek, and he stood in the yard, watching until the rear lights of her car disappeared down the drive.

Again, he wished she'd stayed, but she was right. He needed to handle this, just him and Manny.

Dustin drove his truck to Lucky's Diner with Cece's reminder ringing in his ears. They found plenty of seating outdoors and Manny ordered a third of the menu, claiming some was for Bruce.

Once they settled in with some water for all three of them, Dustin turned to his brother, Cece's advice in his head. "So, tell me what happened with St. Louis and what else has been going on. I've ... I missed you."

After all these years, it was still so hard to admit that truth. Saying, out loud, how much he cared for someone, even Manny, made him feel vulnerable, like he might jinx it. Would that feeling ever go away? Confessing that someone held that connection, trust, loyalty, and love with him felt like pulling his heart out of his chest and letting it walk around, unguarded.

Would he live long enough to ever love without fear?

Manny sighed, his shoulders slumping heavily. "It's been rough, man. I didn't want to get into it in front of your...friend?" He cocked his head, unsure.

"Friend works."

"I know you've always told me to stay busy, always have a job on the burner and money coming in, but I couldn't do that long-distance driving anymore. That's not me. The money is good enough, but I don't want to be miserable for the next forty-plus years. I just...I don't know what I want to do. The fab shop was fine, and I like working with my hands, doing active stuff, but it wasn't a calling either. Truth is, even if I hadn't gotten laid off, I don't know that I would've made it another year."

Dustin scrubbed a hand over his jaw again. "And carpentry and construction are still not an option?"

"That's all you, bro. I can do it short-term, and you know I'll help you out as long as you need me, but forever? Nah. There's so much detail, and some of the people you deal with? I think I'd lose it the first time some customer started yelling at me about a bad decision *they* made."

"Then this is not the line of work for you." At least every other job included talking some client off the ledge about timing or because something they wanted wasn't within the realm of reality.

"But I've missed you too." Manny's gaze met his, the words equally hard for him to say. "It's been a long year, and I tried not to put this on you and handle it myself—"

"That's what I'm here for, Manny. Don't ever feel like you can't come to me. I want to help you. We're all we've got. We have to stick together."

"I know, but I'm not a kid anymore."

"Doesn't matter. You need my help, then I'm going to help you. I have plenty of work here right now, and I can take on more with you on the team. Beyond that, we'll figure something out. Let me sleep on it. I've met some people here in town—good people—who know lots of other people. I can ask around."

Manny's eyes misted as the waitress delivered a chicken sandwich platter, Italian salad, order of half fries, half onion rings, slices of apple and peach pie, and a steak sub wrapped to go. "Thanks," Manny managed to tell Dustin, once they were alone again. "That means a lot."

He dug into his salad, half of a chicken sandwich in his free hand. They sat quietly for a while as he polished off the salad and some of the platter, Bruce getting several bites of chicken. "I may have overordered," he finally admitted.

Dustin laughed. "You think? We can get this to-go though."

"You know…" Manny wiped his mouth and brushed the crumbs from his lap. "You were talking about us sticking together? How we're all we've got?"

"Yeah."

"Not for nothing, bro, but seeing you today, I think you've got a lot more than just me. I hope you know that."

Chapter 15

Y ou ever work at a ranch before?" Sawyer asked Manny.

Manny shuffled his feet a little but looked him straight in the eyes when he answered. "No, sir."

. "He's not afraid of hard work though," Dustin added.

He'd called Sawyer as soon as they'd gotten back from Lucky's Diner. Dustin's intention had been to put out feelers. See if he knew about any job openings in the area. Sawyer had said they always needed extra hands around the ranch. The pay was decent, and he could be flexible with scheduling to accommodate Dustin's work, but it was hot, dirty, outdoor stuff.

Perfect for Manny.

"That's what matters to me," Sawyer said. "We can show you the ropes. All you have to do is listen and learn."

"And it's mostly hands-on? Outside?" Manny asked.

"Absolutely."

"That sounds perfect."

"Good. We start early, usually take a break and get lunch midday, when it's hottest out here, and then start back in the afternoon until we finish. Sometimes it's four or five p.m., sometimes it's sundown. All depends."

The light in Manny's eyes spread warmth in Dustin's chest.

"We can pay you weekly. Oh, and Dustin tells me you got your CDL."

"Yes, sir."

"That's interesting. Can you back a trailer?"

"Absolutely." Manny nodded excitedly.

Sawyer made a noise of affirmation as he nodded, absorbing this detail. "You would be surprised how many people can't manage our big trailers. We started requiring CDLs for insurance purposes."

A truck pulled down the long driveway of the ranch, kicking up dust as it wound toward them.

"Now, who is that?" Sawyer asked aloud. "Is that— I think that's Lyle. The man I was telling you about. Beth's mom's fella."

"Yeah?"

Sawyer held his hand up to shade his face, squinting his eyes. "Yep, red truck. That's him."

Once parked, Lyle strolled over and introduced himself. He'd stopped by for no other reason than to visit and see how Sawyer was doing.

Manny and Dustin shared a look. People up north rarely to never dropped by unannounced, except maybe siblings.

"Listen, I'm going to take Manny around to the stables really quick. Y'all okay here?" Sawyer asked.

"We're fine." Lyle waved him off. "Go do your thing. We can talk shop while you're gone."

"You're the Dustin that Sawyer told me about." Lyle turned to him after they left. "The contractor working on the old Hollyhock house?"

"Yes, sir."

"That's quite the project. Got Cece helping, I heard."

"I do." Not for the first time, Dustin had the impression he was being interviewed as part of some community process.

"She's got a good eye, that Cece. She fixed up some stuff for Anita's condo, got it looking really nice."

"Yes, sir," he said again, unsure of how else to respond.

"Now, did Sawyer tell me you were actually born around here?"

Dustin tried not to react, even as the question shook him. These folks really did talk about everything and everyone, all the time.

"Uh...I was. Back in the nineties."

Lyle studied Dustin through his glasses and then over the top of them. "Mm-hmm. You know, I knew some Longs back in the day."

Had Dustin given him his last name? He was pretty sure he hadn't. But the Shipleys knew it, and Sawyer knew it, so of course Lyle knew it.

"You from over more toward east Texas?"

"Hays County," Dustin answered.

"Yeah, yeah, out east," Lyle continued. "I was telling Sawyer—that is, if you're trying to find some of your kin, and you don't mind—I know some people out that way, still got family out there too, on my Memaw's side. Whole slew of cousins."

Dustin blinked, wishing Cece were here if only to share his shock and confusion. "I don't...I mean I've done a little digging while here, but I haven't found anything. Then, with work getting busy, I haven't had time to look into it any deeper."

"No, I know. And I don't mean to intrude or get up in your business, but I'm saying if you're curious and you really want to see what you can find, I'm happy to do a little poking around. If not, it's no skin off my teeth. I'll leave you to it."

Dustin nodded, thinking how Cece had grown up like this her entire life. Everyone in everyone's business. A person couldn't sneeze around here without half the town hearing they had a cold.

It was equal parts frustrating and oddly reassuring. People only wanted to be helpful, but in doing so, they inserted themselves in your life. For better or for worse, if you grew up within a community, they were a part of you. Forever. With Cece struggling as a child, it was easy to see how that perception of her had persisted, even into adulthood. Everyone in town knew her as the little girl who wore braces and couldn't walk for a while.

Never mind that now she was this strong, independent woman capable of anything she put her mind to. To them, a part of her was poor little Cece. Always.

Her fiery defensiveness made a lot of sense now, her frustration understandable. Even though well-intentioned, people's concern was a double-edged sword.

"You know, I don't want you going out of your way," Dustin answered him honestly. "But if you know someone or find something you want to show me, that would be okay. I'd appreciate it."

"Come to think of it . . ." Lyle snapped his fingers. "I've got a job out that way too. One I won't get to for a bit, and they're getting antsy. Kitchen and dining room remodel. Are you looking for any more work?"

Stunned again, Dustin shook his head. He'd never

expected to have work offers thrown at him in this Texas town. Maybe Florida needed to wait. The work here would probably dry up soon, but surely Richie could wait a little while. The opportunity to be part owner remained down there, but for right now, he had the chance to make money here. "I have my hands full this week, but the inn will wrap up either this weekend or early next week. Let me see where I am when I finish the inn, and then could I let you know?"

"Sure, sure. They're not going anywhere. Good work is hard to find, so they're waiting on me or for me to give them someone I recommend to do it."

"What kind of remodel are they thinking about?" Dustin felt like he was in a fever dream or had fallen into a small-town sitcom where people you just met got all up in your business and then gave you job offers.

"Kitchen and dining room. No additions, just changing up the layout, opening things up. There might be some interior design work too."

"Really?" Dustin considered working with Cece on yet another job. This could make, what? Three more jobs lined up after the inn, not including the house.

"The family will make the final decision on who they use as far as interior design goes. They're particular about what they want, but there's no reason Cece shouldn't throw her hat in the ring. Probably be a nice little paycheck too. These people have money and tend to want the best of everything. It'll be worth your time if you get the contract."

"I would..." Dustin shook his head like he was shaking off the snow. This town operated differently from anywhere he'd ever been his whole life. And he'd been some places. "I'd love to take a look, if these people are okay with that."

"Sure they will be." Lyle patted him on the back. "I'll call them and give them your number."

Lyle didn't have his number. He opened his mouth to say as much, but Lyle was already walking away.

"Don't worry, I can get it from Sawyer," he said, as though reading his mind. Lyle climbed into his big red truck and backed out, pulling down the driveway, leaving Dustin to wonder if their entire exchange really happened.

Chapter 16

"Are you going to tell me where we're going?" Cece turned toward Dustin as he drove east on 290 toward Austin. All he'd said this morning was he had an appointment, and then he'd asked if she would like to come with him.

"Hays County."

"M'kay." She studied his profile. "But we're supposed to be working on Hollyhock. Is there a reason we're going on a field trip?"

He glanced her way. "I've got maybe another two days left of work at the inn, right?"

"Yes."

"And after that, a few weeks, and Hollyhock will be done."

She didn't want to think about that. "Yeah," she muttered, staring at the hem of her T-shirt.

"But in the last week or so, I've been given three different job offers. *Three*, Cece. Without me soliciting or doing anything. Just word of mouth alone. That's unheard of for a contractor my age, let alone a guy from out of town."

Her gaze jerked back to his profile. "So...?"

Dustin gave her a quick glance before staring out the windshield again, his jaw set. "So, I was thinking...what if I were to take those jobs? What if, with you and Manny helping me, at least a little, we had the staff, skill, and hands to line up those three jobs?"

She leaned forward, liking the sound of this.

"We could make good money, help a lot of people out—two of them your future in-laws—and get to work on some really cool projects."

Was she dreaming? Was Dustin considering staying in town longer? Working with her for weeks to come, possibly months?

"I'm listening," she managed.

"There's Garrett and Shelby's nursery and playroom. That we could start later because we have eight months, give or take. That job won't take long, but I know we could make it special for them. Then Sawyer's house. Beth's future home. That will take longer, but think about it. You might have nieces and nephews grow up there. How great would it be to say, *yeah, Aunt Cece helped build our home*?"

Another knot twisted in her throat, making it difficult to breathe. She hadn't thought about their work like that. The potential for creating homes, not just for other people but for her family.

"Then there's this other job Lyle told me about. It would probably be the first on the schedule, depending on their time frame. That's where we're going now. An older couple that lives outside of Austin. They were waiting on him to handle a remodel, but he said they'd welcome a recommendation to consider. He gave them my name. Our name."

"Seriously?"

He glanced at her again, his shock plain. "Yeah, my thoughts exactly. I've got to say, everyone I've met since coming to town is really nice and all, but man, are they nosy."

She covered her mouth to laugh. "We are *so* nosy."

"I can honestly say I've never experienced anything like it, when it comes to people being in my business. The flip side, though, is people helping me grow my business."

"So you're saying we have to be all up in your business before we help with your business?" she teased.

"Pretty much." Dustin laughed.

"I can't believe Lyle might have a job for us though." Cece attempted to process all he'd said.

"At first, I was like *nah*," Dustin said. "When it came to these job offers, I don't have the staff, and that wasn't the plan. But you're so good at what you do, and Manny showed up, so we have more help at least on Sawyer's job. I mean, I'm guessing he'd be okay with Manny breaking to help build his house. I don't know, but I'd be crazy not to at least take on these three, make us all some money, and help your family out."

"I..." She swallowed hard. "I agree. They all sound like great opportunities."

"So, you'd be in?"

"Of course I'd be in."

They shared a smile as he nodded. "Good."

"Tell me about the place we're going. What kind of work do they want done?"

Dustin filled her in on the details of what the grandparents wanted and about the opportunity for some interior decor. That part of the job wasn't a given, but Cece had the chance to make her case for why she'd be the best.

They drove another ten minutes, then she felt the weight of Dustin's hand on her leg. Glancing down, she smiled at the sight of his open palm, reaching for her hand. She laced her fingers through his, some light '70s rock playing softly on the radio.

She could deny it no more. Dustin staying in Fredericksburg meant falling in love with him. She was helpless against it, but even more, she wanted to fall in love with him. Maybe she already had. There was no gauge of comparison. All she knew was the light and joy inside her every time they were together. Excitement and security swirled together in an intoxicating mix. She didn't want to leave his side.

When he left, her heart would break. Fracture into a million pieces. She couldn't imagine ever recovering, but surely she could. She'd been through so much in her short lifetime, and she always managed to survive.

Regardless, fear of a broken heart wouldn't stop her from jumping at the chance of love. Since when had fear ever stopped her? It couldn't. If she'd ever let fear win, she wouldn't be who she was now.

No, if Dustin stayed, she would love him as hard as she could and deal with the fallout when it happened.

They drove another hour before they reached an outlying suburb. Houses sat spread apart, too far away from the hubbub to attract younger upstarts. The neighborhoods had a laid-back feel, the homes fifty years old at the newest. Old oak growth and more stop signs than stoplights.

A left turn took them toward a brick house with big white columns outside.

"What do you call this architecture?" Dustin asked.

"This is Greek Revival." Cece gazed in wide-eyed

wonder at the beauty. "This house is probably more than a hundred years old."

"Really?" He gaped.

Cece nodded. "Likely handed down through generations, knowing this area."

Dustin parked next to a black Mercedes sedan from the early 2000s. The lawn of the home was perfectly manicured, as were the hedgerows along the drive and the topiaries on the porch. Off to the right of the home was a rose garden.

Cece could imagine the owners attentively clipping and feeding their roses. In broad-brimmed sun hats, they'd be ever watchful of any disease or insect that dared intrude on their precious Queen Elizabeth or Mr. Lincoln roses.

"You ready for this?" Dustin asked, about to ring the doorbell.

"I'm so ready." Cece could not wait to meet the owners of such a delight.

A bespectacled gentleman, probably in his late sixties or early seventies, with perfectly cut and coiffed white hair, opened the door. He was wearing slacks and a sweater-vest, and Cece wanted to hug him on sight. The man was the quintessential grandpa.

"You must be the folks Lyle sent," he said.

Dustin made the introductions and Mr. McAlister—Bob—invited them in.

Inside, Bob's wife, Felicia, sat in the living room. Still golden haired, no doubt from the best hair stylist in town, she wore soft cashmere, a huge smile, and perfect makeup. She smelled like gardenias, and Cece wanted to adopt them both, immediately.

"Please sit, sit." Felicia motioned toward the couch. "Can I get y'all something to drink? Tea, lemonade, water?"

"Water would be lovely," Cece answered for them both. No way was she drinking a beverage other than water in this woman's living room. She bet the grandkids didn't even get to bring food in here.

Well, maybe the firstborn, but none after that.

Dustin chatted with Bob until Felicia returned.

"Lyle gave me an idea of what you want to do with your kitchen and living room, but why don't you tell me, in your own words, with detail."

What came next was a very in-depth story about what the McAlisters wanted, and why.

Their three children, two boys and one girl, were grown with kids of their own, and they lived scattered about Texas. They were busy, with bustling schedules, and the holidays and special occasions were their times to reconnect. Felicia, also known as Gigi, had happily volunteered to be the host. The grandparents' home was the most centrally located but needed a refresh. The vision was for a new layout for the kitchen and dining room to accommodate the growing family. They'd toyed with the idea of an outdoor living space, all open and connected and conducive to gathering.

They walked through the existing rooms and Dustin gave them some suggestions, some quotes, and the McAlisters seemed delighted.

"Lyle tells me you do interior decor work." Felicia directed the statement toward Cece.

Dustin's encouragement to believe in herself and her worth rang in her ears. "I do. I've done a few homes and a bed and breakfast."

"What would you envision here? Give me your recommendations."

"Well…" Cece looked toward the kitchen and dining room, the layout fresh in her mind. She let her imagination roam free. "I would highly recommend the outdoor space. You'll need the room, and it will keep heavy traffic out of this living room."

Felicia sighed. "I do get funny about too many people tromping through my living room."

Cece knew it. "And having a living space outside would mean showcasing your beautiful rose garden."

"Robert is very proud of his roses. Now that the kids have moved out, the roses are his babies."

"I'd even consider gas logs out there, for year-round use. If the space is covered, you could easily sit out there Thanksgiving weekend, watch football, eat leftovers."

"Oh, I love that idea, Bob."

"For the kitchen, avoid too much white. You don't want every spot and drizzle driving you mad. I would stick with a traditional style that fits the rest of the home. Stained wood is making a comeback, or you could go with antiqued glaze in off-white. Darker or highly variated marble counter tops, brushed finish on the appliances so all the little fingerprints don't show."

"That is a wonderful idea."

"And I'd be happy to show you fabric samples for classic but luxurious valances. I'd avoid drapes. In the dining room, unless the china cabinet is an heirloom, we could look at doing a built-in, which would give you more space when the table is fully set. I believe Dustin has pictures of a built-in we did recently."

Dustin pulled out his phone and began scrolling. "I do, right here." He passed his phone to Bob and Felicia.

"That is beautiful." Felicia lightly touched the screen.

"We bought our china cabinet, and I'm sure one of the kids would love to have it."

They discussed a few more things the McAlisters had on their wish list, and the rest of the conversation went as well as it'd began.

"I'm going to give you my card," Dustin said. "Think over what we talked about, and I will call you in a couple of days to check in."

"Wonderful." Felicia took his card, studying it a moment. "That's right." She touched the card with the same reverence as when she'd touched the picture on his phone. "Lyle said you were a Long from around these parts."

Dustin's gaze found Cece's. This was exactly what he meant by nosy yet helpful.

"You think you might have some people here?"

"I don't know, ma'am. Maybe. I'd had it in my mind to find out, but with work lately—"

"You could be the baby from that scandal years ago." Felicia clamped a hand over her mouth.

Dustin looked at Cece, but she had no idea what to say or how to make the situation less awkward.

"I am so sorry," Felicia said, lowering her hand. "That was...I'm just...This caught me off guard is all. See, I went to school with Daisy Long. We were friends all the way up until adulthood. Probably until, I don't know, until my children got bigger, and we were so busy we lost touch."

"Daisy lost a daughter," Bob added. "And I think it was too hard for her to be around people who had their families, especially big families."

"She didn't die though," Felicia amended. "Bob, hon, you make it sound like she died."

"Well now, I didn't mean to make it sound like that. I meant the daughter ran off. And that was a huge scandal in town back then."

"No, you're right." Felicia patted him on the leg. "You see, the Longs were society people. Appearances were very important, especially back then. Daisy's daughter started cavorting with a man much older than her, with a reputation for trouble."

Cece wondered when she last heard the word *cavorting* in conversation.

"Daisy did *not* approve." Felicia shook her head for emphasis. "And everyone knew it. They had a huge fight one night, and her daughter left town. I don't know if they ever spoke again after that. The rumors were wild. Daisy's daughter was on drugs, or with child, or both."

Cece glanced at Dustin; his face was set like stone.

"I think Daisy tried to get her to come back for a few years, but there would be conditions, of course. She couldn't stay with that man. Eventually, Daisy and her husband moved to Dallas, and I don't know what happened after that. We drifted apart as friends. It happens when you get older."

Cece stared at Dustin, hoping he'd look in her direction, but it appeared as if his thoughts were a thousand miles away, or decades in the past.

"What was her name?" Felicia asked Bob. "Daisy's daughter."

Bob shrugged.

"It'll come to me." She nodded.

Dustin still didn't react, so Cece set her glass of water down and rose to her feet. "Well, we appreciate your time today. Thank you for meeting with us."

"No, thank you for coming out here." Bob stuck out his hand, and Dustin shook it.

After the pleasantries and goodbyes, Cece led the way to Dustin's truck. Not a word was spoken, but this time, Cece reached for Dustin's hand. She held him the only way she could as he drove.

"You're thinking about what Felicia said." She finally broke the silence.

He didn't look her way but nodded.

"Do you think, maybe...?"

"I don't know," he said on an exhale. "I can't stop thinking about it though. All she knew were rumors, but the last name and the ages would line up, along with this area of Texas. What are the chances?"

Cece shrugged, studying the hem of her T-shirt again. "I don't know, but there is a chance. Is there any way to investigate it more?"

"If Felicia remembers her friend's daughter's name. I know my mom's name. According to the records, I was with her until I was almost two. I got a glimpse of my release papers once, by accident. I don't have any documentation, but it's branded on my brain. I've tried researching her by name alone, but I only reached dead ends."

She noticed he didn't offer up or say his biological mother's name out loud, and she wasn't going to ask.

"Then maybe she'll remember," Cece offered.

"Maybe." Dustin gripped the wheel.

They finished the drive home in silence.

Chapter 17

Dustin pulled into Silva Ranch the next day around lunchtime. He wanted to let Sawyer know that if he was serious about needing a reputable contractor, he'd do it.

Dustin also wanted to check up on Manny without being obvious about checking up on Manny.

All night, he'd thought about family. His biological family had always been a mystery, but could it be unraveling? Manny, his chosen family, was the only person he counted as close as blood.

Did he really want to know about his past? He thought he did, but now that he had the chance, he wasn't so sure. What would it change? He was a grown man. Manny was his brother. The past held the truth, but it also had the power to hurt. He'd had enough of that. He wanted to look toward the future.

He thought about Cece and her sisters, her extended family of Sawyer, Garrett, and Shelby.

Cece's connections spread wide, like a silky web meant to protect and nurture, but one could also get stuck in it.

Dustin's connections were few. He floated from place to place, job to job, with nothing holding him down or in place for very long. He was a survivor, and as such, he went where he needed to survive.

Now here he was, about to stay for longer than intended. He could lie to himself and say it was just about the work, but he wasn't a liar.

Cece.

He wanted more time with her. Whatever happened with her, if he got just a few more weeks, he'd take them. He'd cherish those weeks for as long as he lived and worry about what came next when it came.

Next to him, Bruce stirred.

"Yeah, we're going to see the big, weird dogs again," Dustin told him.

Cece was busy finishing Beth's dress at the inn, and he'd worked on Hollyhock all day. The upstairs rooms, kitchen, and dining room floors were sanded, and the upstairs floors were stained. He left the windows up and screens down to vent and took the opportunity for fresh air and a visit.

"Dustin." Sawyer waved as he and Bruce got out of the car. "Not checking up on Manny, are you?"

"Shh. I'm trying to be sneaky about it."

"Uh-huh. Good luck with that. We're down here by the stables. I'm showing him how to efficiently pitch hay."

Dustin followed Sawyer down to the stables nearest the house, surprised to see Beth there helping.

"I didn't know you worked the ranch too," he said.

"I don't. Not really. Only when I need to get out and clear my head." She smiled. "Plus, Cece wanted to concentrate on my wedding dress and didn't need me looking over her shoulder. Thought it might be best if I skedaddled."

"Cece is making your wedding dress?" Manny asked.

"Basically," Beth answered. "It's my grandmother's dress, but Cece is altering the top and most of the bottom. I would describe it but..." She tilted her head toward Sawyer. "I'll have to tell you about it later."

"That's pretty cool." Manny looked to Dustin. "She does it all. Makes dresses, builds houses, designs interiors. She's a jack of all trades."

A furrow of confusion wrinkled Beth's brow. "What do you mean, 'builds houses'?"

Manny clamped his mouth shut.

"Well, that's mainly the reason I came out here today," Dustin interjected. "Sawyer, I know we looked around your place the other day and you talked about needing someone reputable and trustworthy to finish the job."

"Yeah?" The expression of hope dancing across Sawyer's face was unmistakable.

"We kidded about it being me, but if you're seriously interested, I'd like to bid on the job."

Sawyer leaned his pitchfork against the truck. "You mean it?"

"Absolutely."

Sawyer slid off his gloves and stuck out a hand to shake on it. "Yes, sir, you bet I'm serious. When can you start?"

Dustin laughed, shaking his hand. "I finish at the inn tomorrow. Let me draw you up a quote, and maybe I could get started as early as next week."

Sawyer launched himself forward, hugging Dustin and shocking him stupid. "This is great news. Did you hear that, Beth?"

Dustin patted him on the back too. "You're welcome."

Sawyer let him go. "And you're still thinking a couple of months to finish it?"

"Yeah. I can get started, and I may have another job come up, but if I can have Manny help some on your house, I don't think it'd slow us down much. I might even hire a third person on if things go well. I'll know for sure when I get started. Barring weather events, it'll be around that. I'll pad the date to give us wiggle room. I don't like to undercut a timeline because then people are disappointed, but with Manny and Cece working with me, eight to ten weeks should be about right."

"Wait." Beth shook her head. "Cece isn't building houses."

"Actually, she is. She has been. I mean, she's not pouring concrete or climbing on roofs or anything, but we've put in flooring at Hollyhock. Sanded and stained floors, built cabinets, remodeled the kitchen."

"You had my sister putting in flooring?"

"Beth," Sawyer tried, but it was no good.

Dustin knew that look. He'd seen it in Cece's eyes when she started railing about builder beige paint. Beth didn't like what she was hearing, and Dustin was about to hear all about it.

"My sister doesn't need to be building houses and sanding floors. I thought when she said she was helping out at Hollyhock, she'd be painting trim and sewing pillow shams. Not hard labor."

"She's not doing anything beyond her abilities, and she loves the work," Dustin stated.

"Sawyer's house though—our house—has a lot of work left to be done. Cece could get hurt. What if she fell? Do you know how devastating that could be?"

Sawyer stepped closer to Beth, putting his arm around her. "Why don't we all just take a beat here. Cece isn't going to do anything rash or irrational. She knows her limits."

Beth glared at him. "Have you met my sister?"

"Fair point, but—"

"I won't let her get hurt," Dustin tried. "She really wants to do these jobs with us and—"

"*Jobs?* Plural? What else are y'all doing?"

"A nursery for Garrett." Manny ticked off on his fingers, helpfully. "A house out in Hays maybe, Sawyer's place—"

"Thanks, Manny," Dustin commented sarcastically.

"Sure, man."

"I just..." Beth threw her hands up. "I can't believe this."

"Wait." She turned to face Sawyer. "Did you know about this?"

But before he could answer, she stormed away.

"I'm going to—" Sawyer indicated her direction. "Let me talk to her. I'm sure it will all be fine."

Dustin and Manny watched them go.

"I'm missing something, aren't I?" Manny asked.

Dustin scrubbed a rough hand over his face. "Yeah. I wasn't thinking. Cece's sisters are protective of her, especially Beth, and—"

"Yeah, but Cece is awesome at renovations. Have they seen what you guys did to Hollyhock yet?"

Dustin shook his head. "No, actually. They haven't. I don't think they know what she's capable of. It's like they're stuck with this fragile image of her."

"I mean, we all get hurt sometimes. It's part of life." Manny simplified matters. "I about stabbed myself in the foot with a pitchfork earlier today."

Dustin groaned. "Don't tell me that."

"What I'm saying is, it doesn't matter how protective people are or how careful we are, we're all going to fall down sometime. That's how you learn and grow."

Dustin reached for his brother, clapping him on the back. "I know. Sawyer will talk to Beth." Cece had explained before, how protective her family was over her, but seeing it in action was something else entirely. Protection to the point of smothering her potential. He didn't want to lose these jobs, but more than anything, he didn't want Cece to suffer a bunch of sheltering she didn't want or need.

"I hope this doesn't kill the job," Manny said. "I'm ready to get busy and make some money."

"I'll talk to Cece. We can get this straightened out. How are things going here?"

"Great, actually. It's hot and sweaty work, but Sawyer is awesome. How cool are those horses, bro?"

Dustin smiled, trying to focus on his brother's words. "They're very cool."

"I like it so far."

"Good. That's good to hear." Dustin searched the path Sawyer and Beth had taken but saw no sign of them. "Listen, I'm going to let you get back to work. I'll see you later."

"Later, man."

Dustin went to his car and headed straight for the inn.

He wanted to let Cece know before she heard it from Beth, and he wanted to see her.

She let him in the back of the inn. Beth's dress was hanging high on a rod, Cece working on the hem with small white dots and thread laid out across the floor.

"I'm doing a little beadwork and hemming the bottom, and then I'm done," she explained. "Not too much more beadwork though. Beth isn't the super sparkly type. Just enough to catch the light, add some dimension."

Dustin inspected the dress. He'd only known Beth a short time, but from all that he knew about her, it was the perfect wedding dress for her. Classy, pretty, reserved. Nothing too flashy or trendy. She'd look elegant, timeless.

"I hope you know how amazing you are," he said to Cece, still staring at the dress.

"What?" Her voice trembled a little.

"I mean it." He turned to her. "I was just thinking... something Manny said. You can do *this* with a wedding dress, see houses fully formed as homes in your mind, you have these creative ideas and all this random knowledge about stuff I've never even heard of."

She pinched her lips together. "Thank you," she managed after a moment. "Did you... did you come by just to flatter me and make me all emotional or..."

He chuckled, pulling her close and dropping a kiss on the top of her head. "No. Unfortunately. Here, let's sit."

"Uh-oh." She sat next to him on the couch.

Dustin told her all about the exchange at Silva Ranch, Beth's reaction, his failed attempt at explaining, everything.

"Did she snap at you, big time?"

"No, not big time. She was upset though. I think she's envisioning you laying Sheetrock or shingles, not what you're actually doing. Although, if you really wanted to lay shingles on a roof, I could show you a safe way to do it, though I don't recommend it for either of us. Probably my least-favorite work to do. I hate it really."

Cece took his hand. "Don't worry about Beth."

"You sure? I feel like we're both in her bad books now."

"Eh, I've been in her bad books plenty of times before. I'll talk to her, and if she's unreasonable, we'll get into an argument, have it out, then we'll make up, and I'll do exactly what I planned on doing anyway."

He had to smile. "It's like that, huh?"

She nodded. "I realized, I think on our trip to San Antonio, that I love my sisters, and they love me, and we will be the biggest pain in each other's butts for the rest of our lives. That's just how it is. But they can't stay mad at me forever. It's never worked before, and I don't see it ever working in the future."

Dustin leaned in and kissed her again. First her cheek, then a brief kiss on the lips. "I will say though, between the two of you, you're way scarier when you get mad."

Cece leaned back with a smile. "Then Beth wasn't that mad. Upset? Sure. Annoyed at me? Definitely. Trust me, if she was mad, you'd be here hiding with me in a closet. Doesn't happen often, but when Beth blows a fuse, it's terrifying."

"I'll take your word for it and hope I never witness it." Dustin scrubbed his palms on his jeans. "I'm going to leave you to it with the dress. Get back to work at Hollyhock. You want to come by later?"

"Actually . . ." Cece stood, eyeing the beads on the floor. "I think I'm done for the day. My eyes need a break, and I've had enough of sitting on my little sewing stool. I need to stretch my legs. What are you working on at the house right now?"

"I've stained the living room and dining room floors, and it's drying. I was thinking maybe some of the yard work. Get started at least."

"Sounds perfect." She began packing up her needle and thread.

"What, you want to go pull weeds right now?"

"I would love to pull weeds or just putter around the yard. Anything outside. Plus, I don't want to be here when Beth gets home."

"I thought you said she wasn't really mad, and that you'd handle it."

"She wasn't, and I will." Cece stretched her back with a smile. "But not right now."

Dustin had raked and pulled weeds for what felt like hours. Cece had edged out the existing beds and spread the native grass seeds they'd ordered along the sides and back of the house.

"I think I'm worn out." Dustin groaned as she approached, all but dragging the edging tool behind her.

"Same." She swiped a gloved hand across her sweaty brow, leaving a streak of dirt across her forehead.

Dustin attempted to wipe it clean for her. "We're filthy."

"Probably stinky too. But look at this yard." She turned with her back to the house, the sun dipping lower in the tree line of the drive, coloring the cloud-dappled sky a dusky violet.

The yard looked great. With the weeds and brush gone, the scalloped lining of the flower beds stood out. Manicured hedges gave the house its original quaint, homey appeal. Come spring, the front yard would be full of color. Cece had uncovered iris and tulip bulbs, hyacinths, and daffodils. There were azalea bushes and, along the sides of the house, hydrangeas.

"The original owners must have loved plants and

gardening," Cece said, admiration lacing every word. "They probably spent hours in this yard every weekend, making sure it looked just right. Fresh clippings of flowers carried inside to place in a vase. Can't you just see it?"

Dustin took the edger from her, leaned it against the brick steps, and placed his arm around her. "Now I can."

He turned to face her. "I never would've thought to do all this if it weren't for you. All your talk of using what was already here and creating an ecosystem for native birds and insects. I would've tilled the whole yard and laid down sod."

She blanched at the thought.

"But I didn't, because of you."

Her smile, bright within her smudged face, was radiant. "Good thing I got here to prevent catastrophe."

"Cece." Dustin bent and kissed the tip of her nose. "Something occurred to me today. I think maybe you've been underestimated your whole life."

She blinked. "What . . . what makes you say that?"

"Because I did it too. When I first met you, I wasn't sure what you were talking about. I thought, *who is this girl—young woman—talking all this talk about old houses and revival architecture?* But as the night went on, I realized you knew a thing or two about a thing or two. Now, I know you know a lot. More than most people."

"You think so?"

"I know so. And I get it about everyone being so overprotective. I realize it's because they care, but after Beth's reaction today, I see exactly what you mean. I imagine it gets pretty frustrating."

"So frustrating." She nodded.

For weeks now, he'd convinced himself he didn't deserve Cece. She needed someone financially secure and set up well enough to take care of her. But that's not what Cece wanted. "You don't need anyone to take care of you, do you? Or someone to boss you around."

"I can't stand being bossed around. And I don't want to be 'taken care of.'" She used air quotes.

Dustin smiled, his chest swelling with the warmth he felt inside. "You want someone to stand beside you, do the work with you, and believe in you."

She nodded, biting at her bottom lip. "That's exactly what I want."

He took her hand and pulled off the glove, kissing the back of her hand and her knuckles. "You were the last thing I expected to ever show up at my front door during a storm, but now I can't imagine never having met you."

Cece pulled her hand away, removing her other glove before wrapping her arms around his neck to pull him down for a kiss. "I can't imagine it either."

He kissed her deeply then, his hand slipping to the small of her back to press her close. He kissed her until her breath came in ragged little gasps, their cheeks flushed and hot. He kissed her cheek, down her neck, breathing deeply the smell of her perfume and the outdoors. Cece melted into him, her breath hitched as she dug her fingers into his shoulders.

He wanted to wrap her around him, and never let go. Care for her and cherish her and bring her bliss into the early hours.

"Do you want to come in?" he asked, her eyes burning amber as she looked at him. "We could wash up, and you could stay. Stay the night."

The sly smile she gave him then almost buckled his knees. "I would love to. I thought you'd never ask."

Chapter 18

The morning light shone full blast, right onto Cece's closed eyelids. She grunted, moving the pillow to cover her face.

"Got to get some real blinds in here," Dustin grumbled, pulling the covers over them. "Not paper ones."

"North-facing window," she muttered, attempting to sit up.

"Huh?"

"North-facing window." She rubbed her eyes, slowly waking as she gazed around the room, her vision gaining focus as the last sands of sleep blew away.

She'd spent the night with Dustin.

The recognition, and the memories, sent ripples of excitement through her limbs. She'd spent the night with him, and he had been everything she'd expected and more. Tender and giving, but powerful and ... enthusiastic.

Cece hid a grin behind her hand, as if anyone could see her.

"What are you grinning about?" Dustin asked, sitting up next to her.

Busted.

"The ... um, the window. You were saying about the

window. It's north-facing. Good for houseplants, bad for sleeping in. That area would make a good green space. We should get a nice plant stand, something art deco, and have a little collection with all that morning light. Some thrillers and spillers." She yawned, and then clamped her mouth shut. She'd said "we." "We should get a plant stand," as if it were their house. Together.

But it wasn't.

"I mean, if the owners are plant people." She tried to cover her tracks. "That would be a good spot. It'd be really pretty."

Dustin chuckled. "Are you really grinning and rambling about houseplants at seven a.m.?"

She shrugged, thankful he didn't seem to have noticed her slip. "Among other things. Sorry. Morning person."

"Don't apologize." He leaned over and kissed her cheek. "I am too. I can't form full thoughts about houseplants and lighting, but I do like mornings."

Cece leaned against him, knowing he was more than capable of holding her up. "I love the start of each day. Full of promise and potential. You can get a lot done. But by ten at night, I'm pretty much ready for bed. I don't go to bed because I have stuff to do, but I could."

He wrapped an arm around her, thick and warm. Solid and steady. "I'm glad you spent the night," he whispered.

"Me too." Her cheeks warmed. "But I bet my sisters are going to have questions."

"Oh, oops." Dustin laughed, full and round, filling the room. His smile stole her heart from her chest.

"Hello?" someone yelled from the front of the house, making them both startle.

Manny.

"Yo! Dustin. I got breakfast!"

"Crap," Cece hissed. "All my clothes are dirty."

"Here." Dustin jumped up, hopping into boxers and a T-shirt. "You can wear this over your underwear." He pulled a Lions T-shirt from his bag. It was big enough to hang down almost to her knees.

"I can't not wear pants," she fussed, putting on the shirt.

"I might have some basketball shorts with a drawstring you could pull really tight. That might work?"

Cece held out her hand, and he passed over a pair of blue shorts. Putting them on, she dissolved into giggles. "Please look at me." There was no mirror in the bedroom. "Do I look as ridiculous as I feel?"

She'd gone to bed with her hair wet, and what they'd done in that bed hadn't helped the state of it.

"I mean . . ." He lifted a shoulder. "I don't think you've ever looked hotter, what with the sex hair and you wearing my clothes, but I'm really biased and probably the wrong person to ask."

"Good gosh, just come on." She shooed him toward the door.

They awkwardly entered the kitchen to find Manny standing there, a donut hanging out of his mouth.

"Wow. Hey, guys," he said around the donut. "Maybe I should've called?"

"Shut up and hand over some breakfast." Dustin bumped Manny's shoulder with his. "Where were you last night? I thought you'd slept on the cot in the living room."

Manny finished the donut in two more bites. "Worked late at the ranch. Sawyer let me stay at the big house. That place is *nice*." He grabbed a wrapped item from his bag of goodies, opening it up to reveal a bacon, egg, and cheese croissant.

Cece's stomach growled in interest.

"Guess it was a good thing too, huh?" Manny took a bite of his croissant with a cheeky grin.

"Yeah, yeah. That's enough from the peanut gallery." Dustin stole the croissant from him and took a big bite.

"Hey, man! Not cool."

"I'll make coffee. You want some?" Dustin asked, ignoring his protest.

Manny dug into the bag and pulled out another croissant. "Good thing I got five of those things."

"Jeez, Manny. How much food did you order?"

"Sawyer got all this." He started on another breakfast croissant, guarding it carefully but passing the bag to Cece. "He took what he wanted and said I could have the rest. I got bacon, egg, and cheese sandwiches, some apple cider donuts, pumpkin donuts, and something called a Cowboy Breakfast pastry."

"Oooh." Cece dove into the bag, digging until she found the Cowboy Breakfast. "I'll take one of those." Sausage, vegetables, egg, and cheese, folded into a puff pastry.

Yes please.

"How were things at the ranch after I left?" Dustin asked, frowning as he pulled another croissant from the bag. "Beth wasn't too happy, huh?"

"Didn't seem like it, but Sawyer didn't say anything when he got back to the stables. Guess they talked." He dug around in the bag for more breakfast. "The rest of the day was great though. We fixed a few things in the stables—some gates that needed work, stuff like that—and then Sawyer showed me how to shoe a horse." He excitedly stuffed an egg bite in his mouth. "Coolest thing ever."

"Shoe a horse?"

"Yeah, you..." Manny hopped up to demonstrate. "You get the horse's hoof like this, right? Take off the old horseshoe with these clamp things and a hammer, clean out the hoof, and then put the new shoe on. I just watched this time, but it was so cool. He just kept talking to the horse the whole time, and they let him do it. He said I'd watch him a few times before I could help. The horses need to be really used to you and your voice, your smell. Safer that way."

Manny's enthusiasm was contagious. Cece watched him act out each hoof while she ate.

"Sounds like you enjoyed yourself." Dustin brought them all mugs of coffee.

"I did. I really did. I was there late because he wanted to talk to me about a few things, and he had me drive one of their trailers around town, parking it, backing it up. I think he was testing me." Manny ate another egg bite with a grin. "I did great, obviously, and ended up crashing there. We're going to start later today since it was a long day yesterday."

"I think it's wonderful you enjoyed it so much." Cece smiled. "Sawyer would be a good boss, leading by example instead of just commanding people around."

"Yeah, unlike this guy when I was just a kid." Manny used his coffee mug to point toward Dustin.

"Excuse you." Dustin pointed back with his coffee mug. "I didn't command you, I just made you follow the rules of our foster house. You came in like a wild man, and I didn't want you to get the boot."

"I know, I know." Manny sat back down. "I've got to give you a hard time though. You were tough for a teenager."

Cece pulled her feet up in the chair to tuck beneath her, dying to hear stories from their childhood. As if reading her mind, Manny turned, one hand laid out flat on the table. "When I say he busted my balls daily, you have no idea."

"Dude," Dustin reprimanded.

"See what I mean? I get to the house, right? I'm not even seven, basically a wildling, ready to fight everyone and everything, and the kids already there with these foster parents, they're like…kind of happy. They go to school, they've got clean clothes—not the newest or nicest, but decent. They look fed. This pisses me off even more. Like, who do they think they're kidding? I decide I'm going to pick a fight with the leader." He thumbed toward Dustin. "Get kicked out for sure. Except old coz here won't bite. I'm calling him names; I think I stole his shoes one morning—"

"You did." Dustin sipped his coffee.

"Nothing works. I can't get him riled up. I go to school, mad as a hornet, trying to think how I'm going to throw this house into chaos when I get home. I get off the bus at the stop, and who is there? Dustin." Manny thumbed toward him again.

"I risked cutting school early that day to get to him before he got home."

"He looks down at me and says, 'Come on, little man. Let's take a walk.' Little man." Manny puffed out his cheeks in defiance. "I was so mad at that too, but I followed him. He takes me to a bodega near our stop. We get—I'll never forget this—two hot dogs and two colas, and we walk to the park and eat them. And he tells me, there's no way he'll ever fight me. That I'm half his age, and he's been me. That he came to this house the same way, ready to disappoint these people before they could disappoint him."

Cece glanced at Dustin, his expression warm as Manny told this story. And she could picture him too. All of thirteen years old, trying to wrangle a wild child, be the big brother.

"Thing is, Dustin said they hadn't disappointed him," Manny continued. "They were decent people, and the other kids were all right too. He said if I had two brain cells, and if I'd shape up, follow the rules, and follow his lead, I could be set up in a good situation. But if I kept up with my crap—he didn't use that word—I could be on the street. No hot dogs or soda, no big brother looking out for him."

Dustin's soft smile splintered her heart.

"I'd never had a big brother. No one ever took me to the park to walk and talk and junk. I decided right there, whatever this joker tells me to do, I'm going to play along. But I better get little field trips like this on the side occasionally."

"And you did."

"I did. I think the Marshalls—that was the family who raised us—I think they knew it kept the peace to let us do that sometimes."

"You were so high energy too." Dustin shook his head. "Oh man, if we didn't play ball after school or run around outside just to tire you out, you'd be vibrating by dinnertime."

"I forgot about that." Manny laughed. "I was okay once I got into middle and high school and could play football and stuff, but when I was little, yeah, too much energy. How'd you know?"

"Because I was the same." Dustin set down his coffee mug and turned it between his hands. "You and me? We weren't made for sitting at a desk all day. It drove me crazy. As soon as I was a junior and could sign up for classes at the career center, I jumped on it. They had classes like welding and machine tool workshops. I took a building construction course and never looked back."

"No desk work or homework." Manny nodded. "I did the machine shop classes too. I liked those a lot more than algebra. Guess I'm not really using either right now."

Cece had hated algebra too. She'd much rather be making things or doing something. How had she ever thought bookkeeping might be a tolerable career choice?

"It takes some of us a while to figure out what we want to do," Cece told him. "I'm only now realizing how much I like renovations and decorating. I can't wait to help the McAlisters with their home."

"That's if we win that bid."

"We'll win it." She smiled. "I've got a good feeling about it."

"Speaking of…" Dustin got up and refilled his mug, bringing the pot over to top off their coffee as well. "I haven't told Manny what the lady, Mrs. McAlister, mentioned while we were out there."

"Uh-oh. Sounds serious."

Dustin lifted a shoulder. "Maybe, maybe not." He sat back down. "She knows some Longs from that area, out in Hays County. Said they had a daughter, who—age-wise—would be about right. She ran off with a guy, and all anyone knew were rumors, but one of the rumors was that she was knocked up."

"You don't think—"

"I don't know," Dustin cut him off. "I'm not thinking anything until I have more than rumors to go off of. She said the family was pretty hoity-toity, so a girl, unmarried and pregnant by some guy her parents didn't like? She could've run off and moved around. Maybe?"

Cece thought about Felicia's information. So many things lined up that there was a very real possibility this Daisy person could be Dustin's grandmother.

"Probably won't be anything," Dustin said. "But it's the only thing I've heard that matches the last name, right county, and right age."

Manny sipped his coffee, then put his mug down with a thud. "How crazy would that be if it's her?"

"It would be crazy." Dustin cleared his throat. "I doubt it is though. I don't even know that I want it to be her."

"Why?" Cece asked, shocked.

"I don't know. I...I thought I wanted to know, but if I'm really faced with it, do I want to know all about what happened? When I was a kid, I imagined my birth parents were this great, loving couple. All orphans do. But the truth is, great loving couples don't tend to orphan kids. So then, I figured they were terrible, and I hated them. Now..."

Obviously, it wouldn't be a story full of rainbows and sunshine, but it'd still be the truth. She couldn't imagine not knowing where she came from.

"Now, what?" she encouraged.

"Now I know it could be either of those things. Or both. They might've just been normal people. Normal people in a terrible situation they couldn't change, but regardless, they didn't want me."

Cece swallowed hard, unsure of what to say.

"How is knowing the dirty details going to help me? I've got a good life. Things are clicking along for me." Dustin shook his head. "I'm just not sure I want to complicate things even more with some story from years ago messing with my mind."

Chapter 19

Tell me we're only doing one of these," Manny grunted. Dustin had him helping with the install of the claw-foot tub and shower combination, and the thing weighed a ton.

"You need to bulk up, boy," Dustin teased him. "All that time sitting on your duff has made you soft."

"Yeah, yeah, yeah."

"Bring it over another five or six inches to your right. Little more...okay, set it down. Gently."

"You think I'm just going to drop it like a bag of cement?"

Dustin eyeballed the way the tub fit in the space, ignoring Manny's attitude. "This looks perfect."

They were finishing up caulking the new toilet when the doorbell rang. Dustin sighed gruffly from his place wedged between the wall and bowl. "Who in the he—?"

The bell rang again.

"I don't know, but they're impatient." Manny stood.

Grumbling a few more choice words, Dustin managed to get out and push himself to stand.

"You might not be built for plumbing, bro. You need to be about six inches shorter and fifty pounds slimmer."

"Zip it." Dustin left the bathroom with Manny following him down the hall to the front door.

Through the panes of glass at the top of the door, he saw a man in a dress shirt and slacks, wearing what looked like an expensive watch and sunglasses.

"You getting served papers or something?" Manny asked behind him.

"Not helpful." Dustin shoved him playfully out of the way. "Can I help you?" he gruffly asked the stranger once he opened the door.

"Yes, sir. Hi. I'm Adam Bayne." The man held out a business card. "With Advantage Realty Group. We're a real estate investment company interested in the Fredericksburg market."

"We're not interested in whatever you're selling." Dustin and Manny shared a look.

"No, no." The man smiled. "We're interested in buying real estate in this market."

He didn't even have the house on the market yet.

"We know you recently purchased this property, and we wondered if you'd have any interest in selling it."

"Eventually, that is the plan."

"Eventually, as in...?"

"As in when I'm done renovating it, I'll put it back on the market."

The man's smile grew, unnerving Dustin. "What if I told you we'd buy this house as is, no additional renovations needed?"

"We're listening," Manny answered.

Dustin elbowed him in the arm.

"This would be a cash offer, as is, no inspection or high closing costs."

He stared at this stranger, wondering about his angle. Dustin trusted few people, and none of them were slick salesmen.

"I can see you're skeptical. We want to buy the property next to this and the one on the other side of you along with this property. The other two are land lots."

The picture began to come together. "You want to build on to that neighborhood down the road, develop all this land into residential properties."

"Eventually, yes."

"And this house?"

"Well, the land would be enveloped into the existing neighborhood. The homes are new construction, modern. Not…"

"So, you'd level this house."

"Or you could move it."

Yeah, right, at the cost of an arm and a leg. "I'm not interested in moving the house or having it leveled."

"We're willing to offer you five hundred thousand dollars."

Dustin took a step back, knocked off-balance. Manny whistled long and high.

"Cash offer, like I said. No inspection, no delays."

"But the house—"

"The house won't be here. We want the acreage. If you want anything from the home, fixtures and the like, they're yours to take before the closing."

"You're just going to tear it down?" Manny blurted. "I don't know about that."

Dustin put a hand on Manny's arm to settle him.

"We could sweeten the offer if there's some sentimental tie to the structure itself."

The floor tilted beneath Dustin's feet. *Sweeten the deal* as in even more money. "I'll need to think about this." He managed to get the words out to hopefully get this guy off his porch. He couldn't think with him there. "I don't make decisions on impulse. I will consider your offer though."

"Of course." The man smiled again. "Take your time and consider. We'd like some indication of your thoughts within the week. You have my card."

Dustin studied the card in his hand.

"It's a good offer," the man said. "I think you'll find the market on homes like this in the area won't offer you five hundred. You won't even get close."

Dustin and Manny watched Mr. Bayne walk off the porch and get into his BMW to drive away.

"Five hundred thousand dollars," Manny repeated. "Dude. That's more money than you've ever had in your life."

"I know." That was more than enough to buy into a company in Florida, like he'd planned. There'd be plenty left over to put down on a little house, maybe even have some savings again.

That was the dream, or at least it had been the dream. Now, he wasn't so sure anymore. Maybe his dream had changed and, if it had, what did that mean for him? What would it mean to Cece?

"Yeah," Dustin murmured to himself.

"Not that simple though, is it?" Manny asked.

Dustin stared blindly at the front yard, at the edges of his work with Cece, the earth they'd tilled, some of it by hand, thinking of the seeds they'd planted getting plowed up, never to be seen.

"You think you're going to get more than five hundred for the house if you sell it to a different buyer?"

He shook his head, his gaze returning to the card clutched in his fist. "No, I know that's the most I could hope to get out of this place. That's not it though."

Manny moved closer, quiet for a moment, then, "It's Cece, isn't it?"

"What?"

"Your girl. Cece. You don't want to leave her."

That had always been the plan though. Even when he knew he could stay here longer, finish up extra jobs, and make more money, the end game was still moving on and leaving Texas.

Leaving Cece.

"If that's the issue, then sell the place and stay here. Or take her with you," Manny suggested.

Dustin arched an eyebrow. "It's not that simple."

If he stayed here, what kind of life did he have to offer her? More working and trying to survive from job to job? Hoping they could make ends meet?

"Why not?"

"She'd never forgive me if someone tore down this house, and she has a life here. Family, roots. She doesn't want to leave for Florida. That isn't the solution."

"Then what is?"

That was the problem; he didn't have a solution. He wanted to stay here with Cece, but could he offer her a life, be the person to stand beside her and take on the future together? How could he be the kind of man Cece could rely on when he couldn't even say that he missed her while she was gone to San Antonio or tell her how he really felt?

She should have someone who could put down roots and say he loved her, and he wasn't sure he'd ever be able to do that. He had no real experience, no compass when it came to family and community. He had his foster family for a few years and the people he'd met here, but that wasn't anywhere close to what Cece had, what she'd want.

Plus there was the big elephant in the room: if he sold Hollyhock to some land developer who'd plow it down, she'd never forgive him. But what about his goals? His plans? Could he give them all up?

Dustin shook his head. It was all happening so fast. He needed to think. "You go ahead back to the ranch. We're done here anyway. I'll catch up with you later."

"You sure?"

"Yeah. Sawyer will be wondering where you are. I'm going to..." What? He couldn't work on the house in this condition. He needed to clear his mind, do an activity but not something that took actual concentration or focus. He needed to get out. "I'm going to take a walk."

Chapter 20

Cece finally found Beth at the big house of Silva Ranch. "I've been calling you for the last hour."

"My phone must be on silent." Beth dug around in her purse. "I've been trying to concentrate on the seating chart, and I kept getting distracted."

Cece put her hand on one of Beth's forearms to stop her search. "It's fine. I'm here now."

"Okay." Beth sat down on the sofa, a huge spread of paper on the coffee table with tons of tiny Post-its laid out before her. She sighed heavily.

"Stressed?"

"That obvious?"

Cece leaned into her sister. "A little."

Beth relaxed her shoulders, the shadows beneath her eyes confirming her exhaustion, making what Cece wanted to discuss with her that much more difficult.

"Can I help with any of this seating stuff?" she asked first.

"No. I think I need to stop looking at it for now and come back to it tomorrow."

"Okay." They sat silently for a few minutes.

"I need to talk to you about a couple of things," she finally managed.

Beth shifted, turning toward her. "What's up?"

"Well, first, your dress is finished."

Beth's face lit up as she put her hands together as if in prayer. "It is?"

"Yes, and it's gorgeous and perfect, and you will look like a princess wearing it."

"Oh, Cece." Beth embraced her. "I can't wait to try it on."

"Maybe tonight? Once Aurora gets done at the restaurant? We can have a little sister time, put on our dresses."

"I love this idea."

Just the three of them together, sharing some time before the mad final dash toward Beth's wedding day, would be nice. Once Beth was married, they wouldn't be the Shipley sisters like before, and eventually, Beth would have a home of her own. Leaving only Cece and Aurora to live at Orchard Inn.

Beth may eventually have to hire an assistant at the rate Aurora's restaurant was growing and if Cece picked up more renovation jobs.

"What's the second thing?" Beth asked, as if reading her mind.

"I need to talk to you about something important."

"What is it?"

"You told Dustin, and Manny, and actually Sawyer too, that I'm not capable of remodeling houses as a job."

Beth shook her head, adamant, but said, "I did. I probably shouldn't have said it like that or in front of them, but—"

"*Probably* shouldn't have?" Cece took a steadying breath, trying not to blow her lid.

"You're the one running around building houses and not telling anyone."

"I didn't realize I needed your permission."

"Cece."

"And did you ever stop to wonder *why* I didn't tell you all the details? Wonder why I haven't had you over to Hollyhock to see all the work I've done? Because I knew this was how you'd react."

"That's ridiculous."

"No it isn't. I've been helping Dustin for over a month now. What did you think I was doing over there, crocheting blankets? I've been building things, repairing the house, and you never thought I might love it and want to keep doing it, because you don't believe I'm capable."

"That's not true, I just didn't think you'd want to do that kind of work long-term. I thought you wanted to get into bookkeeping, or help me run the inn or something like that."

"*You* wanted me to get into that. What if I don't want to manage the books for the inn or take your place on the night shifts?"

"That's respectable, safe work."

"What if I want a life of my own though? Did you just assume I'd live here forever, under your care?"

"No! I didn't think that. But I thought you'd want something secure and safe."

"Maybe I don't want to play it safe all the time, Beth."

Beth sat up straighter, her lips pinched together, brow knitted tight like she was trying hard to hold something in.

"Go ahead," Cece urged. "Say what's on your mind. I can take it."

"You should be playing it safer," Beth bit off. "You think I don't notice how you're walking today? You seemed stiffer even walking into this room. You're pushing

yourself too hard. You're tired and worn-out, and it's irre-
sponsible."

"Beth." Cece inhaled harshly through the nose, so
frustrated she wondered if she opened her mouth, if fire
might come out, like a dragon. She wished they could
resolve this issue once and for all. No matter how well
intentioned they were, or how hard they tried to do otherwise, her sisters insisted on seeing her as less than capable
of anything too physical or too intense.

Their worry was sprinkled with pity, not because there
was something wrong with her now, but because they
remembered when there had been. They were old enough
to remember the surgeries, all the concerned looks, the
whispers about the girl with the braces, as though they, as
a family, had done something wrong.

It was stupid, and those people were so ignorant, but
that shouldn't mean that Cece should have to spend the
rest of her life defending her right to take on whatever
challenges she damn well pleased.

"Don't talk to me about being tired and worn-out," she
told Beth. "You're worn-out too, from wedding planning
and running the inn, but you love doing it. It's okay if I'm
tired and a little sore. If it's okay for you, why isn't it okay
for me?"

Beth opened her mouth to respond, then closed it.

"I love doing this work. Can't you see that?" Cece
scooted closer to her sister. "Fixing up homes, renovations. The last few weeks have brought me so much happiness and fulfillment. I need you to understand that. I
know you can."

"I just worry."

"I know."

"I don't think it's the wisest, most reasonable option."

"I know you don't, but Beth...I'm a grown woman. I'm responsible for myself now. I'm not *your* responsibility anymore."

"But..." Beth's gaze met hers, glassy with held-back tears.

"Oh, Beth." Cece wrapped her arms around her sister.

"I don't know how to not worry about you. I don't know how to not worry about Aurora. You're my sisters. I've worried about you both since we were kids because no one else was worrying enough."

Cece swallowed back the pain in her throat. Beth never should've had to take on the role of surrogate parent, but here they were. Trying to unwind the knots of their past. "I love you, sis," she said.

"I love you too." Beth sniffed.

Cece leaned back. "You love me, so listen to me. Trust that I'm not going to do anything crazy or dangerous. I've done this work for weeks now and yes, I'm tired. I should probably go back into physical therapy and tell them my work has changed and I need stretching exercises more than anything."

"Would you do that?" Beth sniffed. "Just to be safe. It'd help with the stiffness, but all this activity is probably really good for strength and mobility."

"It is." Cece nodded. "I feel myself getting stronger every day."

Beth nodded too and pulled her back into a hug. They sat that way for countless minutes, quietly coming to a truce.

"If this is what you want," Beth said, breaking the silence, "then...then you know I'll support you. I only want what's best for you."

"I know you do." Cece finally let go. "Do you want to take a break from all this and go see your dress?"

"I would love to."

"Come on." Cece led the way out of the big house, down the steps and across the gravel and grass toward their cars.

"Ow!" She came down too hard on her left foot into a divot in the ground, probably from moles. As soon as the pain shot up her calf, her leg buckled, making her sit down involuntarily.

"Cece?" Beth rounded her car. "Are you— Cece!"

"I'm okay." Her foot and ankle hurt, but not her leg. Her leg was merely tired, apparently too tired to hold her, a fact she'd never admit. "Of course this happens *now*."

Beth huddled beside her.

"I'm fine. I just sat down. Be careful, there's a hole over here, and my foot found it."

"Can you move it?"

Cece gently wiggled her foot and winced.

"Oh dear." Beth looked around, fretful.

"You are killing me, sis. Really. We just talked about this. I'm not about to die. Relax."

"Well. I know you want me to not care, but I do. Do you think you can stand?"

"Just..." Cece threw out her hands, humiliated, humbled, frustrated, angry, yet thankful her sister was by her side.

Beth stopped talking and let there be silence for a moment. "I'm sorry. Just tell me what you need," she finally said. "Is that better?"

Cece's gaze met her sister's. "Much better. Thank you."

Beth smiled softly. She was trying.

"Can we just sit here for a second? Let me catch my breath, and then I'll try to stand."

"I can do that." Beth settled beside her and crossed her legs.

They sat there for a moment, like two little kids playing in the grass. It was just silly enough to make Cece smile through the pain of her ankle. "Do you remember when you used to play dolls with me in the yard behind the orchard?"

Beth pulled her knees up, wrapping her arms around them. "We used to do that all the time."

"While Aurora turned cartwheels around us."

"Because she was going to be a cheerleader." Beth jerked her head to one side. "A Dallas Cowboys cheerleader."

Cece giggled. "I forgot about that."

"And she tried to talk Mom into buying her short shorts and white cowboy boots. Mom was like, no way." Beth laughed. "Can you imagine Aurora as a cheerleader now?"

"No. I can only see her being a chef. It's too perfect for her. Cheerleaders have to be happy and peppy all the time, and that is so not our sister."

Beth buried her face in her knees, giggling. "Come on, team! Stir that sauce! Bake that bread and dip it in a pot!"

Cece laughed too. Seeing Beth be light and silly, laughing like they were kids, was exactly the balm she needed for her hurt ankle and feelings.

"Okay, let's see if I can put weight on this foot," she said. "Then I'll need to raise it and ice it."

Beth nodded and got to her feet to help Cece up. "Let's go back inside then. We can ice it straightaway. My dress will still be there in an hour or so. You're more important."

Her sister wasn't using this as ammunition for her argument, and for that, Cece would be forever grateful. That was a line you didn't cross.

They made it inside, and Beth helped her settle on the sofa before running to get an ice pack.

"This could've happened to me just as easily," she said, adjusting the pillows under Cece's leg.

"Yeah, but it didn't."

It'd happened to her, right after her brilliant speech on being responsible, trying to convince her sister she should have a life of her own, work with Dustin, and...

Dustin.

She did not want him to see her like this. He'd probably think the worst, like this was somehow his fault, and then he'd never let her work with him again. She couldn't avoid him for the days it'd take for the swelling to go down and her to be able to walk around like nothing had happened though.

What was she going to do?

"Whoa. What happened to you?"

Cece looked up to find Manny standing in the foyer by the living room.

Great. Now there'd be no keeping it from Dustin.

"We, uh, we just had a little run-in with a mole hole in the yard," Beth said. "Icing her ankle a bit so it doesn't swell."

"Oh." He nodded, thankfully unaware of any facts beyond the one that people sometimes stepped in mole holes and tweaked their foot. This was a good sign. "Can I get you anything?"

"No, thank you though."

Manny nodded. "Man, this day just keeps getting worse.

That stupid real estate agent came by and made Dustin get all weird about stuff, I'm late and probably going to make Sawyer mad, and now you've hurt your foot."

Cece's eyes locked with Beth's for a second before her gaze jerked back to Manny.

"What stupid real estate agent?"

Manny blinked at her, eyes big and round as saucers. "Uh...just some guy?"

"Manny." She leveled a look at him.

"Okay, it was this investment realtor guy. Really slick type, you know what I mean?"

"Unfortunately, yes. Go on."

"Well...he came by the house this morning and said he'd buy it for five hundred thousand dollars."

Cece could only stare.

"What else did he say?" Beth asked for her.

Manny laid out the tale of the guy and his business card, his plans to buy the lots next to Hollyhock too, and build a new neighborhood, probably of spec houses, and tear down her dream home.

"Oh goodness." Beth shifted uncomfortably. "Okay, well, um..." She rose to her feet. "I think Sawyer is in the first stables, if you're looking for him."

"Sorry, I..." Manny shifted on his feet nervously. "I shouldn't have said anything. Maybe don't tell Dustin we talked?"

"It will be okay, Manny." Beth walked him out as Cece sat there, speechless.

How could Dustin turn down half a million dollars for Hollyhock? Easily, he couldn't. He wouldn't, and he shouldn't. That much money was more than he'd ever expected.

She shouldn't expect him to do anything but take the offer and run. And he could now. With that kind of money, he could leave Texas tomorrow. Would he really do that?

"Cece," Beth whispered.

That was their house. They'd made it a home together. Sure, it was going to be a home for someone else, but still...

He couldn't let some slimy investment group have it. They didn't care about the area, the community, or anything but the almighty dollar. They'd pack in homes on tiny plots and sell them for at least three hundred thousand each, making millions at any cost.

Even the cost of her dream.

"Take me back to Orchard Inn," she said to Beth. "Take me home."

Chapter 21

Dustin was a sweaty mess when he got back to Hollyhock. He didn't know how long he'd walked. Hours. The effort and outdoors helped some, but he was no more resolved than he had been before. Instead, he had lists of hundreds of reasons to accept the offer and to turn it down. To stay in town and to go.

Rather than beat the dead horse—"Ugh, no," he said aloud. That saying took on more meaning now, rendering it useless as far as he was concerned. Rather than overthink matters and drive himself around the bend, he'd get a shower and get on with his day.

Once cleaned up, he texted Cece and began making a sandwich for lunch. His phone rang right as he was about to take a bite, and he rushed to answer, thinking it was her calling.

The number wasn't Cece's.

"Dustin, hey, it's Felicia and Robert McAlister."

Dustin shook off the fog of his thoughts. "Hi, how are you guys? Good to hear from you."

"We're wondering if you had some time over the next few days to come out and talk to us."

A trip for a potential job was exactly what he needed

today to distract him. He'd have to go without Cece, which felt wrong, but maybe right now, it was for the best. "How about now? I could head over in a few minutes. Would that work?"

"That would be wonderful, as long as it's not too much trouble."

"No trouble at all. I'll see you in about an hour." Dustin ended the call and wrapped his sandwich to go. He hugged Bruce. "Sorry I have to dash. Wish me luck, son!"

He made it to the McAlisters in record time. Between thoughts of Cece and thoughts of the offer running back and forth across his mind, the miles passed in a blur. He pulled up at the—what had Cece called it?—the Greek Revival home around one o'clock. Bob stood outside by the porch with a hand full of freshly cut roses.

"Dustin!" He waved the flowers at him. "You got here quick. Come on in."

Dustin followed him inside, the house as warm and welcoming as before.

"Felicia, sweetheart?" Bob yelled as they walked toward the kitchen. "Dustin is here."

Felicia emerged from down the hall in a flowy dress with long, wide sleeves. The bottom hem brushed the floor.

Cece would say she looked like an actress from the 1970s, floating about her Hollywood home, about to call him *Dustin, dahhhhling*.

"I'm delighted you could come see us on such short notice," she said instead. "Would you like something to drink? Bob, honey, get him some tea. You must be absolutely parched."

"I'm okay, really. Thank you though."

"You're sure?" Bob raised both eyebrows over the tops of his roses.

"I'm sure."

"Suit yourself." He set the roses down on the edge of the island and picked up a set of snippers. "Felicia makes the best sweet tea." He began clipping thorns off the roses.

"Bob, honey, must you do that in here?"

"This is where I always do this."

"Well, at least move them near the sink."

"Yes, dear." Bob moved over to the sink.

"Thank you. Now"—Felicia focused on Dustin—"I suppose we'll get down to it. Firstly, Bob and I want to hire you for our renovation."

Dustin fought the urge to high-five the air since Cece wasn't there.

"Not only do you come with Lyle's recommendation, but your bid is reasonable, and you're easily the most personable contractor we met with."

"Really?" Dustin tried not to sound surprised.

"Don't tell Lyle we said that," Bob joked.

"And Cece. Oh, we just adore her. I can't wait to work with her on the vision of our outdoor space, along with the other two rooms."

"Cece is— You mean, she won the bid for the interior decorating too?"

"Of course. She's a peach, and I simply must work with her."

He couldn't believe it. No, scratch that. He could believe it. They'd be fools not to want to work with Cece.

"She will be so excited to hear this," he said. "We can start next week if you want. Does that still work?"

"As long as we're ready by Thanksgiving."

"You will be." Probably wouldn't hurt to go ahead and try to hire that other hand to help on this job. He'd have to ask Sawyer or even Lyle if they knew of someone who'd be a good fit.

"Secondly…" Felicia pulled out a chair at the kitchen island and held out a hand, inviting Dustin to do the same.

Dustin's excitement drained immediately. He suddenly felt numb, knowing what was likely coming next.

"I want to apologize for how I handled myself the other day," she said. "I got a bit ahead of myself, and, well, sometimes my mouth gets away from me. But I would like to talk to you about my old friend from high school, Daisy. That is, if it's all right?"

He nodded, unable to form a word in response, anxiety quickly setting like cement in his stomach.

"I found my old yearbooks and called a classmate I'm still friends with."

Dustin took a steadying breath. "You did."

Felicia nodded, solemn. "Her married name *was* Long. Daisy Long." Her gaze held his, knowing what this might mean for Dustin. "I asked my friend about what happened, since we'd lost touch. After their daughter left and they moved to Dallas, Daisy's husband passed about five years later. She has since remarried, which is why I could never find her on social media, and apparently, she never did reconcile with her daughter."

Dustin had tried social media too, a couple of years ago, when he'd gotten it in his head to look. Google, Facebook, all the usual suspects. He hadn't had a potential grandmother's name though. All he'd had was the name on his release papers.

"The rumors were true though." Felicia nodded. "The daughter had a child here, then moved north."

Where she'd abandoned Dustin.

"I don't think things went well for her there—the daughter, I mean."

"Nell Long," Dustin uttered the name he'd seen on his release papers.

Felicia frowned. "Her name was Eleanor. Eleanor Long. She must've shortened it legally after she left."

Of course she had. Chances were good she'd changed it several times after that too.

"Word is, she moved around a lot with her boyfriend after they left Texas. I think he was involved with some unsavory people and dealings, if you know what I mean. Drugs and money scams. Then, everyone sort of lost track of her in the early 2000s. My friend didn't know if she'd changed her name again after the boyfriend was arrested or if... you know, if she's no longer with us."

Dustin tried to feel nothing, show no reaction.

"But her mother, Daisy—now Daisy Cunningham— still lives in Dallas."

He nodded numbly.

Daisy Long, now Cunningham, from a well-to-do family, bearing the shame of an unmarried, pregnant daughter, who'd taken up with someone who they probably considered to be low class, then ran away, thinking she'd find happiness but likely only finding heartache.

"If you want Daisy's information, I could get it for you."

"Thank you, but...I..." Dustin managed to shake his head. "I should probably just..."

Not do or say anything rash. His insides roiled with a storm of emotions. Anger, sadness, resentment, along with the conflict of knowing his birth mother had been from a good family once, before it all went so wrong. He had questions, but he also didn't want to know any more. He wasn't sure he could handle it.

Bob cleared his throat. "Why don't you just, uh, think on it for a while? No need to figure it all out now, is there?"

Dustin shook his head again, thankful.

"Of course." Bob went back to working on his roses.

"Thank you for looking into that," Dustin managed to say to Felicia.

She reached over and squeezed his hand without a word.

Dustin got up to leave, and Bob lifted a vase from the sink, full of his peach-colored roses. "Before you go, we wanted to give these to you and Cece. She was such a fan of my roses, and the real joy is in sharing them."

Dustin choked down the knot in his throat and made a hasty exit.

He made it to his truck and down the driveway before tears burned his eyes.

How had things gone so wrong for his birth mom?

Had she had a lot of friends? She'd likely come from a family like Felicia and Bob's. Was his birth father really that bad? Bad enough to split apart a family? How different would his life had been if his birth mother had given up the boyfriend and stayed with her parents?

What if?

He'd worried the past would only muddle his mind, and he was right, but the whirring thoughts weren't as terrible as he'd imagined. He had some answers and even more questions, but at least now he knew something. He knew about his mom.

Dustin was halfway back to Fredericksburg when he

came out of the fog of his past. He immediately called Cece, his call going to voicemail.

He hadn't heard from her all day, and it didn't sit right. They'd been inseparable for weeks, and now they'd gone far too long without speaking.

She would've been busy with Beth, showing her the dress and finishing up wedding preparations, but it wasn't like her to be radio silent all day.

Dustin texted her. Moments later, he got a response, but it was not one he wanted.

I need some time and a little space.

Space?

Everything within him screamed no, but he didn't want to go against her wishes.

Why space? What else had happened? He just needed to talk to her, and then, if she wanted space, he'd do his best to oblige.

After he went by Hollyhock to pick up Bruce, he headed straight to Orchard Inn. Trying not to let concern and his anxiety about the recent news get the best of him, he pulled up to the house and found Sawyer walking down the steps of the front porch.

The inn would open for business tomorrow, so he was likely here helping with the final touches.

"Hey, man." He came down the stairs to greet Dustin. Bruce bounded toward him, happy to see his new buddy. "You looking for Cece?"

The hairs on the back of his neck prickled. "Yeah, why? What's wrong?"

Sawyer came closer. "She's okay, but, um…" His expression said a million things at once. Cece was upset, and somehow, Dustin was the reason. But why?

"Manny told Cece about the real estate investor's offer today."

Dustin groaned. "Dammit, Manny." That was why she wanted space.

"I'm sure he wasn't thinking."

"I know, but—"

"She needed to hear it from you?" Sawyer's expression was pure commiseration, as though he'd been there before.

"Exactly." Dustin ran a rough hand through his hair. "He doesn't think about that though." Because he was a kid who'd never cared for someone the way Dustin cared for Cece. "I tried to tell her. I texted, but then I got called out to the job in Hays County."

"Yeah?"

"We got the job," Dustin said, reminding himself this was good news, and right now, he and Cece should be celebrating, not distant.

"That's great."

"Yeah." Dustin sighed, feeling himself shift into autopilot, going to that place where his feelings receded and walls went up in protection of his heart. "It's great. I'll still finish your house too though."

"I know."

"Listen." He turned to Sawyer, trying to keep the walls down, never wanting to be that person again. Solitary, no connections other than Manny. It hadn't been living. He'd only been existing. "How upset is she?"

Sawyer grimaced. "Pretty upset, but I've seen worse. I've seen Beth more upset, that's for sure."

"I didn't accept the offer though. I don't know that I will."

He cocked an eyebrow. "You're going to say no to a five-hundred-thousand-dollar cash offer? You could have the money in your account by next week."

"No? I don't know."

"Cece knows what that kind of money would mean for you. For anyone."

"Does she know what *she* means to me though?"

After everything he'd experienced the last few weeks, including learning more about his past, the only person he wanted to see, talk to, and share it with was Cece. He cared more about her than the money. If he had to choose, right now, between losing that much money or losing her, the choice was clear. It wasn't even a choice. It was a truth he knew in his bones.

"I love her." Dustin stepped back, stunned by his admission.

Sawyer smiled. "Yeah, man, I know."

Dustin blinked. "Does...does Cece know that?"

"I'm not sure, but it's obvious to any of us who've been paying attention."

Dustin shook his head, feeling like someone had clocked him and rung his bell.

"Did she say she doesn't want to see me?"

Sawyer didn't answer.

"I know how she can get if she's upset."

"She's a hothead, like me." Sawyer kept pacing.

"And she'll rile herself up and make it worse."

"That's why it's good to have Beth in there with her. She's good at keeping us both on the level."

"If I could just see her, talk to her, explain what happened and how I feel."

"I think you need to give her the night. Let her talk

to her sisters and think before you try rushing in to save the day."

Dustin grumbled.

"I know it sounds crazy, but I've learned a few things about Cece and her sisters in the past year. You have to be patient."

Now Dustin was pacing, Bruce right on his heels. "But I'm not patient any more than you're cool-tempered."

"I know, and I'm not patient either, but I had to learn. To try and be better. You can't make a woman hear you out or listen—especially not a Shipley woman—until they're ready. Trust me on this. She's got stuff she needs to come to terms with too. Maybe even things you don't realize yet. You'd do more harm than good if you tried to force your defense."

Dustin stopped mid-step, and so did Bruce. He looked up at the sky, the bright sun skittering behind a cloud.

"I think she's scared more than anything," Sawyer said. "Maybe you both are, even if you don't realize it. I remember when I fell for Beth. I was terrified. Ecstatically happy, but terrified. Love is scary and wonderful. It's supposed to be."

He was scared—even terrified. He'd never said those words to anyone. Not even Manny. But he felt them. Even though he had no idea how he'd provide for Cece or give her the kind of life she deserved, he wanted to try. He wasn't going to lose her over some house offer. She needed to know that. He needed to get a message to her somehow. Tonight.

"Go home," Sawyer urged. "Let her talk to her sisters and think. Cece has a good head on her shoulders and an even better heart. I know it's tough, but you have to trust her."

Dustin nodded. "I will, but I need you to do something for me. Can you do that?"

"What is it?"

He hurried back to his truck and reached inside, grabbing the roses. He brought them back and held them out to Sawyer. "Just give her these and tell her I came by. You can wait until later tonight if you want. Just...will you give them to her?"

Sawyer nodded, taking the flowers. "I'll do it. Y'all are going to be okay."

"You sure?"

"I'd bet the ranch on it."

Chapter 22

Cece stared out the window toward the orchard trees behind the inn. In the kitchen, Beth and Sawyer talked, their voices hushed and hurried.

She sat up, adjusting the ice pack on her ankle before deciding to move it and peek. Her foot and ankle were swollen but not discolored. That was a good sign.

She heard Sawyer leave through the front of the house. He'd had to endure her venting about the investor's offer and how all investment groups were crooks, looking to drain local communities of land, funds, and resources.

Moments later, Beth joined her in the den. "Can I get you anything?"

"A new leg?" Cece frowned.

Beth's expression pained her more than her foot.

"Sorry. Gallows humor. Figured you were used to it coming from me by now."

"I know, but..." Beth sat on the far end of the couch. "This could've happened to anyone."

"You said that already."

Her sister studied her hands before meeting her gaze again. "I'm trying to help. Or at least make things better. I know the timing of..." She indicated Cece's ankle.

"...after the disagreement we'd just had, wasn't great. I don't want you to think I won't keep my word. I promise I'm going to try to back off and let *you* lead your own life. I don't want to fight anymore or have you so..."

"Angry?" Cece offered.

"Yeah."

"I appreciate the intention, sis, but sometimes people need to be angry. I need to be angry. Annoyed and angry and hurt. It's okay for me to upset about this, but it doesn't mean I'm upset at you. You don't have to fix this for me. Just let me feel my feelings, okay?"

Beth pinched her lips together and nodded. "Okay. I'm going to make some tea. Do you want some?"

Cece shifted on the couch. "Is it the vanilla chamomile, and will you put honey in it?"

"You know it."

"I'd love some."

Beth made the best hot tea. She wasn't stingy with the honey, and she used their biggest, thickest mugs, so they didn't burn your hands. Sometimes, she even remembered the little mug cozies that Cece had crocheted last Christmas. They kept your hands safe and your tea warm. Beth was good at remembering the little details. Not for the first time, Cece imagined her big sis would make an amazing mom someday.

She'd probably helicopter a little too much, but she'd be great at it.

"Sorry I'm late." Aurora came in the back, through their family entrance. "We had a party that took forever to wrap up. What happened?"

Thankfully, Beth retold the incident, sparing Cece.

"Are you okay?" Aurora sat on the ottoman next to her.

"Scale of one to ten, ten being the hiking tumble or the time I tried to pierce your ears at home."

Cece laughed, then winced as it jostled her leg. "Don't make me laugh." Secretly, she loved it. Aurora's dry humor hit just right. "Maybe a five?"

"Okay, five isn't so bad. We can handle a five. A five is like when Beth slammed the door on my hand during Christmas break her freshman year in college."

"I did not slam the door on your hand." Beth returned with Cece's tea, having remembered the cozy. "I slammed my bedroom door because you were harassing me, and your hand happened to be in the way. Do you want some tea too?"

"Please." Aurora moved a pillow to hold in her lap. "Do you think you might be wearing sneakers to a wedding again?"

"Probably."

"I don't care what shoes anyone wears." Beth returned with their teas. "I don't really care what anyone wears at all. That's not what matters." She sat on the sofa again.

Cece let the tea warm her hands as she met Aurora's gaze. "Dustin is going to sell Hollyhock."

She scrunched her brow. "Y'all aren't finished with it yet. How can he sell it?"

"The buyer is a developer. He doesn't want the house itself. He doesn't care a thing about the actual house. I looked up the company name Manny gave us. They clear acreage and build multifamily townhomes and houses inches apart from one another, sometimes with additional apartment buildings as part of the development. None of it's affordable though. They'll cram a bunch of plots onto the acreage, and starting price will be like, three hundred thousand."

"Ew."

"Exactly."

"And I didn't even think about the rehab farm near there, Rolling Hills. They can't have a huge development and all that traffic and congestion right near the farm. It'd ruin the whole purpose of the place being an oasis."

"Does Dustin know all this?" Aurora asked.

"I don't know. A simple Google search would show him, so maybe?"

"I can't imagine he'd be okay with that considering all the hard work you've both done."

"They're offering five hundred thousand dollars for the property, *as is*. They'd probably go even higher if Dustin resists."

"Wow." Aurora's eyes went wide. "That's more than I was expecting."

Cece stared at her hands, picking at a nail. "Yep." She didn't want to feel so defeated, but...

This was Dustin's property; he could do whatever he wanted with it. His main goal all along had been to make the most profit possible on the sale of Hollyhock and work for his own company. He'd have a business—a successful one, no doubt—and a life with security and stability. No residential buyer could top what an investment firm might offer. The obvious answer was for him to sell the property and sell it quick.

But they'd worked so hard. The love and attention they'd poured into Hollyhock—now no one would ever get to appreciate it. No family would play in what was guaranteed to be an amazing yard. There would be no Christmases around that brick fireplace with the mantel perfect for stockings to be hung with care. No big meals in the dining room, with the collectible china of their choice proudly displayed in the inset cabinet. No bubble baths in the claw-foot tub.

She sighed, long and slow.

Instead, her dream home would be razed to the ground. A pile of rubble to be hauled off in the back of several dump trucks.

She had every right to be sad. And mad and frustrated and disappointed.

It wasn't just the house though. With that kind of money, Dustin wouldn't even need the other jobs in Texas. She wouldn't get to be a part of all the plans they'd made together. The future, even short-term, they'd laid out as partners.

All along, she'd told herself he'd be gone someday. She'd tried to convince herself that was okay, but it was never okay. She was a terrible liar, and that included lying to herself.

She didn't want him to go, ever.

Cece wanted Dustin to stay right here in Fredericksburg and keep working with her. Stay and see where their relationship went. She imagined it could go wherever they wanted.

"Have you talked to Dustin about this yet?" Aurora broke the silence.

"Not yet."

"Cece," she said softly. "You need to talk to him."

"What am I going to say? *Hey, don't take all that money. Keep working on the old house and sinking money into it, then sell it for half what that guy's offering after you do all that hard work. Don't start that business you dreamed of and would be able to afford with this offer. Instead, just scrape by from job to job, here with me.*"

"Yes." Aurora nodded. "You should say exactly that."

Cece sat up a little straighter and tried not to flinch at the discomfort. "You've lost it. *Stay here and work with me? Give up* your *plans and the life you set out for,* for me? *I can't promise you wealth or anything like that, and it definitely won't be easy, but that's okay because we'll figure it out?*"

"*Yes,*" her sisters said in unison.

"Say exactly that," Aurora insisted.

She shook her head. "No way."

"Aurora is right," Beth agreed with their sister.

Aurora looked at Beth, eyes wide. "Can I get that in writing?"

"I'm serious." Beth scooted forward until Cece met her gaze. "You should tell him what you're thinking and how you feel, or you'll regret it. Trust me on this."

"What do you have to lose?" Aurora asked.

"Everything! Him. My dignity. My sense of self-worth. I'm just going to hobble over there and throw myself at his mercy, and then he rejects me?"

"Okay." Aurora held out her hands. "First of all, he is not going to care about you hobbling. I mean, he'll care, but not in the way you mean, and you know it. Second of all, I can't see him rejecting you. I've been around the two of you. I see how he looks at you."

"But I always knew he'd leave. I told myself I wouldn't get in this position. He was up-front and honest about his plans all along, and I knew from the start he was only here temporarily. For me to come back now and pressure him to have a totally different life isn't fair."

Her sisters listened intently, their sympathetic gazes making it a little easier to get it all off her chest.

"But I started really liking him, more and more every day. He's nice and hot, and he was into me too, so I didn't want to deny my feelings and not spend more time with him."

"Of course not," Beth agreed. "Y'all were obviously into one another."

"It was just going to be for fun though. Then he was so thoughtful and genuine and amazing." Cece swiped angrily at a rogue tear that'd formed on her lashes. No one gave that thing permission to be there. "With his big stupid arms and face, and how he holds me, and how beautiful and perfect he makes me feel."

Aurora reached over and wiped gently at her cheek where another tear had escaped.

"I'm scared." Cece confessed something she never thought she'd admit to again in her life. "I'm never scared anymore, not with what I've been through, but this? The thought of losing him and just...poof, he's out of my life? Forever? It scares me so much."

Beth placed a gentle hand on her good foot. "We know. We've been scared before too."

When she looked up, her sisters were misty-eyed as well.

"Remember when I thought Jude and I were just going to be a short-term rekindled flame?" Aurora asked. "I convinced myself we could just spark up again and then snuff it out when it was time for me to go back to California. Love doesn't work that way though. I thought I had my whole life planned out, and it didn't include Jude or staying in Fredericksburg. But guess what? I was wrong. Plans change, and Dustin's could too."

"Exactly," Beth agreed. "Sawyer was just a distraction from work for me, something to help me deal with all the stress of getting the inn back on its feet. He wasn't what I was looking for, and he certainly couldn't be a priority. Then, I realized how much he meant to me. Enough to hurt me if he ever kept anything from me. Now look at us. If you'd told me the day we met that we would be here now, I would've laughed you out of the inn."

Aurora reached for her tea and took a sip. "You have to tell Dustin how you feel. Not just about the house but about him."

"About all of it," Beth added. "Tell him you want him to stay, regardless of what happens with Hollyhock. You want him here, in your life."

Cece imagined hobbling up the front steps of Hollyhock, pouring out her heart and soul only for it to blow up in her face.

"We know it's scary. We've been in your position."

"What if he still leaves? I could put myself out there, and he could still leave."

"I know, but what if he doesn't?" Aurora asked. "Jude went way out on a limb for me when he told me how he truly felt. Can you imagine how scary that must have been? He'd loved me for years, but he'd thought he'd be holding me back from my dream if he told me. He didn't know my dream had changed. All I needed was to hear him say he wanted me and that he wanted me to stay. I needed to hear that he felt the same. What if your words are all Dustin needs for the two of you to start a life together? What if your courage is the first step?"

Beth produced a tissue from who knows where and passed it to Cece. "It doesn't matter what you thought or said you were going to do when you started all this. You love each other, and that changes everything. You should at least give Dustin the choice. He's given you the benefit of choices since the beginning."

"And believed in you even when we..." Aurora shrugged one shoulder. "Faltered? Just a little?"

"He has a right to decide the life he wants too." Beth squeezed her free hand.

Cece sniffed, wiping at her nose. Her sisters had a point. Even if it meant she'd be ripping her heart out just to let Dustin break it in half, she had to tell him how she felt. She'd regret not telling him for the rest of her life, and she'd sworn to herself years ago she'd never live a life of regrets.

"Okay. I'll talk to him tomorrow."

Her sisters shared a smile.

"Promise?" Beth asked.

"I promise."

Someone came from the front of the inn, startling them from their moment. Sawyer came from the foyer, a vase full of apricot roses in his hands.

"Oh, honey, they're beautiful," Beth cooed.

Sawyer lowered the roses, his expression sheepish. "Um...they're for Cece, babe. From Dustin."

Beth's smile grew. "That's even better."

Sawyer sighed. "Good. Guess I should've thought about how it looked, me walking in here with a bunch of roses. But he came by while I was on my way out. He wanted me to give you these." He passed the roses to Cece.

"They're Bob's roses." Cece sniffed one of the blooms.

"Who?"

"The job we looked at in Hays. The husband grows beautiful roses. Dustin must have gone to see them."

"He didn't want to come in?" Aurora asked.

Sawyer explained, but Cece heard little of it. She

wanted to talk to him, but if he'd come in even moments earlier, the conversation wouldn't have gone well. The flowers, these roses, were all the encouragement she needed to face her future and whatever happened between her and Dustin tomorrow.

She'd rest, maybe she could even go see him without crutches, and she'd put everything out on the table. Whatever he decided after that, she'd accept it. Somehow, she'd be strong enough. And for the first time today, she had hope.

"Thank you, Sawyer." She smiled at her future brother-in-law. "But now you need to get lost so Beth can try on her dress."

Sawyer gave her a wink before walking to the front with Beth to kiss her good night. It took forever for her to return to their living quarters.

"Will you try your dress on already?" Aurora asked, impatiently setting down her tea.

"You should try on the bridesmaid's dress too."

"Yes!" Cece agreed.

"Okay, but let me wash up some from the kitchen. I must keep that dress pristine." Aurora disappeared down the hall with Beth, and after what felt like an eternity, they emerged, Aurora first.

The bridesmaids' dresses were the lightest champagne shade, in flattering chiffon with an empire waist. The soft neutral flattered Aurora's undertones and would do the same for Cece. That was why Cece had picked the style and shade.

"These are perfect." Aurora twirled. "You did great."

"I did." Cece nodded. "The flowers are all candlelight and cream shades too. Chrysanthemums, anemones, and asters. It's going to look so nice together. Okay, Beth!" she shouted down the hall. "We're ready."

Beth stepped out into the living room, a vision in silk and lace.

"Oh my god," Aurora gasped.

Cece clutched her heart. Her sister looked perfect in the dress.

"I love it." Beth blinked back tears. "I…" She took a step forward and turned. "You did it. It's absolutely perfect."

"Cece." Aurora gaped. "This is…" She moved closer to Beth for a better look. "I can't believe you can do this."

Cece shrugged. "I didn't know I could. Until I did."

Beth turned again, looking down at the silk skirt, barely touched with beading and lace. Just enough to give her an ethereal sparkle and texture. "I know you want to renovate houses, but I think you need to consider keeping dressmaking in your repertoire."

"I'll say." Aurora fluffed the bottom of the skirt, watching it fall back into place. "I'm placing my order now for my wedding dress."

Cece smiled, her heart swollen with pride and joy. "I'm so glad you both like it."

"I'd like to take back everything I said," Aurora added, meeting her gaze. "Any doubt I had or anything I did or said that sounded like something other than my full support and belief in you. You are a queen, sis."

Cece absorbed the compliments, letting them sink in and reminding herself not to argue or try to negate their meaning. She was capable, and now others were seeing that. All she had to do was keep going and see where life might take her.

Chapter 23

What little sleep he got was fitful. He'd tossed and turned, thinking about Cece, Felicia's details about his biological mother, the offer on Hollyhock.

But mostly, he'd thought about Cece.

If it weren't for her, he would've never even thought about staying here. If it weren't for her, he might already be done with Hollyhock and on his way to Florida, trying to start a life there, where he knew no one other than his buddy and had nothing but the shell of plan.

Cece had intrigued him from the moment they met. Who was this woman, out in the middle of a storm, sheltering on his porch and then preaching at him about how to renovate his house? Every day, he'd learned more and more about her creative and intelligent mind, her understanding and open heart, and her dry, silly humor. He'd fallen for her, fallen in love. Obviously, there were plenty of opportunities for him in Florida, but there was no other Cece. Not anywhere.

A knock on the front door jarred him from his thoughts. Bruce began barking excitedly, and he knew. He knew in his bones.

"Cece," he said as he opened the door.

"Hey." She barely lifted her hand above her waist.

Shadows darkened her eyes, and her curls were a mess from what he guessed was a sleepless night for her as well.

She was still the prettiest sight he'd ever seen.

"Come in." He stepped aside.

She made it two steps before being greeted by Bruce and his kisses.

"Sawyer told me you came by last night," she said without looking up.

"I did."

"And the roses, they were from Bob's garden?"

"Yeah," he said. "They offered us the job...if we want it, I mean." The answer came out breathier than he'd intended, but having her here, knowing they had a chance to talk—about everything—stole his breath.

She gave Bruce one last pat and straightened. "Thank you for giving me space to think last night."

Dustin shifted as Bruce leaned his full weight on his leg. "Not going to lie, it was tough not to bust in and try to fix things, but Sawyer gave me some good advice. We needed to be ready to talk. Really talk."

For a moment, they stared at each other in silence.

"I made coffee," he offered. "You want some?"

"I could use a whole gallon of coffee." She walked past him, and he saw her favoring her right leg, limping a little.

He bit back the urge to be completely reactionary and over-the-top at even the notion of her being injured. "Are you all right?" he tried instead.

"I will be." She flapped a hand in the air as if to brush off the question. "I tweaked my ankle in a mole hole yesterday. I have the worst luck, but it's a lot better today. Better than I thought it'd be actually."

"You want to sit?"

"Sure."

He brought her a cup of coffee and sat next to her at the card table.

"I'm sorry you had to hear about the offer on Hollyhock from Manny," he began. "I tried contacting you when the guy left and again after I went to see the McAlisters, but—"

"I know," she stopped him. "And it's okay. I'm not upset that I heard about it from Manny."

Dustin stared into his coffee, for the first time unsure of how she'd react to his news. "Not only did we get the McAlister job, but they want you to do the interior decorating."

Cece froze with her mug in midair. "Seriously?"

"Seriously."

"That's . . . wow, that's great news. I mean, like you said, if we decide to do it."

He nodded.

Cece tilted her head. "There's something else though. What is it? What's wrong?"

"Felicia found out more about my mom."

She slowly lowered the coffee mug, her brow etched in concern.

"She talked to an old schoolmate who kept up with— I guess it's my grandmother, Daisy."

"Oh, Dustin."

"My mom left me when I was almost two years old. She moved around a lot before that, and from what I've been able to put together over the years, she moved around a lot after, apparently with a sketchy boyfriend."

"Did Felicia know what happened after that?"

He shook his head. "Not exactly. Sounds like nothing good. She changed her name from Eleanor to Nell before giving me up; she could've changed it again, which makes it even harder to trace. I don't know if she ever married the guy, but apparently, he was trouble. Con artist, drugs, a real piece of work." Dustin lifted a shoulder and let it drop. "Chances are good they're both dead by now."

"Dustin."

"If they were doing drugs in the late nineties and early two thousands? How many people accidentally overdosed then? Meth and heroin? Odds aren't great for her."

"You could probably find out for certain."

"I know." His stomach turned at the possibility of all he might find. Most scenarios went from bad to worse in his mind. "But I don't know that I want to know. Part of me doesn't want to learn the truth."

She sighed. "That makes sense."

"It does? Because I can't make sense of how I feel."

Cece reached for him, her hand on his forearm. She didn't speak but offered him comfort. Letting him know, no matter what happened between them, she was here for him in this moment.

"I'm angry *and* relieved," he finally said. "I've got all this resentment, but I also feel sorry for her. And I'm... thankful. I didn't grow up in that life. Yeah, the foster system was rough for a while, but then I got very lucky. Eventually, I ended up somewhere decent. No one was on drugs, no one roughed us up for the tiniest thing we did wrong. We had strict rules, sure, but I needed them. Then I got Manny, and I grew up."

His life could've taken so many different paths. He imagined his mother staying with Daisy, leaving the boyfriend and raising Dustin with grandparents, in a community that might grow to love and accept them. Then, he imagined his mother not giving him up, raising him in the danger and chaos that had become her life. Not only could she be dead, but Dustin might be too.

"I just…It's a lot to process," he said. "Sometimes, I hate my parents for abandoning me. Who would do that? But then I feel bad for them, especially her, because what must it take to push a person to do that? Was it selfishness or did she know I'd be better off? How could she know? Things could've been worse for me in the system. I know so many people have it much harder. Plus, do I really want to know the answers to all this? It won't change anything. More importantly, I wouldn't want to change anything because it brought me to right here, right now, with you."

Cece's gaze met his, and she swallowed hard, blinking and pinching her lips together.

"Cece." He took her hand. "All I went through, the issues I had being abandoned and then bounced around, that all led me here. Like you said the other day in the field, I am who I am because of my past, and I wouldn't change who I am or this destination."

A tear escaped her eyes and drifted down her cheek. He caught it and wiped it away with his thumb. "You're who you are because of your past too," he told her. "The struggles you went through are why you're so strong. You're determined and pushy because you've always had something to prove. You're independent because you insist on being so. You're a fighter, but so am I, and I love that about you."

Cece grabbed his free hand, bringing it to her lips to place a kiss on his knuckles. She did him in, over and over again, with her soft expression and open emotion. He wanted to scoop her up and never let her go.

"I wouldn't change anything about you or me, even if I could. I think we're pretty damn perfect together and—"

"I don't want you to sell Hollyhock," she blurted.

"What?"

Cece shook her head, making her messy curls wilder. "I know it's crazy of me to ask and that it's a lot of money to turn down, but I don't want you to sell to that investment group. Don't let them destroy what we've built. We can find the right buyer. I know it. And it won't be as much money, but it will still be a lot."

Dustin blinked; his shoulders felt like he had twenty-pound sandbags on each. "What are you saying, Cece?"

"I'm saying don't... don't leave. I don't want you to go to Florida. Please."

He took her hands in his, hoping he wasn't squeezing them too hard.

"I don't want you to leave me," she told him, her voice trembling. "Not in a few weeks or a few months or ever. I...I think you should stay here. With me. Florida isn't that great anyway. There are hurricanes and alligators and...and...I'm not there. You said it yourself—we're pretty damn perfect together. Why should we be apart? There's work here, and everyone loves you. I...I love you."

Dustin reached for her, pulling her toward him until she was in his lap. "I love you too," he said without hesitation, without fear.

He kissed her then, kissed her until she stopped shaking, until the tears on her cheeks had dried.

As scared as he'd always been to form attachments,

to say how he felt, to love someone just to have to miss them—he felt none of that now. All he felt was joy and love and certainty.

"I'm not going anywhere," he told Cece.

"Oh, thank God." She wrapped her arms around his neck, squeezing him hard enough to take his breath. She kissed his forehead, his cheeks, peppering his face until she found his lips. "We'll figure it out," she said between kisses. "Once we make some money on this place and our other jobs, we can save up, and like you said, one job leads to another and another. I don't know how, but I know we can make it work and—"

"No." He stopped her, pulling her hands from his shoulders to hold them. "I meant I'm not going anywhere at all. *We* aren't going anywhere. We're not leaving this house."

Cece tilted her head, blinking as she studied him. "But . . . we don't . . . What?"

"You and the last few weeks have been the closest thing to a home I've ever had in my life. Part of that is this place. I want to live here, live in the now and plan for our future."

"Wait, wait." Cece sent her curls flying again as she shook her head, as though trying to clear it. "Are you saying you're keeping Hollyhock? And you want to live here, with me, like this is our home? Like this would be the house? Our house?"

He laughed, his soul finally so at ease. "Yes. That is exactly what I'm saying."

Cece wrapped her arms around him again, burying her face into his neck. "Yes!" she squealed, though it was muffled. "This the best—yes! Wait." She popped back up again. "But that investment group. Manny said they were going to buy the lots on both sides. We'll be in the middle of their development."

Dustin pursed his lips and shook his head. "I don't believe him. First of all, I did a search, and no one has bought either lot yet. They aren't crazy expensive or that big, so I did a little more poking around online. They'd need Hollyhock, the two small lots, and probably that farm—"

"Rolling Hills?" she asked.

"Yeah, they'd need all of them in order to have enough land for a development."

"Rolling Hills would never sell to that guy. They're big-time hippie throwbacks. They'd hate the idea of a development nearby."

"That's what I thought too." He smiled. "So if we bought at least the lot next to us, they wouldn't even want to. You've still got money saved up, right?"

Cece nodded. "And we'll have more once we finish these next three jobs."

"Plus what I get from insurance for fixing Orchard Inn."

Her eyes widened. "That's right. We could…" Her eyes went wider. "We could really do this."

"We really could." He pulled her down for another kiss.

"And this is what you want?" she asked in between kisses. "It's not five hundred thousand dollars, cash."

"Cece." Dustin caught her chin, looking deep into her eyes. "A life here, with you, is worth more than all the money in the world."

Epilogue

Cece adjusted Beth's veil and smoothed out the back of her wedding dress so it lay perfectly, barely touching the floor. She met her sister's gaze in the full-length mirror. "I told you you'd look like a princess."

"It's perfect." Beth glowed. "You outdid yourself, really."

Aurora joined them in front of the mirror, powder in one hand as she studied them with a keen eye. "Do not get all emotional, or you'll start crying and ruin your makeup before we even leave this bedroom." She blotted the tip of Beth's nose.

Over the last few days leading up to Beth's wedding, the reality seemed to hit them all. This was the end of an era. Beth would live in the big house at Silva Ranch until her house with Sawyer was complete. The three of them would no longer see one another before bed each night and first thing in the mornings. Knowing how much their daily lives would change, they'd been...dare she say, sweeter to one another? Kinder and a lot more sentimental.

Such a huge dynamic change, and it'd snuck up on them.

"Are y'all sure I don't look bloated in this dress?" Shelby turned to the side, smoothing the chiffon over a barely noticeable baby bump.

"If you do that? Maybe." Cece shooed her hand away, grateful for the diversion. "But you're pregnant, not bloated. It's an empire waistline. No one will know you're pregnant unless you want them to know."

"Or walk around like this." Aurora mimicked her holding the dress down over her belly.

"Shelby." Beth turned dramatically, teasing her. "No one is going to be looking at you. Have you seen me in this dress?" She posed.

Shelby giggled. "You're right. You look amazing. I'm just not used to my body doing all these weird things."

Aurora scrunched her nose. "What weird things?"

"Oh, honey, I will tell you later. I've heard it only gets weirder."

A light knock on the bedroom door pulled them from their silliness.

"Girls, it's me."

Shelby opened the door, letting their mom, Anita, in.

"Beth." Anita placed her hands over her heart, her eyes welling up.

"Nope." Aurora rushed over to their mom, fanning her face with a wedding program. "Don't you start either. No one is allowed to get weepy yet. Cece! Say something funny. We can't have a bunch of teary-eyed women going down the aisle."

"Um…" Cece tried to think of something. "Oh! Garrett and Dustin got the dogs matching bow ties for pictures after the reception."

Shelby snorted. "Garrett wanted to get Dodger a full-blown little doggy tuxedo, but Dustin was like, 'um, let's just stick to a bow tie for this wedding and work our way up to dog tuxedos, m'kay?'"

Cece had to laugh, imagining Dustin attempting to wrangle Bruce into a tux. "It was enough of an accomplishment getting most of these men into suits. Maybe we should let the dogs stick with bow ties indefinitely."

"Agreed," Aurora said.

The five of them finished powdering their noses and fixing every hair. They left the private quarters of the inn and checked with the wedding day coordinator Beth had handpicked.

"The coast is clear," Carl, the wedding coordinating wonder, said. "Sawyer is outside, and it's just us in the house right now. Anita, you'll go first, and Lyle will seat you both. Then, we have Cece walking down with Dustin."

Sawyer had graciously asked Dustin to be a groomsman since the two of them had grown so close.

"Next is Aurora with Jude, then Shelby with Garrett."

Beth had decided she wanted two maids of honor and one matron of honor instead of a host of bridesmaids.

"Okay, Anita," Carl said. "You're on."

He opened the front door for her. Lyle waited at the bottom of the stairs. Cece peeked through one of the door's glass panes to see her mother walk toward the wedding guests along the aisle that ended at the foot of the gazebo.

She rejoined the bridal party to find Carl fanning Beth frantically.

"I just can't believe today is finally here," Beth said.

"The next step toward the rest of your life." Cece took her hand.

Beth reached out for Aurora and Shelby until they each had a hand in the middle of their circle. "I'm so happy I get to spend the rest of my life with all of you. For years, I wondered how and if we'd make it, but here we are."

"Here we are." Cece smiled, her lips trembling.

Shelby sniffed back a tear.

"I swear to God, y'all." Aurora dropped her hand. "Stop it right now. Carl!"

Carl came over, flapping a fan around the circle. "That's enough, ladies. Are we going to do this thing or what?"

Beth took a steadying breath and nodded. "Let's do it."

Cece went first, in order of youngest to oldest. She took her bouquet from Carl and walked out onto the porch, where Dustin waited for her at the bottom of the stairs.

Wow, he mouthed silently.

She could say the same about him. He was smartly dressed in a rented tux and looked like a million bucks. He held out his arm, guiding her hand to loop through and rest on his forearm. Cece gave him an impish wink as she linked her arm through his.

He tried to hold back, but she felt his deep chuckle reverberate through his body.

They walked down the aisle of a long cream carpet, with cream chairs on both sides and the gazebo framing the arbor at the end. Once they reached the arbor, they each went to the respective bride or groom side.

Aurora followed, and then Shelby.

Finally, Beth floated down the aisle to the music from the string quartet, she and Sawyer both beaming.

The minister began, and not a dry eye was left among the wedding guests when they got to the vows they'd each written. Sawyer's voice shook as he told Beth how much he'd loved her from the moment they met, and how he cherished her and promised to always be there for her and her family.

Once pronounced husband and wife, the two of them

went back into the inn, the wedding party following right behind them.

Cece and Aurora found Beth in the foyer, while Jude, Garrett, and Dustin shook hand with Sawyer, congratulating him.

"Did I do okay?" Beth asked, breathless. "It felt like a dream, but I'm not sure I'm a reliable source."

"Everything was perfect." Aurora hugged her.

Cece shooed her toward the hall. "Come on back to your room, and I can fix your veil and stuff for the reception."

Beth nodded. "I should probably touch up my makeup too. I made it all the way to the vows before I lost it," she told Aurora.

"I know." Aurora smiled. "You did great."

Cece turned back, approaching Dustin before she hurried off with her sister.

"How'd I do?" he asked.

"Wonderful. And so handsome." She touched the cream boutonniere on his suit.

"I've never been this dressed up. It's not comfortable, but I feel like I look good."

"*So* good. And it suits you." She rose up on her toes and met his kiss.

Later, after the wedding party and bride and groom were introduced at the reception, Cece and Dustin grabbed some food and found a table with Aurora and Jude. Bruce settled under the table by Dustin's feet.

"I think we've decided we don't want a particularly fancy wedding," Aurora announced, lifting her champagne glass.

"No?" Cece tried to act surprised, though she could've predicted that about her sister ages ago.

"No, I think something a lot smaller than this."

"And more casual, probably," Jude added.

"Definitely. We could have everything on the farm, just close friends and family. I don't think I want a particularly formal dress either." Aurora tilted her head as if trying to picture herself.

"Something more candlelight cream, flowy, maybe bell sleeves in something sheer or just lace? Think, Stevie Nicks getting married in the English countryside, except it's you, in a field of lavender," Cece suggested.

"Yes!" Aurora exclaimed as Jude pointed at her, nodding.

"Sounds perfect," he said.

Of course it did. Cece knew what she was doing.

Jude tried a bite of the beef tenderloin and let his eyes roll back into his head. "Good choice on the carving station," he said.

"I like to think so." Aurora smiled.

"Have y'all picked a wedding date yet?" Dustin asked.

Aurora and Jude looked at each other. "During the spring or early summer?" she asked.

"Sounds good to me."

"We just wanted to get through this wedding first," she told Dustin. "Then we can sort out ours."

"I also vote for beef tenderloin at the reception." Jude took another bite.

Their lives were changing so quickly now, shifting into a higher gear. Cece was already staying at Hollyhock a lot more, and Aurora would be married by the middle of next year. All three sisters would move on to new homes and new lives. They'd always have the inn to keep them grounded and together, but now their futures had different and exciting paths.

Beth had found an assistant who was more than happy to stay on the inn premises at night in exchange for what was essentially a free place to live. Beth would still be there every day, running the place, and no doubt Aurora would be involved in culinary oversight from time to time, but it would never go back to the way it was a year ago.

Anita and Lyle approached the table. "May we join you?"

"Of course."

Their mother sat with them as they reviewed all the events leading up to the big day.

"Everything was so lovely too," she said. "The ceremony, the couple, the vows, and the dress." Anita sighed. "My mother would've been so proud to see you girls and what you've accomplished. You make me so proud too."

"She talks about you all the time," Lyle added. "Telling me the latest about the inn and your restaurant. And now it sounds like you and Dustin have another job?" he asked Cece.

"You mean Felicia and Bob's?" she asked.

"No. Another one here in town, after the holidays."

"Oh, you mean the renovations at The Grove?" One of the other inns in town had heard what a great job Dustin did after the storm, so they'd sought him out for some updates on their place.

"That's it."

"We'll work on that into the new year," Dustin told him. "And then may have a couple more after that if discussions work out."

"That's great news." Lyle lifted his tea glass. "Here's to staying booked and busy."

After a few minutes, Beth and Sawyer went to the middle of the dance floor for their first dance.

"Do you want to dance?" Dustin asked Cece once they were finished.

"I don't know if that's such a great idea. My ankle isn't one hundred percent, and I'm not that great to begin with."

"I can lead you through the turns. Or you can just stand on my feet."

Cece laughed, remembering Sloane's comment about Dustin looking like the kind of man who could put you where he wanted.

"What's so funny?"

"Nothing. Let's dance."

He led her to the dance floor for a slow song and held her tight as they swayed to the music.

"If you would've told me weeks ago that I'd be here, dancing and in love with the woman who showed up on my porch to yell at me for buying that house..." Dustin laughed.

"I know." Cece thought back on the day they'd met. "I was so mad at you, and I didn't even know you."

"I'll always be grateful that you decided to give me a piece of your mind."

She giggled against his chest. "I'll remind you of that every time I do it."

They danced to a few more songs and decided to take a break as Beth and Sawyer went to cut the wedding cake.

"Are you ready for cake?" Dustin asked her.

"Always."

He brought her a piece of the strawberry layer, and they sat at a table away from the crowd.

Sloane found them though and hurried over, sliding into a seat. "Have you guys seen that cowboy, about yea tall?" She held up her hand. "Black hat, very yummy?"

"I thought only bad guys wore the black hats," Dustin commented.

"A bad boy? Don't tempt me with a good time."

Cece snorted a laugh with cake in her mouth. "No," she managed. "We haven't seen him."

"I might've seen him inside near the cake," Dustin offered.

"You are a prince." Sloane ran off.

"You *are* a prince." Cece put her chin in her hand and smiled at him cheekily.

"Now, now. Don't flatter me too much. Have I told you how beautiful you look tonight? Every night?"

"Yes, but you can say it again. I don't mind."

Dustin's smile tickled her heart.

"Listen, I…I have something for you. I wanted to wait until we were alone, but now seems perfect." He passed her an envelope.

Cece carefully opened it, wondering if it was what she thought—

It was.

Inside the envelope was the deed to 4 Hollyhock Lane with both of their names listed.

With her savings, and the money he'd made at the inn, they were able to buy the adjacent vacant lot and pay down some of Hollyhock's mortgage. Then, they'd agreed that the money they made on their next three jobs would all be spent on paying down Hollyhock and saving for the future.

Their future. One they would build together.

"This is the best piece of paper I've ever seen." Cece managed to smile through misty eyes.

"I talked to the couple at Rolling Hills too," he said.

"Yeah?"

"You were right. They'd never consider selling, and they never even got approached by the guy. They're happy right where they are and have no plans to leave."

"That's it then. Hollyhock is safe."

Dustin nodded, leaning forward to press his lips to hers. "Mmm, you taste like strawberries and buttercream."

She kissed him again. "Have you used the phone number you got from Felicia yet?"

"You mean, have I called my biological grandmother?"

Cece nodded with a smile.

"Not yet, but...I think I will. I'm thinking I might even try to meet her, if she's okay with that."

She put both her hands on his. "I think that's a great idea."

"Never thought I'd even consider it, but I don't know. I never thought any of this would happen, and now look. I've found my people. Maybe my grandmother wonders about me the same way I wondered for all those years."

"I'm sure she does."

There was a commotion near the dance floor as it cleared and ladies gathered for the bouquet toss. Cece got up and held out her hand to hold Dustin's, leading him to the gazebo.

"Where are we going?" Dustin asked, Bruce right behind him as they left the wedding party.

"One of my favorite places at the inn, and you've yet to enjoy it."

In the evenings, the gazebo was lit with string lights at the edges and small floor lights around the bottom edge. The effect was dreamy and romantic, and it was the perfect place to escape from the crowd.

"You don't want to ...?" He indicated the bouquet toss about to happen over his shoulder.

Cece shook her head and tugged him forward. "I don't need to catch a bouquet to know my future."

"No?" he asked as they reached the gazebo and she sat, patting the seat next to her.

Bruce immediately jumped up.

"Not you," Dustin exclaimed as Cece melted into laughter.

"No," she finally answered him as Dustin joined her on her other side. "I already know it."

"And what does your future hold?" he asked, sitting down next to her.

She leaned against him, taking in the crisp autumn air. "Well, I'm going to live with you at Hollyhock. We'll have a beautiful home, a gorgeous yard, maybe a little garden in the back. We're definitely going to have houseplants aplenty in the bedroom window. We'll renovate houses all over the area, and Bruce will become the most beloved pitty in all of Texas."

Bruce plopped his head in her lap, as though very satisfied with this news.

"Manny will stay with us until he saves up enough to get a place of his own," she continued. "But he'll still come for dinners on Sundays, either at our house or Beth's or at Lavender."

"Mmm." Dustin nodded. "I like the sound of Sunday dinners. Please continue."

"Eventually, we'll need to get some chickens."

"Oh." He laughed. "Will we?"

"And a donkey."

"A donkey?"

She lifted a shoulder in a little shrug. "I've always wanted a donkey and a little barn. We have the space now too."

"Okay, so a donkey. What about kids?"

"As in baby goats or baby humans?" she asked, teasing him.

"I . . . both? I guess?"

"*Both* sounds good to me too."

Dustin chuckled, the sound and feel against her making her think of home. He was to be her home now. Dustin and Hollyhock—and Bruce. Just last year, she could never have imagined finding the perfect man for her.

"Both it is," he said, wrapping his arms around her. "And somewhere in there, do you want to get married or—"

"Sure."

"Somewhere between the chickens and the donkey?"

She nodded. "Obviously after the donkey. We'd want the donkey and Bruce at the wedding."

"Obviously." He laughed. "Will the donkey need a bow tie too?"

"Probably. And we can get married in our backyard. We may have to put the chickens in the barn during the ceremony. That might be a touch too far."

He laughed fully then. "There is no one like you, Cece. I love you, and I can't imagine my life without you."

She turned to him then, leaning against his chest as she gave him another kiss. "Lucky for you, you don't have to."

About the Author

Heather McGovern writes contemporary romance in swoony settings. While her love of travel and adventure takes her far, there is no place like home. She lives in South Carolina with her husband and son, and one Maltipoo to rule them all. When she isn't writing, she enjoys hiking, scuba diving, going to Disney World, reading, and streaming her latest favorite on television.

You can learn more at:

HeatherMcGovernNovels.com
Facebook.com/Heather.McGovern.Author

Book your next trip to a charming small town—and fall in love—with one of these swoony Forever contemporary romances!

THE SOULMATE PROJECT
by Reese Ryan

Emerie Roberts is tired of waiting for her best friend, Nick, to notice her. When she confesses her feelings at the town's annual New Year's Eve bonfire and he doesn't feel the same, she resolves to stop pining for him and move on. She hatches a seven-step plan to meet her love match and enlists her family and friends—including Nick—to help. So why does he seem hell-bent on sabotaging all her efforts?

HOME ON HOLLYHOCK LANE
by Heather McGovern

Though Dustin Long has been searching for a sense of home since childhood, that's not why he bought Hollyhock. He plans to flip the old miner's cottage and use the money to launch his construction business. And while every reno project comes with unexpected developments, CeCe Shipley beats them all—she's as headstrong as she is gorgeous. But as they collaborate to restore the cottage to its former glory, he realizes they're also building something new together. Could CeCe be the home Dustin's always wanted?

Connect with us at Facebook.com/ReadForeverPub

SUNFLOWER COTTAGE ON HEART LAKE
by Sarah Robinson

Interior designer Amanda Riverswood is thirty-two years old and has never had a boyfriend. So this summer, she's going on a bunch of blind dates. Pro baseball pitcher Dominic Gage was on top of the world—until an injury sent him into retirement. Now, in the small town of Heart Lake, his plan is to sit on his dock not talking to anyone, especially not the cute girl next door. But when they begin to bond over late-night laughter about Amanda's failed dating attempts, will they see that there's more than friendship between them?

SNOWED IN FOR CHRISTMAS
by Jaqueline Snowe

Sorority mom Becca Fairfield has everything she needs to survive the blizzard: hot cocoa, plenty of books…and the memory of a steamy kiss. Only Becca's seriously underestimated this snow-pocalypse. So when Harrison Cooper—next-door neighbor, football coach, and the guy who acted mega-awkward after said kiss—offers her shelter, it only makes sense to accept. They'll just hang out, stay safe, and maybe indulge in a little R-rated cuddling. But are they keeping warm…or playing with fire?

AN AMISH CHRISTMAS MATCH
by Winnie Griggs

Phoebe Kropf knows everyone thinks she's accident-prone rather than an independent Amish woman. So she's determined to prove she's more than her shortcomings when she's asked to provide temporary Christmas help in nearby Sweetbrier Creek. Widower Seth Beiler is in over his head caring for his five motherless *brieder*. But he wasn't expecting a new housekeeper as unconventional—or lovely—as Phoebe. When the holiday season is at an end, will Seth convince her to stay…as part of their *familye*?

CHRISTMAS IN HARMONY HARBOR
by Debbie Mason

Instead of wrapping presents and decking the halls, Evangeline Christmas is worrying about saving her year-round holiday shop from powerful real estate developer Caine Elliot. She's risking everything on an unusual proposition she hopes the wickedly handsome CEO can't refuse. How hard can it be to fulfill three wishes from the Angel Tree in Evie's shop? Caine's certain he'll win and the property will be his by Christmas Eve. But a secret from Caine's childhood is about to threaten their merrily-ever-after.